D1375366

Please return/renew this item by the last date shown. Books may also be renewed by phone or internet.

🖥 www.rbwm.gov.uk/home/leisure-and-culture/libraries

☎ 01628 796969 (library hours)

☎ 0303 123 0035 (24 hours)

his gimlet eye for the foibles and nuances of human behaviour. A huge success'

WILLIAM BOYD, author of *Any Human Heart*

'With shiny-sharp humour, Luke Kennard takes us down the dark alleys of longing in the domestic setting'   *Sainsbury's Magazine*

'*The Answer to Everything* is that rare thing: a book with a brilliant twist which also happens to be touching and hilarious'   ISY SUTTIE, author of *The Actual One*

'Savagely funny, very highly recommended'   *Bookseller*

ALSO BY LUKE KENNARD

POETRY

The Solex Brothers (2005)
The Harbour Beyond the Movie (2007)
The Migraine Hotel (2009)
Planet-Shaped Horse (2011)
The Necropolis Boat (2012)
A Lost Expression (2012)
Holophin (2012)
Cain (2016)
Truffle Hound (2018)
Notes on the Sonnets (2021)
Bad Sermons (2021)

FICTION

The Transition (2017)

The Answer to Everything

Luke Kennard

4th ESTATE • *London*

4th Estate
An imprint of HarperCollins*Publishers*
1 London Bridge Street
London SE1 9GF

www.4thEstate.co.uk

HarperCollins*Publishers*
1st Floor, Watermarque Building, Ringsend Road
Dublin 4, Ireland

First published in Great Britain in 2021 by 4th Estate
This 4th Estate paperback edition published in 2022

1

A catalogue record for this book is
available from the British Library

ISBN 978-0-00-844454-9

Set in Bembeo Std
Printed and bound in the UK using 100%
renewable electricity at CPI Group (UK) Ltd

MIX
Paper from
responsible sources
FSC™ C007454

This book is produced from independently certified FSC™ paper
to ensure responsible forest management.

For more information visit: www.harpercollins.co.uk/green

The Answer to Everything

●●●

— Can we take a step back for a moment and look
  at what we're actually doing?
— Of course. *Falls off cliff*
— That's funny. You're funny.
— [This message has been deleted.]

1

The boys were asleep, the youngest in the nursery because she was trying to wean him again, and the oldest lying next to her in the double bed. When she heard the stairs creaking Emily made sure Matty was breathing regularly and tiptoed out of the room. Steven often complained that they never managed to finish a sentence or talk about anything other than the children. She felt she should probably make an effort to rectify that. She adjusted her hair in the reflection of a family portrait in the hallway, undid a button on the shirt she wore for pyjamas.

Steven looked surprised when she entered the living room, then shifted from the middle of the sofa they were halfway through paying for.

He was holding his phone and the *News at Ten* was on quietly in the background.

'You're up,' said Emily. 'You okay?'

'Yeah,' said Steven. 'Thought I'd try to get to know another room.'

'Lay down some precious memories. Drink?'

'Nah.'

* * *

Their new home was small, but the kitchen was by far the largest room – something Emily wasn't used to after the galleys of rented Victorian terraces. It was fitted with piercing halogen lights, angled, she supposed, to flatter your utensils as if they were museum exhibits. She unscrewed a half-empty bottle of red wine and filled a glass to the brim so that she had to crouch over the work surface and inhale the first sip before picking it up.

'It's hard to really make a new build feel like it's *yours*, isn't it?' she said, letting her voice echo in the hallway before she re-entered the room. 'It's like trying to personalise a … car or something.'

'We can paint if you want.'

'What colour?' said Emily. 'Black?'

'If you like.'

'I don't know what you'd have to do – you could buy antiques and art and framed prints and they'd just look out of place. You don't feel that, do you? I'm not saying I'm not happy.'

Steven raised his eyebrows.

'Well, I should hope not,' said Emily, in a low voice. He smiled at her. 'I am happy,' she said. 'I like that this is actually *ours*, too, even if it feels like a mock-up in a department store … I'm proud of us.'

'Well, that's something,' said Steven.

'Happy wife, happy life,' said Emily.

'You can stop doing the voice now.'

'I wasn't doing the voice. God, I don't really want to go back to three days a week,' she said, stretching her wine glass above her head then bringing it back to her lips. 'I mean I'm probably squeezing three working days a week

2

into two days anyway because that's how it works, but if I had to *be* there for an extra day and I was getting *paid* for an extra day they'd probably make me do *four* days' worth of work and the money would only go on childcare, so I'd be losing a day with the children – they'd be losing a day with me – for what, exactly? I'm sorry, this is boring.'

'No, I'm just tired, sorry.' Steven stopped pinching the bridge of his nose.

'Everyone's tired,' said Emily. 'If you're talking to someone, they're probably tired. What's wrong?'

'Do you feel like you *need* to go up to three days a week?' said Steven.

Emily took another small sip from her wine glass, followed by a gulp.

'It's really hard to grab a buzz from red wine sometimes,' she said. 'I need to rethink my whole approach, get some gin.'

'Mm,' said Steven.

'But then you need tonic water and ice and lemons and the whole thing is just … a whole thing. Real commitment.'

Steven, she could see, was playing an online pool game on his phone. She watched as the cue ball followed the black into the bottom left corner pocket.

'Shit,' he said.

She looked at the television. Local news. Someone had been stabbed, but not in their immediate vicinity.

'Oh my god, that's the biggest spider I've ever seen,' she said.

The spider had emerged from under the pine television table, its legs offensively thick, knees arching above its head.

It paused in the middle of the room as if taking in the new information.

'It's like a classic childhood spider,' said Emily. 'We're barely in here at night – it's probably his domain now.'

Steven looked up and then went back to his phone.

'Just leave it,' he said. 'It'll scuttle away.'

'No, we need to establish a boundary,' said Emily. 'Set a precedent.'

She stood and picked up an abandoned mug from the bookcase but it still had dregs of tea in it from the morning.

'Agh,' she said, and put it back.

'Where are you going?'

In the kitchen she selected a mug embossed with a stylised Dutch cityscape, returned to the living room and looked around, irritably. The books were too thick and the postcards were too narrow. In the drawer she found a fifth birthday card for Matty from last year. Treading as softly as she could, Emily circled the spider, approached it from behind and gently but swiftly brought the mug down on top of it. One of its legs protruded from the rim like a rogue hair, but disappeared when she slid the card underneath. She carefully picked up the trap.

'Could you open the—' said Emily. 'Never mind.'

She held the card, spider and mug to her stomach with one hand and opened the high window with the other, then lifted the card and mug above her head, slowly, as if performing a religious ritual. Once her arms were outside she shook them both hard. It was too dark to assess the situation, so, still holding it at full extension, she turned the mug to face her, screamed and dropped it out of the window so that it smashed on the tarmac.

'Emily, what the hell?'

'I'm sorry,' she said, 'I'm sorry. It didn't come out of the mug and I panicked. I'll deal with it in the morning.'

'Since when do you scream like that?' said Steven. 'You'll wake up the boys.'

'Fuck's sake,' said Emily, looking out of the window. 'I loved that mug.'

'Do you want me to?'

'Actually, would you?' said Emily. 'They could cut themselves.'

Steven sighed and left the room. He came back holding a dustpan and brush, wearing a coat over his pyjamas and flipflops over his socks.

'Strong look,' said Emily.

She put on her coat as she listened to Steven scraping up the pieces of mug from the path. Then she walked through the front door and stepped around him.

'I'm going to take a walk.'

'You're what?'

'Just around the block.'

'We don't live on a block.'

She walked to the edge of the estate, where a shoulder-height fence with no gate gave onto a tantalising copse of silver birches. In the half-moon light it looked like a linocut of a forest. She called her mother.

'I'm sorry, Mum. Are you awake?'

Always well-calibrated, her mother quickly interrupted the pleasantries and asked her what was wrong. Had she ever, Emily asked, staring above the pines, felt lonely?

'Of course.'

'But in your marriage?' Emily said.

'Irritable, maybe,' her mother said. 'Sometimes for months.'

'He barely talks to me,' said Emily. 'And when he does it's like he's desperate for it to be over.'

Was there anything, her mother asked, that she wasn't telling her?

There wasn't, Emily said. She told her everything, she knew that.

'And you're feeling okay?'

'I'm feeling confused and sad.'

'In a way that …'

'Topically. I'm rationally and legitimately confused and sad.'

'Yes, yes, I understand, darling.'

Her mother went silent long enough that Emily wondered if she'd lost signal and took the phone away from her ear.

Then her mother said, 'Sweetheart, sometimes you need to count your blessings. I don't say that lightly. I'm not dismissing the way you feel. You have a husband who loves you, who loves the children, who doesn't drink, or not much, anyway, and who doesn't gamble. Sometimes you're going to feel bored and lonely because that's what being alive is like. There are going to be whole *epochs* of your life which are like that and you have to learn how to weather them.'

'Okay,' Emily said.

'There, you see?' her mother said. 'That's the spirit: okay.'

She lay in bed next to Matty staring at the white ceiling and the blue-white effulgence cast across it by the LED streetlights. She wanted an uneven old ceiling, preferably with wooden beams so she could play constellations with the knots. Then she could have used the knots to count her blessings. She wanted warm, impractical light. Oil lamps. It was fussy to want things like that, but it seemed to her that the whole estate, not just the individual, identical houses, had been designed by an artificial intelligence as an adequate storage solution for humans, with no intuition as to what it really meant to be alive.

So weather it, she thought. Weather it good. She gently pulled the duvet away from Matty to cover her feet. She could hear a distant siren, which she always found comforting behind triple-glazing – like a thunderstorm. Someone else's problem. She watched the five-year-old's pretzeled form, tangled up in the duvet, his Pokémon T-shirt rucked up around his waist. She put one hand on his back.

2

In the house across the road Elliott stood at the window of his living room inhaling watermelon-flavoured vapour from an electronic cigarette. He had been pacing from the kitchen to the living room and back again for half an hour, but must have resolved something unconsciously because now he had stopped. Tomasz, his son, did that too, and, if you tried to interrupt him or asked him if he was okay, he would say crossly that he was *thinking*. Elliott watched as the lights went out in number 24, and he was going to go to the kitchen to check the time on the oven when he felt a presence behind him. Alathea, when she needed to, could move through the house like a ghost.

'Inside?' she said.

'I cracked the window.'

'I know – it's freezing.'

'It's just water vapour.'

'And nicotine.'

'Which gets absorbed by my lungs.'

'And by your children.'

'Mostly my lungs.'

'I know,' said Alathea, 'that it's not a comfortable thought, that your actions could harm others. But will you go outside? When you want to do that?'

'Okay,' said Elliott. 'Sorry.'

She was standing in the doorway. She must have been up writing client notes as she was still dressed for work. Her feet were bare.

'You look great.'

She laughed.

'I was being sincere.'

'I feel gross,' said Alathea. 'But thank you.'

She was holding a passport and a pair of scissors.

'What's this?' said Elliott.

'I was going to cut up your passport in front of you,' said Alathea, 'but the vaping distracted me.'

'Why were you going to do that?'

'Threaten to, I mean,' said Alathea. 'Because I'm extremely suspicious of you.'

'Oh dear,' said Elliott. 'Because of Polly?'

'The more I think about it,' said Alathea, 'the more extremely suspicious I get. I mean it's not that you didn't tell me – I don't expect you to tell me everything you're doing, I expect you to say work ran late. But really, if you were just grabbing a drink or a bite to eat after work, which is fine by the way, wouldn't you have gone some-where closer to campus?'

'What, like Chicken Dot Com?' said Elliott.

'That's true,' said Alathea. 'Polly is a classy girl.'

Elliott laughed through his nose.

'Wouldn't you have gone somewhere more convenient than the Ethiopian restaurant in the middle of the indus-trial district on the other side of the city?'

'I really like that place,' said Elliott. 'It's one of a kind.'

'Oh yeah, no, it's great,' said Alathea. 'And I suppose the

fact that you tell everyone they *have to try it* probably increased the chance of a mutual friend being there on a Friday night.'

'That's true.'

'Who noticed that you clocked him but didn't go over to say hi.'

'Because,' said Elliott, 'of how it might look. Polly had an article accepted so we were celebrating. I honestly just couldn't be bothered to explain anything. The thing with *me*—'

'What's the thing with you?'

'—is that if I was genuinely trying to hide something I'd probably have come straight home and told you I'd seen Robert and that I was out with Polly. I'm very calculating.'

'But maybe you assumed Robert wouldn't say anything.'

'What *did* Robert say? Fucking Robert.'

'Do you ever think about taking *me* out for dinner?'

'All the time,' said Elliott. 'But we can't.'

'No,' said Alathea, 'because I'm imprisoned by the children you impregnated me with.'

'Hahaha.'

'Hahaha. Like a fairy-tale princess.'

'We *both* are.'

'It's funny how easy it is to do so much damage, isn't it?' said Alathea, turning the passport over in her hand. 'I think that's what I've learned. Most of what's required of you in life is *not* doing things.'

'Not so funny,' said Elliott. 'You could take one step off a pavement on a busy road and that would be the end of everything.'

'Do you think about that often?'

'One little step. You'd have eulogies about how you weren't always an easy person, but god they miss you so much. Seriously, what have I done?'

'When's the conference again?'

'Not until next month.'

Alathea opened the passport and cut a tiny slit into the cover.

'Please,' said Elliott.

'No begging,' said Alathea. 'Come on.'

Elliott looked around the living room and picked up a small glass foot from the mantelpiece. There was no fireplace or even a gas heater, but they had had the mantelpiece installed because it didn't really feel like a living room without it. It was a cast of their eldest son Tomasz's foot from when he was four weeks old. Elliott weighed it in his hand. It felt too hard and solid to break unless he dashed it against the pavement. He glanced out of the window.

'Oh, you're good,' said Alathea.

'We could just talk about this. If you want to tell me what's wrong.'

'You have two tickets,' said Alathea. 'Polly?'

'No. Maurice is broke,' said Elliott. 'I got his flights and he's paying me back at the end of the month. On payday.'

'Silly Maurice.'

'Silly. Maurice.'

'So useless with money.'

'He's the wayward younger brother I never had.'

Elliott approached her and placed the foot in her hand. She dropped the scissors and tossed his passport onto the sofa. He attempted to take her in his arms, but she stiffened.

'Hey,' he said.

'Okay,' said Alathea. 'I'm sorry.'

'You don't have anything to apologise for.'

'No, I suppose I don't.'

'I took Polly out for dinner, I didn't tell you about it and I'm sorry,' said Elliott.

Alathea kissed him. 'Just you wait,' she said.

He made up his bed on the IKEA futon in the corner of Tomasz's room. He kicked some Lego bricks under the bunkbed then arranged the bears, the monkey and the soft Mario which had fallen over and kissed Tomasz on the forehead. He lay down on the cement-firm mattress and put his hands behind his head.

The ritual had started on their honeymoon in Brittany nine years ago. Alathea's parents owned a holiday cottage in Quimper. A beach hut, really, Alathea had told him, but he wasn't surprised to find it palatial. In a way it was a good sign that she still wanted to keep it going. It was a sort of breakthrough, boded pretty well.

They argued a lot on their honeymoon. When Elliott fussed about arrangements changing – they had tried to meet up with another couple, also on honeymoon, I mean who *does* that? – or insisted on getting to stations long before departure, and Alathea would tell him that, Oh my god, he reminded her of her father. Elliott took great offence at this. When he looked back on his life before children, he couldn't believe he'd ever felt stressed or rancorous about anything, but whenever he thought back to anything specific, lo, he'd been pissy and irritable anyway.

On the third day they were arguing on the Max Jacob Bridge and Alathea reached into Elliott's inside pocket, took out his wallet and threw it into the river. Elliott calmly looped Alathea's J. W. Anderson Pierce handbag off her shoulder and threw it in after the wallet. It bobbed a little then started to take on water and sank with a gurgle. Whether they both confused their excitement for arousal he wasn't sure, but the way Alathea had kissed him on Max Jacob Bridge really stayed with him. She dug her nails into his upper arms. When she let go, Elliott took off his shirt and jeans, climbed into the river and swam out. He retrieved the handbag but couldn't find the wallet. He was getting cold and, anyway, retrieving the bag and not the wallet represented something of a victory; Alathea took off her coat for him to use as a towel, shivered in her white blouse. Since then, the mutually-assured-destruction approach to affection had proven something of a thrill, sustaining, even. They had developed certain rules. No rough stuff aside from the destruction of property and collateral hurt feelings; no breaking the fourth wall.

Elliott took out his phone and, despite there being nothing, as far as he was concerned, to hide, he changed the password on his email account.

3

When Emily answered the door a small man with sandy hair and a strong jawline was leaning against her doorframe.

'Emily, right?' he said. 'Sorry to bother you. You settling in okay?'

'Oh, hey,' said Emily. 'Yes – thank you.'

He was wearing climbing shorts and a faded Metallica T-shirt.

'I'm David and I'm the … Ugh. I'm the "chair" of the allotment. We're not *recruiting* or anything, we just wanted to let you know we're here, but really you can just ignore us and get on with your lives – everyone's busy.'

'It sounds lovely,' said Emily.

'I want to make it very clear that we don't expect you to get involved at all, but.' He crouched to pick up an open basket of vegetables and small, russety apples. 'We still like to offer a little welcome package. And if you or your partner ever wanted to …'

'Ooh,' said Emily. 'Pretty. Thank you.'

'They're not allotments in the traditional sense, it's just one tract of reclaimed scrubland. Volunteers are always

14

welcome. But if you'd rather just … buy stuff from the farm shop, that's also fine, nobody judges.'

'It sounds great,' said Emily. 'Do you want a tea or coffee?'

'No, god no,' said David. 'I don't want to impose.'

'You wouldn't be.'

'No, I'm going to go,' said David. 'I'm a big fan of privacy and leaving people alone. You should never get to know your neighbours *too* well. There's various info in here.' He gave her a small brochure bound in recycled cardboard. 'Other than that, very nice to meet you, Emily. Send my best to your family.'

He extended a hand, but Emily was holding the gift basket and the leaflet, so he withdrew it, smiled and gave her an awkward half-salute before ambling away. Emily put the basket on the kitchen counter, tossed a courgette in the air and caught it, then flipped through the brochure. Emergency phone numbers, details of the recycling and refuse-collection system, statistics about solar panels, where to pick up the fobs for the car pool and how to book one of the communal electric cars for the day. The local primary school was rated 'Good' and volunteers developed and maintained a 'nature walk' of less than forty minutes' duration (even at child pace) to allow safe and straightforward access.

'Steven?'

Steven was on a stepladder in the living room installing high shelves to store Emily's books. She took a deep breath and felt momentarily euphoric that they were allowed to make the house look however they wanted it to, knock through walls, hang paintings. It was something she'd long ago dismissed as a bourgeois fantasy but, it turned out, desperately wanted. He had already installed her icons in the eastern corner of the room with a small corner cabinet to keep candles and incense and she felt moved, momentarily, by him having chosen to do this first. As if to say, I know your faith is the most important thing to you; and even if it's not, I know that you'd *like* it to be and I want to acknowledge that. Not that she'd been to church in years, in spite of asking him to convert for her before they could get married. It was still sweet and considerate. She'd been caught by that before; some unambiguous sign of love and devotion which nonetheless didn't seem to come with any verbal or physical affection even if she fished for it. But you judge people on what they *do*, not what they *say*. Her mother liked to remind her how important that was.

'Steven. It looks great.'

He turned and smiled at her with three screws in his mouth.

'I married someone who can put up shelves,' said Emily. 'It was touch and go for a few years.'

Steven turned back to the wall and screwed in another bracket.

'My first boyfriend couldn't even light a match.'

'Mmhm.'

'But I married a big old unreconstructed man who can put up shelves.' She stood at the side of the ladder and rubbed his thick calf muscles and he didn't react. 'Even if he doesn't seem to like me very much.'

'Of course I like you,' he murmured through the screws.

'Not enough to drop the drill on my foot and kiss me,' said Emily.

'I can kiss you once I've put the shelf up.'

'No,' said Emily. 'Girl can't have everything.'

4

It made no difference how early he got up or whether he'd made the lunchboxes in advance: the weekday mornings were a bleary-eyed cyclone constricting around the house. He'd get distracted by something – an article on his phone, a pattern in the clouds – and suddenly they needed to be out of the door and everyone was still in their pyjamas or eating their third bowl of cereal and he'd lose his temper.

'We have ten minutes. Can we please concentrate on getting dressed? I shouldn't be having to help you. Tomasz, why did you tear that up?'

'I hate it.'

The sofa was surrounded by scraps of what had been an A4 felt-tip drawing of a farm with a deer-like creature staring outwards at the viewer in abject confusion.

'I loved it. I was going to put it up in my office.'

Tomasz looked sad.

'I can repair it with Sellotape,' said Elliott. 'It's beautiful, Tomasz, you shouldn't destroy your work.'

'He doesn't like excessive praise,' said Alathea.

'Well that's the only kind of praise I know how to give,' said Elliott. 'Tomasz, trousers, now.' He stooped and held up the little black chinos for his son to step into. 'I said *now*, third time. Ally, can you get Dimitry in the buggy?'

Dimitry had ground a paste of biscuit and saliva into the corner of the living-room carpet and been confined to a small ball pit where he wept bitterly.

'I have to get going.' She rattled the electric car fob on its chain.

'So do I.'

'Imagine I've died or left you or something,' said Alathea.

'Hahaha. Yeah, okay. No, wait, don't go now, it's that horrible woman.'

'Oh no,' said Alathea.

They watched an old woman walk slowly past their house with her little dog scuttling behind her.

'Give it five minutes,' said Elliott. 'I don't want you to run into her at all.'

Alathea growled.

'So,' he said, 'you can get Dimitry in the buggy.'

'Looks that way.' She walked into the hall and he heard her saying. 'Okay, beautiful boy, you're going for an adventure, stop crying. I know. Keep *still*.' Then sounds of a struggle.

'Shoes,' said Elliott. 'Shoes, shoes, shoes, shoes.'

'He kicked me in the *face*,' Alathea called.

'Dimitry, do not kick your mother in the face,' Elliott called back. 'It's all clear, Ally, if you want to escape.'

'*Thank* you,' said Alathea, slipping her shoes on. 'Is it going to rain, do you think? I can't find the waterproof for the—'

'Ally, last night—'

'Oh, I'm completely over that,' said Alathea. 'Say hi to Polly from me.'

'I have no idea if she's even in today.'

'Well, if you see her.'

'I wanted – Tomasz, for the love of god, put your *socks* back on.' He looked at Alathea and she tilted her head to one side. 'For fuck's sake,' he said.

'You have neither the time nor the inclination to have an affair,' said Alathea. 'I know. You're desperate for female company and compensating for my lack of warmth.'

'That's …'

'I mean do what you have to do, Elliott. Just follow the rules and include me. Goodbye, gorgeous, be good.' She ruffled Tomasz's hair and he grabbed the hem of her jacket. Dimitry thrashed around in the buggy and said he wanted Mummy.

'I'll see you later, darling,' she said.

5

When Emily woke up ten minutes before the alarm she thought Who am I where am I what day is it? The white curtain inflated and deflated against the open window and the details of her life and circumstances shimmered vaguely, like a retreating dream. If there was time for a shower – and usually there wasn't – this helped a little: I appear to be some kind of amphibian. If you're lonely, she had read somewhere, you have longer showers to make up for the lack of warmth in your life outside of the shower. Everything was a metaphor.

She could hear the television on downstairs, a child laughing and a man's voice saying, 'Don't spill it.' Who *were* these people?

She had a private joke with herself on dissociative mornings like this: she would splash water on her face, look up into the bathroom mirror and say, 'Oh boy,' like Dr Sam Beckett in *Quantum Leap*. Ziggy says you're a thirty-five-year-old mother of two and there's an 86 per cent chance things are going to go horribly wrong. So what do I have to do, Al? Meh. We'll have to wait and see how it plays out.

Was the concept of *Quantum Leap* – she couldn't quite remember – that if Dr Sam Beckett *didn't* manage to correct his host's egregious mistake in the last minutes of the final act of each episode then he'd be stuck as them forever? Was that the horrible punishment she used to pray, as an eleven-year-old, that he'd avoid every week?

She checked her phone. Thursday. Not one of her working days. This might have made her feel at ease. She tried to think of the last time she'd felt at ease and she thought: childhood. Leaning against the radiator with a bowl of cereal watching *Quantum Leap*. But now any downtime felt like going on a holiday you didn't deserve, a sense of work unaccomplished like an itch in the very centre of the brain.

The kettle was still hot, and ticking quietly as the metal contracted, but it was empty, and she resented Steven not having made her a cup of tea. A little thing. Irrelevant. She filled it up again.

Matty was sitting too close to the television eating a bowl of Coco Pops and watching *Paw Patrol*, a show he had grown out of but still enjoyed in the mornings. Even a small child could feel nostalgic. Steven was looking at his phone and, when he didn't look up and say good morning or ask her how she'd slept, she elected not to ask him either.

She was in the playground with Arthur, encouraging him to brave the slide and catching him at the bottom when he shot down it like a ball bearing in his all-in-one suit. Before he left for work Steven had said *Love you*, absently. He hadn't *touched* her, but it was something. Even if I love you had become a kind of hush between them, a sanding down, the soft rasping hush of sanding down. Something compulsive—

'Arthur, *wait*, don't stand up on the slide.'

22

Something compulsive said in place of anything else, we must, we mustn't, please, but then what else, in the end, was there to say?

Somebody was watching her. A figure by the playground's blue railings.

'*Good* boy – that was so brave.'

'Fast,' said Arthur.

'Was that fast? That was so fast.'

Emily looked over her shoulder. She saw an older woman with a small black Scottie dog. She was wearing a long waxed coat. She beckoned, holding up a hand and curling her fingers three, four times as if gathering the air between them. Emily's instinct was to ignore her, but that felt rude when they'd clearly seen each other, and when something had already undeniably passed between them. That was being alive – constantly sending out packages of information like the background operations of a computer; you didn't know what they were or how they'd be received. And even if the woman was mad, or lonely, or madly lonely Emily didn't suppose it would cost her much to indulge her for a few minutes.

'Come on, Arthur.'

As she got closer to the red railings the woman smiled thinly and said, 'I believe you lost your mobile telephone by the tennis courts.'

'My what?' said Emily, checking her pockets.

'Mummy?' said Arthur, tugging her skirt.

'Climb up,' said Emily. 'You can do it.'

'Here.' The woman handed her phone over the fence and Emily felt momentarily self-conscious about its purple glittery cover.

'*Oh* my god, thank you so much.'

'No, don't thank me,' the woman said. 'Magda.'

'Emily. Ugh. It's really kind of you – you've saved my life.'

'You sound so amazed,' said Magda. 'Do you mean to say you *wouldn't* retrieve someone's purse or phone if you saw them drop it?'

Magda's dog sat as still as a garden ornament. Emily looked at it until she saw an eyelid flicker.

'No, of course I would,' she said.

'Perhaps some people wouldn't,' said Magda. 'They're quite fascinating. Whether it's indifference or active antipathy. Some people might see you leave your handbag on the train seat beside you and think, *Ha!*'

'It would have ruined my whole week to lose it,' said Emily, 'so thank you.'

'Cancer,' said Magda. 'Is that right?'

'I'm sorry?'

'Your sign.'

'Oh,' said Emily. 'It's not something I really think about. Yes, as it happens.'

'Well, no, me neither,' said Magda. 'I can usually tell within a minute of meeting someone, but it's all optional, really.'

'That's so funny,' said Emily. 'How can you tell? How could you tell I was …'

'Can't *do* it.' Arthur was trying to climb onto a spring-mounted unicorn.

'I'm coming, Arthur. Can you do his?'

'I wouldn't dare,' said Magda. 'You're new here?'

'A few weeks,' said Emily. 'No, a month or more now. We're still unpacking, haha.'

'I've always found,' said Magda, 'that I could never completely unpack, wherever I went. But then I travelled a lot.'

'Oh yeah, tell me about it,' said Emily, taking two steps back towards Arthur and hoping Magda would take the cue to say goodbye.

'I've lived here for years now, of course.'

'Thank you so much for finding my phone before a … teenage drug dealer.' Emily helped Arthur onto the unicorn and he began to rock with some pace and an alarming arc. 'Arthur, slow *down*.'

'Oh there aren't any,' said Magda. 'Not for around a decade, I suppose.'

'Ha, yeah,' said Emily. 'Not until the babies grow up.'

'There was something,' said Magda, 'that I wanted to tell you when I saw you, but it's faded like a dream.'

'Well,' said Emily, smiling politely, 'I'm here quite a lot.'

'Perhaps it will come back to me.'

'So you can let me know.'

'Yes, unless it's too late by then,' said Magda. 'You laugh a lot.'

'I'm a very happy person.'

'You may go now,' said Magda. 'You needn't be polite.'

'Well thank you again,' said Emily. 'Honestly. And it was nice to meet you.'

'Honestly?' said Magda. 'Goodbye, Emily.'

Emily wondered if she gave off some pheromone that attracted weird people and made them feel entitled to say anything they wanted to her. But, on the other hand she *had* dropped her phone. And maybe her date of birth was listed on it somehow. And she nevertheless felt much more certain of who she *was* than she had in the morning.

'What a nice lady finding Mummy's phone,' she said to Arthur. She picked him up and held his cheek to her face until he tried to squirm free.

'Who is she?'

Emily turned and watched Magda walking swiftly across the park, the little dog trotting to keep pace with her heel. She tried to think of something to say, but children were always asking you who people were and it never felt like any answer you could give would really satisfy them.

Before she started peeling potatoes for the shepherd's pie, Emily opened the pictures file on her phone to send a photograph of Arthur in the park to her mother. She flicked back through the day's photos, stopped and returned to the beginning. The most recent item, after a photograph of a used train ticket, was in fact a film of 0:32 minutes' duration. She hit Play. In the footage Emily was pushing Arthur on the swing in the park, her expression vacant, staring, not at her son but into the middle distance. She was disturbed by how unhappy she looked – in her memory they had laughed and played together and *bonded*, but in the film she looked by turns bored, distracted and thoroughly pissed off. It made her feel a little sick, and it unsettled her that Magda would have filmed her as she approached. She called Steven and heard his feet on the stairs.

'You okay? Did you cut yourself?'

'I saw a woman in the park,' said Emily. 'She's called Magda. She gave me my phone, but …'

'You what?' said Steven.

'She told me my star sign. It's a bit weird.'

Steven looked concerned. 'Do you need to have a lie down?' His voice implied *another* lie down, as if she'd only just got up, as if he'd kept a running tally of past lie downs.

'No.'

'You saw the …' He looked really irritated. 'A woman told you your star sign and gave you your phone.'

'Yes. Look, let's start again; I was in the park with Arthur – she filmed me.'

'Did you get enough sleep last night?' said Steven.

'*No,*' said Emily, regretting she'd mentioned it at all. 'But I'm okay. Thanks.'

'You're not … hearing stuff?'

'Agh. No. I'm not *hearing stuff*. I'm literally just trying to tell you something that happened.'

'I'm not trying to piss you off,' said Steven. 'What we agreed, and what we agreed we didn't need to put in writing because that just felt insulting—'

'Because what are you going to do, wave a contract in my face that says I'm crazy?'

'Exactly. We agreed that you'd always tell me if you started feeling … weird again. So I appreciate you telling me.'

'Well that's great. You can stop holding your head in your hands.'

'Unrelated headache,' said Steven. 'Everything I read said that there has to be clear communication between us.'

'I hate those books,' said Emily. 'I'm not a case study.'

'Not just books,' said Steven.

'What then, fucking Reddit?' said Emily.

'You'll keep telling me?'

'You'll be the first to know. I mean if it's coming, it's coming,' said Emily. 'Hiding behind a sofa doesn't stop the storm.'

'I know.'

'But it's not. I feel fine.'

'Good.'

6

'Who was that man?'

'Some people,' said Elliott, 'aren't as lucky as us, and they don't have anywhere to live.'

'They don't have anywhere to *live*?' said Tomasz. 'Do you know him?'

'No,' said Elliott.

'Why was he bleeding?'

'Well, you heard him,' said Elliott. 'He said that he fell.'

'And why did he have spots all over him?'

'Sores. He's probably ill,' said Elliott. 'If you don't have anywhere to live, it's easy to get ill.'

'He said, *Sorry to bother you when you're with your kid*,' said Tomasz. 'That's me.'

'Maybe he was worried he'd upset you.'

'Why did you give him money?'

'Because he didn't have any. He said he needed to get a train.'

'Where to?'

'Somewhere else.'

As they walked Elliott waited for some expression of empathy from his son, but instead Tomasz looked faintly amused.

'It's sad,' Elliott persisted. 'And I gave him some money to make myself feel better, not because I'm good.'

'You *are* good,' said Tomasz.

'It's nice that you think that,' said Elliott. 'And in the end I suppose that's what matters. But really, Tomasz, I think you're just being kind. How was school?'

'I don't remember.'

'Hahaha.'

'I *don't*.'

'It was *today*. Nothing bad happened? What's that on your uniform?'

'Paint. Can we go to the park?'

Elliott sat on a recycled wooden bench and closed his eyes – the baby had been up most of the night. He stirred whenever he sensed Tomasz at his side, to open a bag of Mini Cheddars or commiserate over the box of raisins he'd spilled. Otherwise he maintained just enough focus – as if checking a rear-view mirror – to make sure his son didn't injure himself. It was best not to hover anyway – you ended up holding them and lifting them over everything as if they were a ceremonial object; they'd barely have a chance to learn to walk.

Today, though, he found that his gaze was drawn repeatedly back to a woman by the swings, who he recognised as their new neighbour from the estate. He'd seen her a week ago outside her front door, stamping on a cardboard box to flatten it, and he'd almost gone to say hello, to be neighbourly, but then he asked himself *why* and thought, because you're attracted to her, and that's a disingenuous reason to be neighbourly, and by that point she had given up trying to get the box any flatter and gone back inside.

That afternoon she was pushing her toddler on the second swing and making faces at him whenever he approached so that he screamed with laughter. She was wearing a light-blue V-neck jumper and black jeans. A neutral outfit that allowed him to imagine her in a range of different clothes – red-carpet premiere, cocktail bar, royal navy. A fantasy which arrived unbidden but still made him feel embarrassed for himself.

Judging that he had maybe looked at her for too long, Elliott glanced back at Tomasz, who was trying to go down the slide at the same time as two of his friends, then at the trees at the far end of the park, and then back at Emily.

This wasn't really a problem, was it? You're going to see people you think are pretty all the time. He wasn't a creep, and unexpectedly finding someone very attractive was human, right? What are you going to do? Freud believed the *inhibition* of scopophilia could lead to actual disturbances of vision. A jet of multicoloured stars from the top of the climbing frame.

'Daddy?'

'What?'

'Can you open this?'

'Where did you get it?'

'It was Hailey's birthday.'

He peeled the lollipop. 'Strawberry,' he said, pointlessly.

He looked back at the woman. Another quieter part of Elliott cautioned that this was one of the thousand subtle chasms every day contained. What you *do* is exercise some self-control. How many jumpers had she tried on before finding one that looked so effortlessly good on her? Probably this was the first one and it just happened to be perfect. What you *do* is check some emails on your phone. He looked away from Emily and then looked back again. This went on for a few minutes before Emily suddenly made eye contact with him and frowned – briefly enough that he could write it off as an accident or something he might have imagined; but didn't he do that with any information he didn't want to take in? Something had passed between them and he felt ashamed of himself and didn't look in her direction again until Tomasz tugged his sleeve and asked if they could go *home* now?

The next day, after school, he sat on the same bench, opened Tomasz's ziplock bag of rice cakes and looked up to see the same woman pushing a buggy towards the playground gate. She was wearing a long, fitted overcoat. A tall, well-built, bald man walked closely beside her. Elliott started, as if caught, handed Tomasz the rice cakes, took out his phone and opened the weather app.

He had been worrying all night about staring at her, and whether it had been obvious he had been staring at her; that she had noticed and construed it as unwanted attention. That was a disingenuous thought – it *was* unwanted attention, and whether she construed it that way or not was irrelevant. Had she noticed him looking at her at all – and how could she not have noticed? – Elliott felt sure now that it had probably made her feel uncomfortable. It's not nice being stared at, particularly being stared at the way a caged leopard might stare at a bleeding chunk of steak on the other side of the bars.

Of course, this wasn't something one broached in conversation, so his actions had forced her to ask her large husband to accompany her on the school pickup – *Let me make one thing very clear* – and Elliott was, it turned out, deep down, regressive and unreconstructed enough to get the message. Good men tried to pull exactly the same shit as bad men; they just felt more guilty about it. Which was even worse because you had to deal with their shitty behaviour *and* the fact that they felt bad about it. Maybe they should all freeze their sperm and commit mass suicide.

'It's Elliott, isn't it?'

'Sorry?' said Elliott. 'Yes, Elliott.'

'I think we live opposite you,' she said. 'Emily. We just moved in.'

She unclipped her son from the buggy and her husband pursued him across the playground.

'Oh!' said Elliott. 'I thought I recognised you yesterday.'

'Yesterday?'

'I was trying to place you,' he added.

From this point on he would look back on staring at Emily the day before without shame; he would believe *himself* that he had only been trying to work out how he knew her; he was exonerated and it was all thanks to her.

7

It was a cold morning and Emily was sitting outside her house wearing a coat over her nightdress and shivering with a cup of coffee which billowed with steam like a stage-prop cauldron. She'd been getting up early every day since the move, between 5 and 6 a.m. It wasn't that she was uncomfortable – with the money they'd saved on moving somewhere cheaper they'd bought nice beds and expensive mattresses which were delivered in rolls like cinnamon buns and which, when you cut the cord, unfurled and expanded, hissing. She liked being outside. She felt, for the first time, a sense of belonging and of ownership and it was nice, for an hour or so at least, to enjoy that by herself. The houses had small paved yards instead of gardens, but there was a common lawn, of sorts, between the roads. Some saplings. The committee was planning to develop it and had emailed an artist's impression.

Arthur was still asleep in her bed and it was fifteen minutes before she needed to wake Steven and Matty for work and school. She was watching the sunrise and heard the distant ring of a bell striking seven. She looked across the road at number 37, Elliott and Alathea's house, looking for signs of life.

She had marked Elliott and Alathea out immediately as people she wanted to know: they seemed intelligent and funny and attractive. Although in fact, all she could say for certain was that they were attractive, and maybe that was enough; the rest could be inferred, hoped for, projected if necessary. They had two boys, of similar ages to her own, and it was strange to live opposite this mirror image of her own family. The estate's online directory told her that Elliott was a senior lecturer in Fine Art and Alathea was a psychoanalyst. In the playground Emily had recognised Elliott from his photo in the directory. Unlike the smiley, badly lit snaps of the other residents, Elliott's photo looked like a professional headshot, in profile, gazing soulfully – or, she fancied, a self-conscious parody of soulfully – into the middle-distance, the cover of an alt-country solo album. Alathea's photo was less polished – pointedly so? – but she still looked intimidatingly glamorous, half-scowling, half-smirking in a summer dress and sunglasses, a baby on her lap. Emily had only hesitated to introduce herself to Elliott yesterday in the playground because of past disappointments. The best parents she met before they moved had children her boys wouldn't bond with, so there was never a pretext to see them. It wouldn't necessarily be that they didn't *get on*, rather that they didn't *exist* for one another. They might play side by side in the same room but wouldn't even acknowledge one another's existence and if, on a later occasion, she asked Matty if he wanted to see Alastair or James or Cheyenne, he'd look at her like, *Who?*

The online directory was weird. Emily hadn't got around to entering information for her or Steven yet, so once a day her phone would ping and remind her: *Don't forget to tell us who you are!* She wasn't sure who had set up this initiative but supposed it had something to do with the car pool and the allotment, some progressive aspiration to be a different kind of housing which fostered a sense of community. It was a 'reclaimed' estate, upcycled from aging low-spec newbuilds. If they were shabby they at least had the unspecific glow of being ecologically sound; an aura of virtue provided by customisable wooden slats on the frontages. So what had once been a tract of land full of rows of identical, small, white, detached houses, with access to a motorway overpass and little else, was transfigured by a vision of a more communal, cheaper way of living, environmentally friendly, ethically sound, ambitious to recruit the kind of residents who went for that sort of marketing.

Primarily, though, they were marketed for their low cost, and the fact that they quite literally couldn't afford anything else was something Steven had repeatedly reminded her of when they were first being shown around, whenever Emily opened and closed a plastic window and said something like, 'They are a bit small and crummy, aren't they?'

In the living room there had been a hole in one of the plasterboard walls, which could have been a misplaced hammer blow or a fist. She stood in front of it with Steven for a beat too long.

'That's actually fairly easy to repair,' the agent told them.

'Meh,' said Emily. 'I have a Peter Greenaway poster I can stick over it.'

In the main bedroom she had opened and closed the integral cupboard doors to make sure they weren't just sheer to the wall, Western facades. When she opened the second cupboard a square of light-pink paper fluttered out and landed on her shoe. It was a hand-written note.

Thou art so true
that thoughts of thee suffice
– *Donne*

That was sweet, she thought. It was nice to think that the house's former owner was a fan of Donne, that the kind of people who lived in these houses wrote down bits of Donne sometimes. She folded it and tucked it into her wallet as a lucky charm.

When they made an offer they had had to provide character references, which surprised her as she'd assumed once you were buying somewhere you could be as awful within it as you wanted.

She was about to dash the dregs of her coffee into the gutter when she saw the first-storey window of Elliott and Alathea's house open and the figure of a woman clamber up and then perch on the sill. The woman hesitated, turned and lowered herself down so that she was hanging from the windowsill by her hands. She was wearing a grey-checked shift dress and knee-high boots. Emily crossed the path.

'Alathea?'

'It's further to the ground than I thought,' said Alathea. 'Oh god, I can't hold on.'

'I can catch you.' Emily put her coffee cup on the ground.

'No – I'd hurt you.'

'You can't just fall – you'll break your ankle or something.'

'Shit, I think the sill is giving.'

'Try to land on me.'

Emily held out her arms.

'It's very kind of you,' said Alathea, 'but I'd hurt both of us instead of just me. Fuck, I'm going to fall.'

'I'm going to catch you.'

'Don't.'

Then Alathea dropped down the wall of the house and fell backwards into Emily's arms, who staggered and fell over with Alathea on top of her. Emily hit her head on the grass and her teeth crashed together. Alathea rolled off Emily, holding her knee, and then she laughed.

'Owww. I'm so sorry. Are you okay? You probably think I'm insane.'

'You're bleeding.'

'It's just my knee. I caught it on the … Oh, my god, I'm sorry.' Alathea, having got to her feet, helped Emily up and then took out a tissue to dab the cut on her knee.

'Is everything okay? Were you trying to escape?'

'To escape, yes. The fucking front door is stuck,' said Alathea. 'The main bedroom is the only window big enough to get through – those stupid letterboxes these houses have downstairs. I have to go to work.'

'Is … your husband away?'

'Elliott. He's sleeping. So are the boys. You know some-times you just want to get *going*?' said Alathea. 'A morning without getting covered in cold baby porridge. No lunch-boxes, no tantrums. If you wake everyone up it's … you're *in* the morning then, and there's nothing you can do about it.'

'No, I get that.'

'And I really just wanted to get to work.' She tentatively took a few steps. 'And I seem to be fine, so yay. Are you all right? I'm really sorry – what an introduction.'

'Oh, god yeah, don't worry about me. I'm Emily.'

'Alathea.'

'I looked you up,' said Emily.

'Well, thank you for breaking my fall, Emily.'

'Do you want me to call someone about the door?'

'No! Elliott can deal with it,' said Alathea. She readjusted her jacket. 'Oh fuck, I left my phone inside. Never mind.' She started walking away, then looked back. 'That was really stupid of me and I'm sorry.'

'I hope you get to work on time.'

'Thanks to you,' said Alathea.

After pouring Matty's second bowl of Rice Krispies, Emily stood at the front room window and opened its top pane – which she supposed *was* too small to climb out of. She looked back at number 37. Arthur was temporarily happy in his highchair with a sliced banana and she could hear Steven typing on his laptop upstairs, starting the day's work in the corner of the bedroom before he got to work, which annoyed her – that he was so permanently not-to-be-disturbed. He was a speech therapist. He counselled people out of their stammers or lisps or silences all day and then, when he was at home, wrote reports on their progress.

Elliott, wearing skinny jeans and a torn pink T-shirt, was already ushering Tomasz and Dimitry, the latter leashed on some Thomas the Tank Engine reins, out of the door.

She heard him say, 'Come *on*, Tomasz.'

Without thinking she opened her front door and ran across to him. His children were still loitering in the threshold.

'Elliott!' she said. 'You're setting off really early.'

'Oh hey. We're out of fruit,' he said. 'So we have to stop on the way.'

'But your door's working now?' she said.

'I'm sorry?'

'I had to help Alathea down from the window.'

'What?'

'I saw her an hour ago and she said the front door was stuck.'

'You helped her down from the *window*?' said Elliott.

'She was stuck in the house so …' It occurred to Emily that she was betraying some obscure but significant confidence.

'She's crazy,' said Elliott. 'The door's a bit stiff. I mean she's stronger than *I* am. Tomasz, come on, you can choose *one* toy to bring with you.'

'Maybe it swelled overnight or something,' said Emily. 'Sorry to bother you.'

'Agh, sorry,' said Elliott. 'I'm distracted. I'm very sorry you had to help my wife climb out of the window.'

'I really don't mind,' said Emily. 'Any time.'

'Listen, why don't you all come round to eat on Friday – I know Alathea's been meaning to invite you. It would be great for the boys to meet each other properly.'

'Meet their doubles,' said Emily. 'It's funny they're the same ages isn't it?'

'Oh, you didn't hear?' said Elliott. 'You're the perfect neighbours. We ordered you from a catalogue.'

Emily pursed her lips at him.

When she got back to the kitchen Steven had dressed Matty in his uniform and asked her what was going on and she said it was nothing – they had an invite for dinner on Friday. Steven said he was running late, kissed the boys on the forehead and left.

They crossed the lawn at six on Friday, Steven jaded from work and complaining that he just wanted to lie down. Emily might have acquiesced to this normally, but damn it she wanted to make a good impression and she wanted her husband with her. She told him, in the same breath as she told Matty, who wanted to play on the computer, that he was coming whether he liked it or not.

'Both of you.'

'Both of you,' Matty repeated, sternly.

Alathea and Elliott had two bottles of red wine open to breathe. They had prepared wholemeal pizza bases and provided eight small bowls of toppings for the boys to choose from. Emily's sons enjoyed decorating their pizzas, overloading them with cheese and olives and tomatoes, but then wouldn't eat any once they were cooked. Which was embarrassing; embarrassing to have to apologise for them and explain how picky they were, embarrassing to watch Alathea's children sit up straight and devour two home-made pizzas each, and embarrassing when her children complained about being hungry later on. But she was more bothered by Steven being offensively quiet.

She felt she had to compensate by being extra chatty. When Elliott matched her she was grateful and felt as though she could say more or less anything.

'So what's this about?' she said. 'Everyone I've met here so far is interesting or does something weird or has some kind of creative side-hustle.'

'I make earrings,' said Elliott. 'Alathea runs a meth lab.'

'I play bass in a band called Meth Lab,' said Alathea.

'Math rock. Insufferable. None of this is true, by the way. But yeah,' he said. 'It just seems to have evolved that way. I don't know. We ran out of places in cities to convert into bougie hellholes so we moved onto housing estates.'

'Ha!'

'And you shall know us by the trail of olive stones. I don't think there's anything planned about it. Maybe there is. It was just a fucked up little estate of nineties newbuilds going to seed.'

'Built to the lowest specifications,' said Alathea.

'And it could have just been steamrolled and sold to a luxury condo developer, but someone had the idea to … upcycle it. Insulate the houses properly, make it all kind of eco-focused, stick up some wooden panels.'

'Attract the aging hipsters,' said Emily.

'Blech,' said Elliott, 'But I think that's incidental. You're not allowed to have your own car – a lot of people would find that very off-putting. And the kind of people who *don't* find that off-putting are the kind of people … who …'

'I love it when he tries to talk about class without offending anyone,' said Alathea.

'It's not as if it's an … artists' colony,' said Elliott. 'Which would be, like, horribly exclusive and also just kind of lame.'

'Don't use lame like that,' said Alathea.

'Sorry,' said Elliott. 'I watched a lot of American sitcoms growing up. But then I'm naturally cynical and actually' – he took a swig of wine – 'it has so many genuinely progressive things, right? All the recycling. The little fleet of eco cars with their charging ports.'

'Which you *need*,' said Alathea, 'if you ever want to go anywhere other than an overpass or a ring road.'

'That's not true,' said Elliott. 'You just have to get used to walking a bit more.'

'Right, because we all have so much time on our hands,' said Alathea.

'The nature walk's lovely.'

'Elliott likes to forage.'

'We've been here nearly three years and contributed precisely nothing, but increasingly it seems to attract people who *care* about shit. And it's so cheap,' said Elliott. 'Anton – he lives in the identical house by the pond – Anton used an award from the Arts Council as a *deposit*. I mean someone like Anton should, by all rights, be dead. No, but then there's the recycling and the allotments and the farm shop.'

'Exquisite Crops,' said Emily.

'I mean for fuck's sake, right?' said Elliott. 'But actually it's so great and it has the potential to make the whole estate completely self-sufficient within the next century or so. If the whole country isn't completely underwater by then. Steven what do you do, are you a writer?'

'I'm a speech therapist,' said Steven.

'Ohh,' said Elliott. 'Something actually useful.'

Steven shrugged.

'I mean that's what the world needs,' said Elliott. 'I used to have an appalling stammer. It's kind of gone now. I replaced it with, like, bad diction.'

When they were briefly alone together in the kitchen to choose the third bottle of wine, Emily noticed Alathea was walking with a slight limp.

'You *did* hurt yourself,' she said.

'Oh, I banged my ankle,' said Alathea. 'It's fine. It was so gorgeous of you to try to catch me. The moment you did that, I thought, *This is someone I could really be friends with.*'

Emily laughed. 'That's what I've been getting wrong all these years.'

'And generally speaking I don't like women.'

'I should have tried to catch more people. You don't like women?'

'I don't mean ... I mean it's easy with boys, isn't it?' said Alathea. 'They either fancy you or they don't. Every interaction derives from that *one* thing. God knows what women want from you, ever, really. It's very suspicious.'

'What happened with the door?' said Emily.

'The door? Elliott had it repaired,' said Alathea. 'Rehung it or something. He's actually surprisingly efficient with things like that. Is Steven okay? He's really quiet.'

'He is really quiet,' said Emily. 'I'm sorry.'

'No, no, don't *apologise*, Jesus,' said Alathea. 'Have you just had an argument or something?'

'No,' said Emily. And then she started crying.

'Oh, darling, hey,' said Alathea, putting her hand on Emily's arm.

'No, no, agh,' said Emily. 'I'm sorry. It's completely nothing. Ignore me.'

'You know you can tell me,' said Alathea. 'If something's wrong. Even if I'm off-duty.'

'I'm tired and I'm being an idiot,' said Emily, sniffing and shaking her head, quickly. 'Which is probably Steven's problem too. There's nothing wrong. Ignore both of us.'

Alathea opened a cupboard, took out a bottle of port and poured some into a mug.

'Drink this, quickly,' she said. 'I find it smooths your emotions out into a ... still and placid surface.'

'Thanks,' said Emily.

'I'm glad you're here,' said Alathea. 'The boys are playing together – can you believe it?'

It was almost nine when they got back, 'Two hours past your bedtime!' she said to Matty, who rolled his eyes. She was drunk enough to find the lapse in routine amusing and told him he could watch an episode of *The Magic Schoolbus* with Arthur while they got their pyjamas on. She went to Steven in the kitchen where he was pouring two beakers of squash. It was an effort to speak to him but she managed to say, 'Do you have to be so rude and unfriendly?'

'Sorry?'

'Is it so hard to make an effort? When someone takes you into their home, entertains your children and puts you completely at ease. Is it really beyond you to respond with more than yes and no when they try to get to know you?'

'I didn't have much to say,' said Steven. 'Sorry for not being better company.'

She wasn't sure how to respond, and couldn't tell if he was being passive-aggressive or if she'd hurt his feelings. So she just said, 'I need more from you than this,' and took Matty upstairs to read him a story.

8

'Don't dry up while I'm washing up,' said Alathea. 'I experience it as an erasure of my labour.'

'Fair,' said Elliott.

'Just go and sit on the stairs and listen out for Dimitry.'

Her phone went *bloop* and she dropped the knife she was rinsing and dried her hands. Elliott looked at the screen before she picked it up.

'Jonathon Connell,' he said.

'Yep.'

'Jona*thon*.'

He watched her fingers working quickly and then the phone went *bloop* again and she started texting again before fiddling with the side of the phone and putting it in her back pocket.

'New beau?'

'Nah. Chiropractor. Same building. You know who I think *you* like, though?' said Alathea. '*Emily*.'

'Oh, hush.'

'Ha, you're blushing. No, I think you have very good taste – she's lovely.'

'Yes,' said Elliott. 'She's objectively lovely, like thousands of people.'

'Thousands,' said Alathea. 'Do you think you could love a thousand people? You were doing that thing when you were talking to her—'

'When all of us were talking.'

'That thing where you lean forward on the table. I wanted to put a candle in between you and usher her husband out of the room.'

'Alathea,' said Elliott. 'Don't.'

'You don't think it'd be fun?'

'Don't do the Disney-villain thing.'

'I said I thought she was lovely. If nothing else you could probably make her happy, pay her a little attention.'

'Or we could all be friends,' said Elliott. 'It's nice having friends.'

'That's obviously what I'm talking about,' said Alathea. 'I'm going to text her.'

'They literally just left.'

'Yes, but you have to consolidate these things.' She dried her hands again and read from her phone as she typed. *Emily, babe, it was so lovely to meet you when I wasn't indisposed by hanging from a windowsill, although perhaps in a way we are *all always hanging from a windowsill.* Talk anytime. Love, Axxx.* There.'

'I forgot about that,' said Elliott. 'What on earth were you doing?'

'The door!' said Alathea. 'It wouldn't open at all – it's made of some weird expanding wood. These houses are so silly.'

'I haven't noticed it sticking at all.'

'If you want to make me happy,' said Alathea, 'you can look into getting a new door.'

'I don't know what the problem is,' said Elliott. 'As far as I can tell it opens, it closes, it's a door. If it's an issue for you I'll just get a ladder installed under the bedroom window.'

Alathea checked her phone and put it back in her pocket, then she picked up a chopping board and dipped it in the sink.

'Take him into school on Monday,' she said. 'And talk to Emily – she's sad.'

9

Emily held a permission slip which she had ticked and signed in orange felt-tip. Matty's book bag was looped around the handlebars of his scooter. She kept one hand on Arthur's buggy and one foot on the scooter to stop it rolling away while Matty ran around the playground shouting. Every time he turned to his friend they shouted in each other's faces and laughed before running off again. Emily alternated between watching them run and looking at the sky above the low roof of the building where the reception class were taught. Bare branches against the sky: this, more than any other natural sight, had always caused her to feel grateful – she could forget that she felt awkward or nervous and just trace the pattern with her eyes. *I am glad that I am alive and that I am looking at this.* The other mothers, she'd heard, had set up a WhatsApp group where they exchanged vital information – upcoming school concerts; mufti days (the word 'mufti' made Emily want to retch); social events for parents; gossip, presumably. She wanted nothing to do with it but was still disturbed that it existed. Maybe they talked about *her.* Maybe they thought she was unfriendly and stand-offish, even though she wasn't the one making encrypted closed networks and pointedly not inviting Emily to join.

Every morning everyone around her chatted and smiled and seemed so natural it was as if they were following a brilliantly revised script, where she still had a working draft, and all her parts were non-speaking anyway. It was a familiar feeling: food would stop tasting of anything, the things people said would stop making any sense. She'd learned to tread water and cast around for the nearest flotsam or jetsam to grab hold of. She traced the network of black branches then looked at the school gate. She saw Elliott, his head down as if trying to remember something. Or memorise something. His hair looked wilder than usual, as if he hadn't been to bed.

Matty was by her side again, red-faced and out of breath. He had taken off his coat and, when he handed it to her, she held it out and put one of his arms back into it.

'Come on,' she said. 'It's cold, Matty.' Then he ran away again.

Elliott, like most lecturers she had met, affected a distracted, even put-upon air most of the time, but he was capable of sudden and intense charm, all the more engaging for its intermittence. He seemed, in these moments, profoundly grateful to have clicked with someone, relieved to have found a kindred spirit. Oh, god, she thought.

As he approached, pausing to let a double buggy past, she could see the cloudy, faded stains on the shoulders of his black jacket. Yoghurt or banana or baby sick. Tomasz was still holding his hand. It was sweet, but then it shouldn't really be remarkable if someone was an attentive father, she supposed – it ought just to be standard. 'He's got all my neuroses,' he'd told her, proudly, on Friday.

When Elliott made eye contact with her she felt like shouting and laughing in his face and chasing him around the playground.

He smiled. 'Hello, trouble,' he said.

10

Elliott found the school gates surprisingly testing. He worked less regular hours than Alathea, so it tended to be his duty. It was like socialising distilled to its component parts. Ten minutes, distracted by the daily crisis of confidence his son was going through, the smallest of small talk, micro talk, momentary allegiances with people whose names he kept forgetting but who nonetheless seemed far more real than him. You had to prepare something to say in advance. The easiest thing was just to look kind of thwarted. Not so much that people would think you had a drinking problem, but enough to convey a sense that you were struggling bravely with the work/life balance and just about keeping it together. That was acceptable and close enough to the truth to be easy to exaggerate. Everyone his age seemed shocked by parenthood, as if they'd lacked the basic ability to project forwards before entering into it. And maybe, like him, it was the first time they'd ever had to exert themselves in anything other than minimising their own discomfort.

Tomasz was crying.

'Tomasz, what's wrong?' he said.

Like weddings. There was such an obsession with the beginning, something small and finite and perfectible that it left little or no room for the actual life that was to follow. Had he expected, had they *all* expected, for the babies to stay babies? To be the parents of some tiny babies for forty or fifty years and then cark it leaving a planet crawling with babies?

'Tomasz?'

He picked him up, struck by how tall his son had so suddenly become, but Tomasz struggled to be put down again.

'Well what *is* it, then?' he said. Start each day with several small failures. 'Anyway, you've stopped crying. Are you okay?'

He was relieved to see Emily rather than her taciturn husband standing alone in the playground with her foot on a scooter, staring disconsolately at the sky as if in some form of prayer. He never managed to walk to school with her and Matthew because he was always running late. Emily looked, in that moment, like a woman standing on a cliff awaiting the return from a perilous sea voyage of … It bothered him that he found that attractive. What a stupid thing to think of.

Tomasz took his hand. Elliott gave him an encouraging squeeze – a gesture which, though private and invisible, always felt a little affected to him, an American dad in a movie: *It'll be okay, champ, keep your nose clean*. He all but dragged his son behind him as he marched to Emily.

11

Why had he called her *trouble*? Was that just something he said to people if he liked them? Nobody had ever called her *trouble* in her life. *Was* she trouble?

'Hi,' she said to Elliott.

She realised she was still holding the permission slip and would have to try to hand it in when she came back to pick Matty up. Arthur squirmed in his buggy.

She watched Elliott crouch to the ground and whisper something in Tomasz's ear, then he hugged him and watched him walk through the school doors. Elliott got to his feet and staggered slightly.

'All in,' said Emily.

Elliott was trying to smooth his hair down.

'It's a shame they're in different classes,' he said. 'They got on really well on Friday. Are you busy? Do you have time for a coffee?'

'Oh, always,' said Emily.

'Seeing as we're in town,' said Elliott. 'I swear, the walk from the estate, I've lost over a stone in the last year.'

They walked to a little street of furniture shops and franchise cafés.

'Let's go to the one where they give you free milk for babies,' said Elliott.

Arthur sat on her knee and chewed a hard, flavourless gingerbread man. Elliott bought her a latte and sat opposite her with his macchiato.

'Isn't there that thing,' said Emily, 'that nobody has the little white calcium deficiency marks on their fingernails anymore because we all drink so much milk in our expensive coffees?'

Elliott checked his nails.

'Well, I'll be,' he said.

'Major change of habit within our lifetime, Elliott,' she said. '*So* much milk.'

Elliott took a tentative sip. 'So you work, what, three days a week?'

'Two.'

'And you teach drama, right? Ally was telling me.'

'Yeah,' said Emily. 'Drama, theatre studies. Year 7 through the sixth form. It's … fine.'

He took another sip of his coffee and his face lit up.

'It kind of amazes me that teachers don't *hate* academics,' he said. 'I could never do what you do. I come out in hives if I have to give more than two seminars in a day.'

'It's not so bad,' said Emily.

'No, it *is*,' said Elliott. 'I know it is. You probably teach more in two days than I do in a term.'

'So are you not making any work at all at the moment?

* * *

56

Bored in bed the night before, feeding Arthur every forty minutes, she had googled Elliott and found that he'd exhibited at the Venice Biennale and had work in a number of private collections. Some big three-panel paintings of people with very lost expressions in vast unfriendly landscapes – she liked them. It was funny, it struck her as funny, that a visual artist could be both completely successful and essentially unknown outside of a tiny circle of wealthy specialists. I mean literally nobody gives a shit. Your pieces could sell for six-figure sums, but whatever: they're weird, difficult, awkward, pretentious. Nobody wants to see it. It was like poetry, but with money.

But right now, he'd said in an interview with *Art Monthly* that Emily had read on her phone at 1:40 a.m., *I feel like I need to focus on my kids*. So this was him, two years later, focusing on his kids. He had taken a senior lectureship in the Fine Art department at the local university. *Less travelling, less distraction*, he said. *It's not as if anyone's desperate for my next work.*

'You're *kind*, aren't you?' said Elliott.

'What?'

'Do you know how many people take an interest in someone else's work if they're not being paid to?'

'Well, I have an ulterior motive,' said Emily. 'I'm hoping you can get me access to the uni library.'

'I mean why *would* they? Whole scene is a confidence trick.'

'You're disillusioned.'

'Yeah,' said Elliott. 'No. I don't know. World's ending, Emily. That's totally fine, by the way, I'll give you my login and you can just have a look around the catalogue and tell me which books you need.'

'You're quite … cheerful for someone who's lost all belief in his life's work.'

'No use moping,' said Elliott. 'I'm trying to get better at interrogating my own privilege.'

'Oh boy.'

'I thought that teaching might be a way of—'

'How *is* your privilege?'

'It's great. I thought it might be a way of … getting out of the way, you know? But …'

'You're not working on anything?'

'I get to write articles. I know a bunch of editors, so it feels … effortless. Which means it's worthless. But it's a platform, right? I'm reading.' He undid his jacket and then did it up again. '*Researching*. But I abandoned my last project in my first year of lecturing. It was a whole thing about gun silencers – I got really fascinated by gun silencers.'

'Oh,' said Emily. 'Yeah, I guess they make quite an interesting sound. *Paf.*'

'As a theme, I mean,' said Elliott. 'And in genetics, a silencer is a DNA sequence which … actually I didn't get very far into that. You have to be kind of a magpie.'

'Yeah,' said Emily. '*Caw.* Is that how they sound? Are they silent?'

Arthur dropped his gingerbread man and tried to twist off her lap. Elliott picked it up and brushed it off.

'Here you go, Arthur. A little knowledge is a dangerous thing. Anyway, at the moment I don't feel like I'm ever going to make anything ever again.'

'Oh, don't say that.'

'I can't honestly say *I'd* have studied Fine Art for nine grand a year.'

'*I* think about that,' said Emily. 'I don't think I'd have done drama and English.'

'Joint honours?' said Elliott.

'Yeah – everyone *hated* us. I think I'd have done law or something. Broken my dad's heart.'

'St Martin's,' said Elliott, making a dismayed face. 'The last year group not to pay fees – ugh, we still had *grants*. I had friends in the year below who were like, *Fuuuuuck you*.'

'Oh, I paid a tight three grand a year,' said Emily. 'How old *are* you, exactly? You look about twenty-eight.'

'I mean why would you *not* study Fine Art?' said Elliott.

'Well, if you weren't very good at it, for instance,' said Emily.

'The good thing is, while I don't really know what art *is* or what it's *for* anymore, I get to keep busy with admissions and plagiarism cases and paperwork and talking solidly for two hours at a time while a hundred teenagers stare at me with open hostility.'

'Do you get girls writing messages on their eyelids like in Indiana Jones?'

'Oh, god, no,' said Elliott. 'Ha. I'm a joke to them.'

Arthur, tired of the gingerbread man, had progressed from grousing to openly wailing. It was getting louder and people were looking.

'Sorry,' she said. She unbuttoned her top and undid the clasp of her nursing bra. 'I haven't weaned him yet. I know I should have done by now, it's ridiculous. Do you mind?'

'Oh, please,' said Elliott.

He stared at a poster of coffee beans pouring out of a hessian sack.

'Arthur, Arthur, don't bite.'

'Ally really struggled with …' He seemed to think better of it. He listened to Arthur's gentle suckling, watched the subtle nod of his head. 'There's a Picasso sketch …' he said. He briefly made eye contact with her.

'Woman with Nose On Side of Face?' she said.

'No, it's just a really beautiful naturalistic one of a mother breastfeeding,' said Elliott. 'I'll look it up.'

Emily carefully sipped her latte from above Arthur's head. It was room temperature now anyway. Elliott was checking something on his phone. She watched him jab at it endearingly with one finger, like an ape. Then she realised someone was staring at her. His mouth open, half a toasted cheese sandwich in his hand, the man was wearing a padded blue gilet and glaring at her. It was hard to say whether he was old, or just in his forties and a bit fucked up. When she made eye contact he shifted in his chair.

'Would you mind not doing that?' he said, and, even though he was staring directly at her, it took her a moment to realise he was talking to her.

'I'm sorry?' she said, too quietly.

'I'm trying to have my lunch.'

Emily swallowed. Elliott slammed his tiny espresso cup into its saucer and turned around in his chair.

'*What?*' he said.

'Elliott,' said Emily.

'I wasn't talking to you,' said the man. 'I was asking your wife if she could put her tits away. This is a café. It's disgusting.'

'*You're* disgusting,' said Elliott.

'Plenty of mother and baby groups she could go to,' said the man. 'Or just somewhere more private.'

'Well, I'm afraid we don't have a modesty shield,' said Elliott, standing. 'But I can make you a … *being a cunt* shield if you like?' He stood in front of the man's table and held his jacket open like a screen. 'Enjoy your toastie.'

'Don't start on *me*,' the man said. 'I'm just in here having something to eat. I'm having a bad day.'

'Well it's early yet,' said Elliott. 'And to be clear, I'm doing this so that my friend doesn't have to look at *you*. Let me know if I can shield anyone else from you. Millennials, European nationals. I'll give you my card.'

'Um?' the barista had come round from behind the till. The café was silent and everyone was looking over. 'Is everything okay?'

'One of your customers is harassing my friend,' said Elliott.

'I'm not harassing anyone,' said the man. 'I'm trying to enjoy my lunch.'

'It's … what, half nine?' said Elliott. 'Who has lunch at half nine?'

The barista stood there, passing the surface cloth from hand to hand.

'He seems to think it's not acceptable to nurse a child in public,' said Elliott.

'And he's been swearing at me, fucking this, cunt that,' said the man, 'since we started talking.'

Emily was standing now, Arthur whimpering on her shoulder. With one hand she started to load bags onto the back of the buggy, which then capsized, hit someone else's

61

table and knocked a half-eaten triangle of shortbread onto the floor.

'For fuck's sake,' she said.

'Ask anyone,' the man said. 'They heard him.'

The other patrons of the café took this as a cue to return to their conversations.

'Oh, all of you can go to hell,' said Elliott.

'It really pisses me off,' he said.

'Oh, Elliott, honestly.'

They were walking down the street, Emily still carrying Arthur and pushing the empty buggy.

'I'm sorry. Can I take that?'

'No, it was sweet,' said Emily.

'You're shaking.'

'I'm not shaking.'

'I wasn't trying to … like *save* you.'

'I know.'

'Here, let me,' Elliott took the buggy. 'Fucking people in this stupid country. I wasn't trying to make a point. I was just angry. I'm sorry. You know in Europe … They kick the dogs and make a fuss of the children. Here you could breastfeed a dog and people would probably be fine with it.'

'He was just some sad old man, Elliott,' said Emily. 'Just some nutter, eating a sandwich.'

'I feel like it looked like I was trying to make a big deal out of it, which I really wasn't, I'm sure you can look after yourself, I just lost my temper and I'm sorry.'

'Elliott,' said Emily. 'Stop it. I appreciate it.'

'Okay. I'm sorry for "making a scene" though. I made a

scene. I didn't mean to make a scene. You're still blushing.
I'm sorry.'

'It's fine.'

In her keenness to reassure Elliott, Emily had barely
admitted to herself that she felt, in all honesty, very embarrassed about the whole thing, but it was also a novelty –
and perhaps it was this that made her put the work in – to
feel that someone was on her side.

'Just come to ours for coffee next time. Alathea has at
least eleven different coffee machines. Arthur can play.'

12

'Not working today then?' Alathea punched her on the shoulder.

'You sound like my hairdresser,' said Emily. She let Alathea go in front of her through the narrow school gate. 'I only teach Mondays and Tuesdays.'

'Oh sweet,' said Alathea. 'I'm never in my practice on a Wednesday so we should … hang … out?'

'That would be lovely.'

'Otherwise I'm just walking around and around in circles until he falls asleep.'

'Do you want to come to ours? Arthur, hush.'

'Arthur and Dimitry,' said Alathea. 'Like two little old men playing backgammon outside in a Cold War novel. Names are funny, aren't they?'

'Dimitry, Tomasz,' said Emily. 'Do you have some Eastern roots?'

'No, we're just pretentious,' said Alathea.

They walked back towards the estate. Alathea said the long walks were therapeutic, that all human beings had frustrated nomadic genes.

'You look tired,' she said, looking Emily in the eye as she fumbled with her keys.

'Thanks,' said Emily.

'Sexy but tired,' said Alathea. 'It suits you. Bad night?'

'There are good nights?'

Matty and Tomasz were at school and Arthur and Dimitry had both fallen asleep in their prams – the only place they ever napped during the day – so Emily and Alathea drew the curtains and parked them by the book-shelf. They were both drinking black coffee in Emily's living room. Emily had just painted it a slightly less fake-teeth shade of white and the smell was pleasing, medicinal. It was unusual for the toddlers' naps to synchronise, and rare to be able to finish a conversation. They talked about teething and sleep-training.

'It goes in cycles,' said Emily. 'When Matty was small you were weak and stupid if you didn't do it and now with Arthur you're evil if you do. The place is such a state – I'm sorry.'

'What are you talking about?'

'You've made your house look so classy – it's like completely different on the inside and ours looks like … a community centre—'

'You've *just* moved!'

'—during flood-relief efforts.'

'One of Elliott's old friends is a French polisher,' said Alathea. 'They were at St Martin's together. Happiest man I've ever met – never needs to think about art again. Just *rubs* things forever and they become beautiful. I can put you in touch.'

'I think this is just my nature,' said Emily. 'Motherhood shoved out any aesthetic sensibilities I used to have.'

'I feel bad saying it, but it's *so* boring sometimes, isn't it?' said Alathea. 'I mean I love them. It's terrifying how much I love them, but oh my god, babe.'

Emily topped up their coffees.

'It's epically boring,' she said. 'Some days I feel like micro-dosing LSD just to …'

'Oh, I'm always half-cut on port,' said Alathea. 'You can drink port any time of day – it's like Ribena.'

Emily could sense Arthur starting to grouse before he'd made a sound. She shot up, unclipped him from the buggy and came back in with him on her shoulder, his face tucked into her neck, sobbing.

'Oh, baby boy. Did you have a bad dream?'

'Look, he's falling asleep again,' said Alathea. 'Aw.'

Emily arranged herself on the sofa so that Arthur could sleep on her chest.

'You want me to get a straw for your coffee?' asked Alathea.

'No, it's fine. I'll just lie here and turn to fat.'

'Oh, fuck off,' said Alathea. 'There's nothing to you.'

They were silent for a while and Arthur sank back into sleep. The allotment committee were in the process of shipping in some fully grown trees, their roots compressed in a ball of netting. Already, from the striplings, you could hear birdsong. Emily closed her eyes.

It was funny, wasn't it, Alathea was saying, that their families mirrored each other so directly. That she and Emily had gone part-time, doing two or three days a week. I mean they *could* have stayed full-time and their husbands could have dropped down and done all of the ferrying and nose-wiping.

'I do see Elliott quite a lot,' said Emily. 'Steven maybe does one drop off a year?'

'Oh don't get me wrong,' said Alathea. 'He's very flexible. I just mean I had a full-time job too, you know? And when it came to it, the idea of me keeping the same hours wasn't even on the table – we didn't even discuss it. Default position.'

'We didn't discuss it either, really,' Emily said.

'Some families are probably a lot more progressive.'

'True,' said Emily. 'But some families probably spend half their income on childcare. *Or* their parents do it. Everyone games the system and acts like their very specific circumstances are normal.'

'I mean I'm as bad as anyone,' said Alathea. 'When there's a dad at a Stay and Play I'm all: Aw. Poor guy. This isn't for you.'

'When Steven walks Arthur to sleep he says people look at him like his wife must have died,' said Emily. She laughed, suddenly. 'He read all these books about fatherhood. You know, the sort of books that say, *Don't expect it to be anything like it says in the books.*' She wiped a tear. 'It was sort of endearing.'

'Adonis over there,' Alathea gestured over the road. 'Dude's fucking surgically attached to the Baby Bjorn. Last week I saw him sweeping the roof with his baby strapped to his chest. And I'm all … Do you think he'd carry *me* around in woman-sized Baby Bjorn?'

'Hahaha.'

'Because I'd like that.'

'What does his wife do? Have you met her?'

'I think she's pretty high in some kind of tech start-up.'

'Ohhh,' said Emily. 'Well that explains that. Slumming it.'

'Slumming it up.'

'Millionaires with holes in their shirts.'

'How's Steven?'

'I don't know, he's okay.'

'Ha,' said Alathea. 'Yeah, Elliott too.'

'Steven just seems angry all the time.'

'Men tend to.'

'Oh, no,' said Emily. 'I don't want to get into that kind of stereotyping – it just makes everyone worse.'

'Men work on a points-based system,' said Alathea, 'like the International Baccalaureate.'

'See? Already you sound worse.'

'Like, I had an affair, *but* I just sorted the recycling. And you're *still* giving me a hard time.'

'And women are more like A-levels.'

'Sure. Like your A in Household Maintenance doesn't make up for the E in Fidelity. No Oxbridge for you, pal.'

'Since the boys were born … I mean I'm not blaming the kids or anything.'

'Oh, god no.'

'I adore them,' said Emily. 'I'd kill for them. They're all I think about. But it's as if they've *absorbed* whatever love we had between us.'

'Right.'

'Ugh. As if love is a … liquid. Like it's a finite resource. That's a stupid metaphor.'

'Well, maybe it *is* a finite resource,' said Alathea. 'Genetically. They've probably done tests on mice or fruit flies. On a cellular level …'

'I don't want my cheap metaphors literalised,' said Emily.

'On a cellular level love probably gets generated overnight and depletes throughout the day.'

'Thanks all the same, science.'

'Maybe we should go on dates in the morning. Once they've extracted the … DNA from the fruit flies we'll just be in love with each other all the time.'

Emily sighed. She liked being able to sigh in someone else's presence.

'If someone had asked me in my late twenties if I was happy I think I would have said yes,' she said. 'I think I had a good base-level happiness. But now I think I'd have to say that I was terribly unhappy. Isn't that awful? I want for nothing and I'm unhappy.'

'Oh we're *all* terribly unhappy,' said Alathea.

'I don't know why they don't teach you that at school,' said Emily. 'It must have got cut from the curriculum at the same time as Greek and Latin. Magnets are fun, triangles are weird, you're all going to be terribly unhappy.'

'Curriculum?' said Alathea.

'They don't teach you about citizenship, they don't teach you about taxes and they don't teach you that you're going to be terribly unhappy.'

'Oh, at mine they did,' said Alathea.

'They did?'

'We learned *all* about how shit works. Also Greek and Latin.'

'Ohhh,' said Emily. 'That kind of school. I never like to assume.'

'No, don't worry,' said Alathea. 'I sound posh and I *am* posh and I feel terribly guilty about it.'

'I don't think you should feel guilty.'

'No, well, there's not much point in that, is there? It's about doing something constructive. I take plenty of clients who can't pay. And I get to tell them they're not sad because they're poor.'

'Is that true, do you think?'

'They'd be just as sad if they were billionaires. And they'd be sitting there with someone like me trying to work out why that was.'

'So,' said Emily, 'and sorry if this sounds rude, but what are you doing … here?'

Alathea laughed. 'What's wrong with here?'

'Are *you* slumming it? You and Elliott? I mean it's great,' said Emily. 'And I'm very glad you live here. But isn't it a bit below your—'

'Ohhh,' said Alathea, 'we had to move quite suddenly – bit of a messy situation I'll tell you about when I'm drunk sometime. But really we had a lovely house ever so slightly above our means … Elliott hadn't even been made permanent yet – we had some cash-flow problems and the last thing I wanted was to go back to my parents for help. Nobody ever talks about how complicated it can be having wealthy parents – they're not necessarily going to help you and you don't necessarily want to ask.'

'No.'

'You can end up as fucked as everyone else. The more we looked into it the more this place seemed like a fun stopgap until we got our shit together.'

'Oh,' said Emily. 'I mean, yeah.'

'But one evening about a year ago I was driving home from work and I got this feeling of … warmth as I entered the estate – it felt like home.'

'This is our first house,' said Emily. 'I know it's cheap-as, but the deposit wiped us out, so we're still sort of … adjusting. Saving up for a nice table. Wood seems to be more expensive than gold these days.'

'Well, you've done really well then,' said Alathea. 'I'd love to feel more like I'd actually achieved everything on my own terms. Do you want a table? You can take ours when I replace it – you'd be doing me a real favour.'

'That's … really kind.'

'I mean it. But anyway, my parents were in the process of retiring when they took an unexpected hit – account was mismanaged, something fell through. They're fine but of course they made a massive drama out of it. They had to move to their third home on the Gower Peninsula and of course they apparently still have to work, which means we see them about once every six fucking months. I could really do with a date.'

'You can leave the kids here!' said Emily. 'Go on dates!'

'Oh, you're sweet,' said Alathea. 'Maybe we could arrange some kind of regular exchange.'

'Yeah,' said Emily. 'Except Steven doesn't *like* anything. Theatre, cinema, music. Restaurants make him feel sad.'

'Well, just leave the kids at ours and you can go home and have sex,' said Alathea.

'Ha,' said Emily.

'He likes *that*, right?'

'Well …'

'Fox like you. No?'

'You're the only person who's ever found me that attractive, Alathea.'

71

'Bullshit,' said Alathea. 'Have you considered, Emily, that he might be a bit depressed?'

'I think he's just a grumpy sod.'

'People never think fatherhood … I mean a lot of men really struggle and it doesn't get talked about.'

'He's really good with the kids.'

'Hmm,' said Alathea, as if that was quite beside the point.

'When Matthew was born,' said Emily, 'I had pretty bad post-natal depression.'

'Oh, you poor thing, that's rotten.'

'I say pretty bad,' said Emily. 'I mean it was bad. It was severe. For six months I was completely unhinged. And then again with Arthur … I feel as though Steven's never really forgiven me.'

'*Forgiven* you?' said Alathea. 'Jesus, Emily. It's not like—'

'I know, that's not what I—'

'That's completely irrational.'

'Is anything rational?' said Emily. 'Anything that any of us feels? I'm sure he doesn't *want* to resent me. I'm sure he'd much rather be in love with me.'

'Of course he loves you,' said Alathea. 'Who wouldn't?

13

Marketa and Stefan, a couple of graphic designers who lived at number 17, had invited them over for a house-warming party. Emily said, Oh, but the kids and Marketa said, No, no, everyone has babies, that's one of the reasons we moved here, it's great. The ground floor of their house was open plan and minimal. Piles of pastel-coloured suit-cases lined the walls for storage. There was a vast lightshade in the centre of the ceiling which looked like a giant wasps' nest, glowing ominously.

'Wow,' said Emily. 'It's like a show home. I mean … sorry. You really don't have crap just everywhere and I'm envious.'

Marketa laughed at her and her white-blonde bob shook like a pompom.

'For us it is ideal,' she said. 'Because we are terrified of disorder.'

Emily looked around the room. She counted twenty Criterion residents. The table was laid with a pile of paper plates and three giant bowls of pierogi with various fillings and five dishes of brightly coloured pickled cabbage with different herbs and seeds.

Steven immediately skewered a dumpling on a fork and ate it.

'You like it?' said Marketa. 'I make the best pierogi.'

Please don't, thought Emily. Please don't ask him for some demonstration of gratitude or basic politeness. He won't do it. He won't. But actually Steven, although more or less completely silent, ate three plates of pierogi with several ladles of cabbage. This seemed to satisfy Marketa more than any verbal praise or validation.

The walls were clear and white except for a sharply framed painting of the estate in the hallway. It was pale, washed-out, almost, but with very clean lines – it could have been the street she was on right now, but judging by the position of the birch forest, it was maybe her own. Past the houses there was a single figure in a long coat with a small black dog.

'You like?' said Marketa.

'It's calming,' said Emily.

'Stefan's,' said Marketa. 'He doesn't believe me when I say he's good. He sees it as technical drawing.'

'Is that Magda? The little person?'

'I don't know,' said Marketa. 'Who is Magda? Oh wait, I think I know who you mean. I think it just needed something there.'

Eight children were watching a stream of *SpongeBob SquarePants* in a purpose-decorated TV room with no breakables or sharp corners. The walls were dark blue and stencilled with constellations. Ugh – why did she and Steven never do things like that? Their entire home was just a scree of broken plastic toys. Why were they so low functioning in comparison to everyone else? The gloom threatened to engulf her, so she went to the buggy at the back of the room where Arthur was asleep and adjusted the blanket. Matthew sat quietly in a row between Tomasz and Marketa's daughter Lily, all of them transfixed by the screen, occasionally turning to laugh at one another or repeat one of Patrick or SpongeBob's lines.

'Are you okay, Matty?' Emily stroked his hair. He ignored her. He was right, as children always are about that sort of thing. Why was she even asking? She could see that he was okay. All she wanted was some kind of permission not to feel guilty about drinking wine and socialising in the other room. Why was she asking a five-year-old that? 'Good boy,' she said. 'Come and get me if Arthur wakes up, okay?'

Emily topped up her white wine in the kitchen and saw her husband sitting with Alathea and Elliott around a Romanesque mosaic table in the corner of the double living area. She sat with them, tried to lean against Steven, but it was as though he wasn't there, so she sat up straight. The conversation had turned to Jenny, who lived with her two teenage daughters in number 45 – the house with the sparkly pink slats, she ascertained. It matched her phone cover. Every other weekend their father would arrive in a black 4x4 and drive the girls away, returning them on the Sunday evening wearing brand new outfits. Textbook, was the general feeling. Arsehole.

'The thing is,' said Alathea, 'there's probably going to be less and less of that, isn't there?'

'What do you mean?' said Elliott.

'We could never afford to divorce. It's beyond impractical.' She took a handful of vegetable crisps, picked out the beet-root ones and gave them to Elliott. 'It's literally impossible.'

'I don't know,' said Elliott. 'I could get a little bedsit in town. Throw up some movie posters. All I need is a laptop and a kettle.'

'Get into heroin, maybe. Look at him, dreaming. Even a little bedsit,' said Alathea. 'How are you going to meet the rent on that while paying our mortgage and child support? What would you eat? I mean I could take the boys and move back to my parents', I suppose. Move in to their two-bedroom cottage full of ... glass sculptures. I'm sure they'd be thrilled.'

'Haha,' said Emily. 'You two.'

'I'm serious,' said Alathea. 'You get to a certain point and divorce is as much of a luxury item as a ... fucking yacht. Stable of ponies. We actually need to readjust our most basic expectations.'

'People a lot poorer than us,' said Elliott, 'get divorced all the time.'

'Yes, and the state looks after them?' said Alathea. 'I mean is that what happens? I don't even know. Anyway, I don't think we qualify for that because we're middle-class professionals.'

'Ally expected more out of life than this,' said Elliott, smiling.

'All the good that's done us.'

'Her mother warned her not to marry down.'

'Oh, mother foresaw everything,' said Alathea.

'She'd occasionally look up from her copy of *How to Spend It* to dispense some pretty sage advice,' said Elliott.

'I'm not really being serious,' said Alathea, grinning at Emily and Steven. 'You two couldn't afford to separate either, right?'

'Shit, it would be a nightmare,' said Emily. 'And, I mean, the children, you know? It's here or the Salvation Army.'

Steven tore a strip of paper off his stubby bottle of beer. 'And here's pretty good,' he said.

At this point Emily leaned into him again, quite over-whelmed by a burst of thankfulness for his eating three plates of pierogi and saying one small thing which wasn't negative. She felt electrified when he put his hand on her arm.

'Oh, don't get me wrong,' said Alathea. 'Here's great. I love it.'

14

Emily had five tabs open on her laptop and a pile of mock exam scripts to mark, but when her mother called she was halfway through level 178 of *Candy Crush: Soda Saga* on her phone and she felt momentarily annoyed when it disappeared.

'Hello?'

'Emily – is everything "okay" still?'

'Of course,' said Emily. 'You?'

'Oh, I'm fine, thank you. My shift doesn't start until four. Dad's in the garden.'

'You're checking in.'

'Is that what they call it?'

'To make sure I'm okay. Mum, that's sweet, but I'm fine – today's fine.'

'I'm not hovering,' said her mother. 'I can be concerned without hovering.'

'Yes,' said Emily. In her head the game continued: the twinkly soundtrack, the soft tactile appearance of the coloured sweets she'd been rearranging until they popped and disappeared. 'Yes. I have a lot of work and I'm anxious about it, but who doesn't – who isn't?'

'Sometimes you call me and you're quite distressed, and

then you calm down, but I'm left wanting to make sure that you're actually okay.'

'Do I *do* that?' said Emily. 'That doesn't sound like something I'd do.'

'And then you get salty.'

'I do not.'

'So you can see this as a form of aftercare. Are the boys all right?'

'The boys are great.'

'And Steven?'

'He seems hale and hearty.'

'If I can come over – I'm on call quite a lot this month, but if I can look after Matty and Arthur and give you some time together …'

'No, oh god, it's fine, don't.'

'Because you know it's important that you get at least *some* time together as husband and wife. You need to check in on each other.'

'*Do you still love me?*'

'That sort of thing.'

Husband and wife still struck Emily as something of a novelty after eight years.

'Something that I like about Steven,' said her mother, 'is that he never really bears a grudge or any resentment about anything.'

'Yes, he's like an Etch-a-Sketch, shake him and he's blank again.'

'Do you remember that terrible muddle we got into when the kitchen was being extended? I was quite unreasonable with him, and when he'd been kind enough to help us.'

'Actually, I don't think I remember that at all,' said Emily.

'No, you were quite depressed. Really, I started talking to him as though he was an employee – I still feel bad about that. But with Steven, he just …'

'He resets.'

'It's called forgiveness. He has strength of character. You know when you were first together, I thought he was altogether too quiet and I—'

'Yes, you used to say *You're too quiet* to him.'

'I certainly didn't.'

'*You're too quiet, I never have any idea what you're thinking.*'

'But it's actually …'

'Really put him at ease, Mama.'

'He's thoughtful and he's kind and he doesn't need to go to great lengths to demonstrate that. Eventually you see him for who he is and it's *good* and constant, and I don't know if you appreciate how rare that is.'

'No, I *do*,' said Emily. 'No bullshit.'

'And that's important, in the end,' said her mother. 'Once our thin veneers of charm have worn away. You know most of the patients I work with have very little of themselves left …'

'Mum.'

'You hate me talking about my patients.'

'I just don't want to hear about people dying in terror and misery right now.'

'I was building,' said her mother, 'to a life-affirming moral conclusion.'

'I know, in your Radio 4 voice.'

'That was *Thought for the Day*,' said her mother. 'Well, darling, I'm glad you're happy.'

'Ugh, I didn't say I was *happy*.'

'You can only be as happy as your unhappiest child.'

Emily laughed as if her mother had been joking.

'Love you lots.'

15

The Criterion Gardens playground was deserted, as if something terrible or brilliant had happened and Emily hadn't heard about it. Was it that people barely left their houses? That was supposed to be the case if you listened to the commentators, everyone terrified in their living rooms and barely moving, but reality rarely mapped onto the narrative. There was a child-obesity epidemic but Emily didn't recall seeing a single obese child since she'd been at school herself. Matty and his contemporaries were too thin, if anything. It was another thing that just didn't seem to apply, of which they'd opted out. They had chosen to live among the skinny children.

She could see Magda walking her dog on the path opposite and wondered if she could avoid talking to her, but Arthur was toddling in her direction and no matter how she tried to redirect him he turned and pursued his route to the wilderness area — some vestigial memory of blackberries — and it began to seem inevitable that their paths would cross.

'It's Emily,' Magda said.

'Hello,' said Emily. 'Aren't you hot? I'm just out with Arthur.'

'So I see.'

'As far as I'm aware I haven't dropped anything today,' said Emily.

'After we talked last time,' said Magda, 'it came back to me, what I felt I had to say to you.'

'Oh, really?'

'You have a sweet nature.'

'No, I don't think so,' said Emily, smiling.

'You need to be careful,' said Magda. 'How are you feeling? In this little purgatory?'

'Oh, it's hardly purgatory,' said Emily. 'I feel very lucky to be here.'

'Hmm,' said Magda. 'What do you see as the point of it all? What would constitute a good life, for you?'

'Are you a writer?' said Emily.

'Oh, dear no, absolutely not.'

'Sorry,' said Emily. 'It's just everyone I've met so far has been … something.'

'My husband was a poet. He died five years ago.'

'I'm so sorry.'

Magda seemed pleased by this. 'Yes, there's little worse than being married to a poet. Everything is material.'

'That's not—'

'Of course. But one could really choose anything. To account for the best and the worst. Astrology, psychoanalysis, religion.'

'Logical positivism,' said Emily.

'Order,' said Magda. 'There are really innumerable systems with which one could reinterpret the same life.'

'Mostly,' said Emily, 'I just try to get through each day. Arthur come back!'

'I know that's not true,' said Magda.

'Well it's more of a patchwork,' said Emily. 'I admire people who seem to be able to commit to one thing. But I think mostly you believe what's familiar or what seems to be true. Lightly.'

'Until things get desperate,' said Magda.

'Is this what you needed to tell me?'

'It came back to me while I was going through his papers last night. Bob's. He wrote these tiny stalactites of poems. He was fairly well thought of in the States.'

She gave Emily a scrap of paper, a photocopied text, the font blurry at the edges.

so write
to let it be written
that he wrote of her
to mistake
the vista
for the painting
for her
regarding the painting

'That's pretty,' said Emily. 'I'm sorry – I have to follow Arthur. It was lovely to see you, Magda.'

'When we are going to take a journey,' said Magda, 'we prepare for it, but in ways we barely even notice.'

'Oh, I'm not going anywhere,' Emily waved and walked backwards a couple of steps before turning.

'I don't think she really told me anything,' she said to Arthur.

* * *

Elliott was approaching the playground with Dimitry, taking his arm when he stumbled in his training shoes. Elliott was dressed unusually smartly, in jeans which matched the colour of his jacket so that it almost looked like a suit.

'Hey you,' she said. 'I brought a flask of coffee.'

'God, Emily,' he said, quietly. 'Why were you talking to that mad old bitch?'

'Elliott!'

'What? She's awful.'

'You don't sound like yourself. She's actually quite interesting – cuts straight to big talk.'

'I hate her.'

'Why?'

'She scares Tomasz. Like deliberately – glares *theatrically* at him when we walk past. Why would you want to scare a seven-year-old? So I just say, loudly, *Ignore her, Tomasz, some people are very troubled.*'

'Wow,' said Emily. 'That's not very nice. I don't know her or anything – she just helped me when I lost my phone.'

'When we moved here she turned up at our house on the second day and said her old neighbours used to let her cross through their yard and throw her bag over the fence because it's a real shortcut when you're carrying shopping, so she was checking that that was still okay and we were like, Well no, it's not okay, sorry, we don't want people walking through our yard. And then she did it anyway, so we had to confront her again. It really upset Ally.'

'Ugh,' said Emily. 'Okay, that's weird.'

'I mean we could have just *let* her, I suppose. I just—'

'No, you have every right to want some privacy in your own home.'

'Right? And ever since then it's like we're her enemies.'

'Which means it's probably best for me to stay on the right side of her.'

'Or ignore her altogether,' said Elliott.

'I can't,' said Emily. 'I can't ignore someone if they're trying to talk to me. I can't do it – it's too rude.'

'*She's* rude,' said Elliott. 'But no, I get that. I can't do it either.'

'Obliging twins,' said Emily.

'Yeah, it's one of our tragic flaws. High five.'

'How are you today?'

'How *am* I?' said Elliott. 'I've got some marking which I plan to complain about a lot. Other than that it's just a day, really. I can't believe they keep on coming.'

'Oh, they *do*.'

'Just one after another. I got that book you wanted.'

He handed her a library paperback reinforced with thick clear plastic.

'*The Disinherited Mind!*' said Emily. 'It's so sweet you remembered.'

'I skimmed through it. It's a riot. We live in a state of mental and spiritual impoverishment and, because truth is so degraded, art has to fill in the gaps, but it's not up to it. So we're screwed.'

'I'll read it fast and get it back to you.'

'No, keep it,' said Elliott. 'Someone in the library likes me and they just automatically cancel any fines I accrue.'

'Is that how you go through life?'

'What?'

'With a charm exemption.'

'Oh. Well, as much as possible.'

'Never paying your dues.'

He took the flask and poured a capful of coffee, then balanced it on the fence post and added something from a silver hipflask.

'Not so far.'

16

When Elliott entered the kitchen to make a second pot of coffee Alathea was leaning against the sink trying to unlock his phone.

'You've changed your passcode.'

'It prompted me.'

'Hmm. Remind me who Donna is?'

'A colleague,' said Elliott. 'My boss, in fact. They made her take head of department.'

'Uh huh. Does Donna always sign off with three kisses?'

'That's Donna.'

'Affectionate.'

'Inappropriately so.'

'Are you feeling all right?' said Alathea. 'Do you need to sit down?'

'I'm quite all right, Al.'

'I don't really expect honesty, Elliott. You involve me, is the rule. You know that. I was curious as to what you'd said to her that would make her reply *I know. xxx*. Work stuff?'

'We're dealing with a problematic student.'

'If it was something like *I could never leave Alathea and the kids*. So I thought I'd *check*, but you've changed your passcode.'

'Ha,' said Elliott. 'Yeah, it prompts you to change your passcode once a year. Ally, I know there's nothing I can do to make you trust me if you don't already, really—'

'There is. You can tell me your passcode.'

Alathea held his iPhone over the sink, which was full of soapy water from washing up the kids' breakfast things. A single Coco Pop floated among the continents of bubbles.

'Oh no,' he said, rubbing his face. 'Not now.'

'Is that close?' she said. '*I'll always love you, Donna? I know. xxx.*'

'Don't be a child, Alathea,' he said.

'Oh, I'm going to be a very *bad* child,' said Alathea.

Elliott crouched to open the second drawer by his knee. He rifled through it and pulled out a meat mallet. It had a wooden handle and a silver cube-shaped head with metal spikes on both sides, like a weapon in a comic book. He stood, threw it in the air and caught it by the handle. Alathea looked at her new iPad, charging from a wall socket, camouflaged against the black worktop. She pursed her lips.

Elliott raised the meat mallet.

'I have photos I haven't backed up,' said Alathea.

'That's good. Maybe you should give me my phone.'

'Client notes from the last four days. Films – I know you don't care about them because you're the only one who's allowed to be creative.'

'I hate that word.'

'You're a *creative*, Elliott.'

'I especially hate it as a noun.'

'I mean I know how it works. One day I get to publish an autobiography about what a terrible person you were, but until then.'

'I've never been sure,' said Elliott, 'what it is I'm supposed to have done to you.'

'No, you're right, it's fairly subtle. I never really liked the name Donna, it's one of those names …'

Elliott turned the meat mallet – which they had never, to his knowledge, used to tenderise meat – as if to inspect it.

'But the thought of you saying it – I imagine you say it to her quite a lot because you like saying women's names. To them. You work them like a politician. It's quite cute. Say it.'

'No.'

'Say Donna.'

'I'm not saying it.'

Alathea pretended to fumble the iPhone over the sink and caught it again.

'Say Donna, three times, and I'll give you your phone and you can continue your conversation with her.'

'Nope.'

'We'll say nothing more about it. You might want to set her some guidelines – no messaging unless you instigate it, that sort of thing.'

'This is a fairly boring misunderstanding.'

'Then you can really get her pining for you. Say it? Donna?'

Elliott shook his head.

Alathea, without breaking his gaze, plunged the iPhone into the water, holding it down as if she were drowning it.

Elliott said nothing, and let nothing flicker across his face, although he could – and this both troubled and delighted him – feel himself getting hard. He brought the meat mallet down in the centre of Alathea's iPad's screen. It didn't do very much so he raised it and struck the iPad again, then a third time, harder, so that the glass shattered.

Alathea's breathing was short. She looked at him, then she looked at her cracked iPad. Elliott struck it with the mallet again. Tiny crumbs of silver glass dusted the work-top. She bolted from the room. He heard her feet on the stairs.

'I'm not chasing you, Alathea,' Elliott raised his voice. 'No running, no touching.'

'I didn't mean to run!' she called from the landing. 'I'm going to throw your iMac out of the window.'

'Oh, for god's sake.'

Elliott glanced around the kitchen. If you couldn't find something of a similar monetary value it could be compensated by sentiment. There were some crystal champagne flutes on top of the cupboard – the original set had been a wedding gift, but Alathea had already replaced them with a completely identical set after last time.

His legs were shaking but he did his best to walk calmly up the staircase and hoped she hadn't heard him stumble on the top step. When he opened the door to the study Alathea had opened the window wide and was holding, with some difficulty, his 27" iMac two floors over the concrete yard. It was still switched on and displayed his inbox and a work email he was halfway through writing.

He laughed.

'Intel core i5,' she read from the back of the screen. '8GB RAM, 2TB Fusion Drive, AMD Radeon R9. Could you get the plug for me?'

'I have a lot of work on there, Alathea.'

'That's a shame. Oh—' She pulled the power cable out of the back of the screen. 'Never mind – it came out this end.'

Elliott scanned the shelves and pulled off Alathea's first edition of *Anne of Avonlea* by L. M. Montgomery.

'I think this is roughly equivalent,' he said. 'It's in unusually good condition for … was it 1909?'

'You'd know,' said Alathea.

'Yes, paper anniversary,' said Elliott.

'You've always been uxorious.'

He opened the book in the middle and fanned it out. He began to force the hard covers open a little wider – a susurration and a crack.

Alathea gasped and looked as though she might burst into tears. She leaned out of the window and hoiked the iMac onto the ledge.

'Don't make me—'

'Rules,' said Elliott. 'No *don't make mes*.'

'Okay. I'm calling your bluff.'

'Really?'

Elliott bent the covers back so that they were touching, clamped them in one hand so the pages fanned out like a rolodex and ripped out a handful.

'Fuck,' said Alathea, lifting the iMac over the ledge. She half threw, half dropped it out of the window. The crack was surprisingly loud.

Elliott wrenched *Anne of Avonlea* in two, tearing it down the spine. The sunlight picked out the cloud of dust, the frayed green threads.

They looked at each other, their chests rising and falling.

Elliott placed the two pieces of the novel on the desk and walked to the window. The iMac was lying in two bits, face up on the patio, a lightning crack across its vast screen.

'Do you want to finish it off with the mallet?' he said.

'No,' said Alathea. 'Just do me over the windowsill. God, what's the time?'

'Two forty-five.'

'Oh my god,' she started undoing her belt. 'Quickly.'

It was three-fifteen but the school doors were yet to open and Emily stood shivering and not talking to the other parents who stood in groups of three or four or five. She took a fragmented tissue out of her coat pocket and tried to blow her nose. She felt congested and self-conscious and the moment to make introductions seemed to have passed some time before they moved to the area, allegiances formed, codes agreed. She wasn't sure who to blame – either she had developed social anxiety, or she was surrounded by unfriendly people. Where was Elliott? Or Alathea?

Matty was first out when the doors opened and he flew at her and wrapped his arms around her leg.

'Hello, gorgeous. You've got a sticker.'

'For being silent,' said Matty.

'That's good.'

'Can we get a treat?'

'Okay.'

'And can we get one for Tomasz?'

'If you can bear to wait.'

One by one the children were paired up with their custodians until all that remained was Tomasz. He stood holding the corner of his teacher's coat, looking sad.

Emily was about to go over and say something when Alathea sprinted past her and stopped, one hand supporting herself on the railing, saying something to the teacher. Then she scooped Tomasz up while he was in the middle of taking off his rucksack so that he dangled it along the ground as she staggered back to Emily.

'Hey.'

Alathea was red and breathing heavily. It was the first time Emily had seen her looking anything other than well-turned out and collected. Even after falling from her son's window she had the air of somebody who *ought* to have just fallen from a window.

'Ally, are you okay?'

'Gah,' said Alathea. 'I hate being late. It's terrible.' She put Tomasz down. 'I'm sorry, baby. I need to recover from the run.' She turned to Emily. 'Thank you so much for waiting with him.'

'Sure.' Emily cleared her nose. 'You know I can bring Tomasz back if you ever need me to.'

'That's sweet.'

'Did something happen?'

'No, I got held up with a phone call. I lost track of time. Silly Mummy.' She ruffled Tomasz's hair.

17

After a while you stop pushing for something. Maybe that's unfair. Maybe you need to just keep saying what you want, keep driving on the same road. But that's not what you do. You find an alternative route.

Steven was tapping his phone more intently than usual.

'Are you okay?'

'Yeah,' said Steven. 'No. Mum was attacked by another resident.'

'Attacked?' said Emily. 'Oh my god.'

'She's okay.'

'Should we go over?'

'I'll go after work tomorrow,' said Steven. 'I'm just booking the little car. You don't need to.'

'I *want* to go with you. I want to be a supporting, loving wife.'

'No,' said Steven. 'No, I know you do. It's good of you. They can't deal with the boys so only one of us can go anyway.'

'And she doesn't like me, I realise that.'

'It's not really *her*,' said Steven.

'She hates me.'

'She doesn't even know who you are.'

'That makes two of us.'

'Em.'

'No, of course, I don't take it personally. Steven, I'm so sorry.' She put her hand on her husband's shoulder and he smiled as if amused by something.

'It's fine.'

'Look, this is horrible and you're stressed. I'll take the boys to Alathea's and you can catch up on work,' said Emily. 'Or just have a rest.'

'Oh,' said Steven, brightening. 'Okay. Great.'

Matty and Tomasz made aquarium dioramas for school – a project Emily had completely forgotten about but it was okay because Alathea had a whole cupboard of craft materials – while Arthur and Dimitry smeared glitter glue over a dozen pieces of paper, and now they were watching Disney's *Aladdin*. Emily sipped her fourth glass of prosecco and then noticed that Alathea was gently snoring next to her.

'A whole new woooooooooorrrrrld,' Emily sang along, softly.

'Hey,' said Elliott, taking Emily's arm.

'Don't you *dare* close your eyes,' she sang at him. Then she stood and followed him out of the room.

'You can tell me some of the books you wanted from the university library.' He grabbed a piece of paper from the art table and folded it in two. 'If I can find something that isn't a glitter-glue pen.'

'Oh, here,' said Emily, going through her pockets. She handed her pen to him; he turned it over and inspected it from every angle.

'You chew pens,' he said.

'What?' said Emily. 'Oh, god, sorry, gross.'

'The Pentel V5,' said Elliott, 'if I'm not mistaken, has – or *would* have – a small clear plastic dome on top of the lid, containing a tiny rubber colour-indicator. It's missing.'

'Uh huh. I chewed it off.'

'I mean, the potential for choking and/or tooth-chipping, given the compound inserts and position of the metal pocket clip' – Elliott flexed the metal pocket clip in front of her – 'makes the Pentel V5 one of the most dangerous pens on the market for the orally fixated. But that removable tip.' He whistled. 'Irresistible.'

'I'm clearly a connoisseur,' said Emily.

'You can't really beat the classic biro, though,' said Elliott.

'I hate writing with biros,' said Emily.

'Me too,' said Elliott, 'but they make for some great chewing. The standard biro has that little plastic plug in the end, you know. It takes a while to work it out, worrying the edges with your teeth, gnawing the clear outer casing – it can take a day or two of making marks against that – when all of a sudden it slides out against your front tooth. And then you just have a chewing orgy.'

'If you get it into a certain position you can get it stuck to the end of your tongue, like a sucker,' said Emily.

'You certainly can,' said Elliott. 'God, it's like I'm chewing one now.'

'And you chew it and chew it until it's flat, until you flatten the stopper against the … shaft of the stopper,' said Emily. 'And then the side splits so you can't get it stuck on the end of your tongue anymore.'

'Do you like to lean back on chairs, as well?'

'This is some weird school fetish, isn't it?' said Emily. 'You want to dress up as a teacher and tell me off.'

'No, not at all,' said Elliott. 'I'm relieved to find a kindred spirit. I'm never happier than when I'm leaning back on the rear two legs of a chair, chewing the end of a pen.'

'A choking fetish, then.'

'No, choking is a real fear,' said Elliott. 'I mean I haven't really worked through that yet.' He paused. 'I appreciate how it looks, leaning back precariously with the equivalent of a pop-gun in your mouth, but that's not—'

'No, okay.'

'The biro stopper, yeah, once you've lost it, which you always do eventually.'

'Oh yeah, eventually it goes.'

'I mean, I feel like we can be totally honest here, the first couple of times the stopper falls on the floor, you get down on your hands and knees and you look for it, find it and stick it back in the end of the pen, admonish yourself for the disgusting habit and within minutes you're chewing it again.'

'Blech,' said Emily.

'But true,' said Elliott. 'And the floor germs are good for the immune system. Now, the *lid*, the biro lid with its plastic pocket clip, which you can worry and weaken and then just tear off like a lion ripping the leg of a gazelle, the lid you've probably lost ages ago.'

'The lid is long gone,' agreed Emily.

'So,' said Elliott, leaning forward and speaking in a conspiratorial whisper. 'You chew the end of the biro casing itself, even though it's brittle and comparatively pleasureless. You chew it until it cracks into these *flints* of plastic – really rich-tasting plastic. It's how I've always imagined stunt glass would taste. If you ate some stunt glass.'

'And you chew it even though sometimes you get a bit of your lip caught between the cracks in the plastic,' said Emily.

'Yeah, that really hurts,' said Elliott. 'You maybe snap a couple of the fragments in your mouth, but you always spit it out, the shards. The saliva-soaked shards of plastic.'

'There's not much pleasure in the shards,' said Emily. 'And you've broken off quite a bit of the casing and that leaves some of the tubing of the biro *proper*, the thin tube of ink with the nib on the end, jutting out like a bone sticking out of a broken leg. And you start biting off pieces of the tubing.'

'The soft, soft tubing,' said Elliott, closing his eyes.

'That's the real, I don't know, the *yolk* of the biro, right?' said Emily.

'And you chew the pieces you bite off until they're flat, and you discard them one by one,' said Elliott. 'And you always go too far or, I don't know, the residual suction creates some kind of vacuum and the ink squirts into your mouth. Tastes like a hot coal.'

'Oh, god, I've *done* that,' said Emily.

'We've all done it,' said Elliott. 'It leaves a black mark on your tongue. Number of times I've tried to scrub that off, the mark and the taste, scrub that away with a toothbrush.'

'Ugh,' said Emily. 'What's wrong with us?'

'This is just textbook Freud,' said Elliott. 'I've never studied it or anything, but the orally fixated adult – and you're orally fixated if you were either under- or over-fed at your mother's breast, so it's not uncommon – the orally fixated adult is extremely emotionally manipulative when it comes to getting what they want.'

'Ouch,' said Emily, who had always feared that she might be extremely emotionally manipulative. She had taunted herself with it so much that it had come to be easily dismissible as self-cruelty, but the thought that it might be, after all, true made her feel dizzy for a moment.

'Only it's not so bad,' said Elliott, 'because all they really want is oral stimulation. So, for instance, I might emotionally manipulate you into giving me a lollipop.'

'How would you do that?'

'Just by dropping hints at first,' said Elliott. 'But then I'd get kind of passive-aggressive about it.'

'I'll be on my guard.'

'You should always be on your guard against the orally fixated,' said Elliott. 'The symptoms, just so you can look out for them, are garrulousness, drinking to excess, smoking. And absent-mindedly – like it's the brain's default position – seeking oral stimulation at every opportunity. Pen chewing, for example.'

'Agh,' said Emily. 'I do *all* of those.'

'Why did you let me fall asleep?' said Alathea, appearing in the doorway. 'The boys might have drawn on me.'

Emily felt as though she'd been caught in something and put the pen back in her pocket.

'You need to rest,' said Elliott.

'Oh, gosh, it's way past Matty's bedtime,' said Emily.

18

Emily was cooking pasta for a bake. The kitchen had steamed up, but when she tried to open the window the handle gave a loud crack and she found that she couldn't close it again. She opened her laptop, looked up *criterion gardens repairs* and hit the first result. The screen was filled with a cartoon beaver wearing a yellow hard hat. Mild colours and no outlines, the visual code for soft, trustworthy, designed in a very expensive studio. *Uh oh!* it said, in a speech bubble. *Has something gone WRONG?* Below the happy, purposeful beaver, smaller text in the bevelled font of a vegan-soup carton: *The properties of Criterion Gardens are cost-effective and align with the highest ecological benchmarks, but fixtures and fittings may not always live up to our high standards. That's why for just £79.99 a month we offer a comprehensive patch-up service so you never need to worry … Our dedicated team will be with you within 24 hours of receiving a report.* She wondered whether to run the cost by Steven or just to go for it, as signing up for the service seemed to be the done thing, like paying for hold luggage. Eighty pounds a month was plenty though, so she should check it with him. In the meantime she needed to go out, so she wedged a bag of rice between the handle and the window frame to keep it in place.

Exquisite Crops had opened a small café which mostly served heritage beetroot and radish-based dishes, fairly unadorned to allow the beetroots and radishes to speak for themselves. Alathea, on a working-from-home lunch break, took Emily and Arthur while Dimitry was at nursery. Arthur kept standing up in his highchair until Emily gave up and took him on her lap, where he squirmed. She hadn't done the straps up. A highchair had straps to prevent a baby from falling out, not to restrain a badly behaved toddler.

'Poor thing,' said Alathea. 'He has a cold.'

'All of us always have colds,' said Emily, holding a disintegrating napkin to Arthur's nose. 'Blow.'

'You know, with Elliott …' Alathea was saying. 'I mean let's be honest, having kids sabotages everything. You have to abandon your relationship as you knew it and it's best to admit that that's very painful rather than pretending everything's fine.'

'Yeah,' said Emily. 'But you two joke with each other all the time.'

'We're mean to each other,' said Alathea. 'It's not a joke.'

'It's been years since Steven and I even slept in the same bed.'

'Oh no, really? We tend to do the musical beds thing too. Tomasz has terrible dreams.'

'I feel like I'll be co-sleeping forever—'

'Do you … You don't have to answer this, but do you manage to spend any intimate time with each other at all?'

'—I'll be in their university halls. Do we have sex?' said Emily.

'It felt rather blunt just asking.'

'Like not at all,' said Emily. 'Like not even at all.'

'Ah.'

'Weeks went by, then months. He's just tired and stressed and I think if I pushed him against the wall and stuck my tongue in his mouth he'd call the crisis team.'

'God, Emily,' said Alathea. 'I mean you need affection, you need *something*.'

'I'd pay you a hundred pounds if you'd kiss me and stroke my hair a bit.'

'Oh, you just have to ask,' said Alathea. 'Have you talked to him?'

'Is that something people do?' said Emily. 'Talk about their problems? Honestly express their desires?'

'Not often,' said Alathea. 'I'd be out of a job.'

'Ha!'

'Being afraid to ask for what you want, what you need,' said Alathea. 'That's not really fair on yourself or the other.'

'I'm not afraid,' said Emily.

'So why don't you talk to him?'

'I'm resigned.'

'Men are like children,' said Alathea. Emily rolled her eyes. 'No, they are. They hate change, and they hate having to share you. The good ones are just about able to keep that in check, but it's still there. Elliott's, what, seven years older than me and he's like a little boy. But, you know, he does the laundry does the fucking washing-up without being asked to, so there's that.'

'He's a good boy.'

'*Such* a good boy.'

It was almost too embarrassing to think about her dissatisfaction. She envied Alathea and her straightforward, openly unreasonable disappointment. Alathea wanted and lacked the kind of things she could mock herself for. She wanted a big house in a fashionable district of the capital, a 'good' school for her children, an au pair so she could work full-time, a massive, intimidating black 4x4.

'And I mean living with such low overheads here for a while makes that a realistic long-term goal, but maybe it's all bullshit, really, and I'll just end up on antidepressants.' Then she remembered that Emily had been clinically depressed and apologised for being insensitive.

'Oh, no, don't worry,' said Emily.

'No, it was crass of me,' said Alathea. 'But I mean, all those *kept women* sitting in their immaculate country houses waiting to pick the kids up from tennis or cello or whatever while their husband commutes home with his £6,000 a year railcard. They probably *are* on antidepressants.'

And what did Emily want? Why did she feel, permanently, as though she were waiting for a train that wasn't arriving at a station that no longer operated? It didn't seem fair to blame Steven for everything, but she also couldn't help thinking that he might ameliorate her general apprehension and sadness with the occasional kind word or affectionate gesture, both of which were less likely if she blamed him for everything. More accurate to say that it wasn't *helpful* to blame Steven for everything.

'You seemed to be getting on better the other day,' said Alathea.

'Yeah,' said Emily. 'I don't know.'

'Only the one who wears the shoe knows where it pinches,' said Alathea.

'Ha.'

'It's an old Jewish saying so of course it's supposed to be about wives, but it can really be applied universally. Are you coming to the meeting?'

'What meeting?'

'The allotment,' said Alathea.

'Oh,' said Emily. 'I don't tend to … I'm not really a joiner.'

'It meets every other month – it's a really good idea to go,' said Alathea. 'It's mostly just allotment business, but they also talk about the park, the cars – it's like a little town hall in the fifties.'

'I don't think I have anything to contribute,' said Emily. 'Aside from sneezing.'

'You're too civic-minded,' said Alathea. 'Committees are where you complain! Even if nothing's wrong.'

'I don't have anything to complain about either.'

'That way nobody asks you to do anything and they're eager to placate you. Emily, seriously, I understand you've come to accept very low standards. You're grateful for basic functionality. Try to be more like our parents' generation. Get really pissed off about something totally inconsequential. That guy extending his house even though we all quietly agreed not to make major structural changes – what's being done about him? That stupid woman with her fighting dogs. Do we have to wait for them to eat our babies or can we establish some basic yardsticks for acceptable behaviour? Do you want the whole community to become a— The thing about this laidback, laissez-faire model is that it only works when people are nice.'

Emily thought about the dog running around in the park the other day when she was kicking an inflatable Harry Potter ball with Matty. She wasn't good at identifying breeds, but it looked like an overworked muscle with teeth.

'I suppose,' she said.

The allotment team met in an open-plan show home at the mouth of the estate. They walked there together. It was bustling – the interior walls of the former show home had been removed and the walls were decorated with patterned tapestries which seemed to have been woven out of straw. People gathered in knots to chat as if it were more a party than a meeting. Two tables held carafes of cloudy apple juice and flatbreads surrounding bowls of beige dip. Emily saw David, the chair who had given her the welcome pack, surrounded by people in the far corner. He was wearing a child-like light grey tracksuit and looked a little fraught. He caught her eye and mouthed *Help me*. She widened her eyes at him. Poor David. Then she recognised a young couple from Marketa's party and smiled at them.

'Okay!' David shouted and clapped his hands. 'Okay. Shall we get started? Let's get started.'

Arthur was being impossible.

'I'm just going to be a disturbance,' she whispered to Alathea. 'I'll try to walk him to sleep.'

'Oh, babe,' Alathea sighed. 'Okay.'

'You know what it's like.'

'You should really take him to nursery every day,' said Alathea. 'Get some of your life back.'

'I'll build up to it.'

'Well, I'll fight our corner, Emily.'

'Thanks,' said Emily, uneasily.

'Steven, don't you think it's funny,' said Emily, 'that we pay for a music subscription service that gives us access to every song in recorded history along with every new song that gets released every day, but the only things I listen to are the records I had on tape and CD when I was a teenager?'

Steven said that they could cancel it.

'I don't want to cancel it,' said Emily. 'Although actually it would help to pay for the house-repair subscription, so maybe we *should* cancel it. It's just *funny* that I could choose literally anything … that faced with almost *infinite* choice I keep choosing the same thing.'

Steven said he supposed it was funny, but from an evolutionary perspective it made sense to choose familiar things because they were confirmed to be safe. Then he stretched and said he was knackered.

It was 10 p.m. and she had a pile of year 8's workbooks to mark. She set up a workstation on the kitchen island, dimmed the spotlights and made a cup of peppermint tea. She plugged a tiny speaker into her laptop and googled 'best new music'. It was nice that so many people were still bothering, even if there wasn't so much money in it any more. And there was plenty, she acknowledged, that was worthy of her attention, that she could give herself over to, make an effort to get into. But nothing new made her feel as centred and transported as being fifteen years old, sitting in the corner of the dining room in the glow of her parents' giant midi-system playing R.E.M.'s 'E-Bow the Letter' over and over again, and singing along with Patti Smith's part until her brother told her to shut up. What was Elliott into? Men loved telling you what to listen to and he was probably no exception. She imagined a teenage Elliott making a mixtape, or waiting to press the Play and Record keys (the Record key heavier, crunchier) – waiting for the right song to come on the radio. No, he'd have pressed them in advance and hit Pause so there'd be less interference when the song came on. She pictured him hovering over the Pause key, imagined him peeling the thin sticker and applying it to the blank cassette, writing her name.

Her laptop speaker made a low buzz which resolved into static and feedback.

'What the fuck?' she said. She checked her phone. Nothing. The noise stopped. Her heart was beating fast. She stirred the cup of peppermint tea and pressed the teabag against the side. She opened the first workbook. Then she imagined Elliott in his sixth-form uniform, putting the cassette in his bag. The speaker buzzed again. 'No,' she said.

She imagined waiting at the top of the hill that led down to her own school – she had no idea where he'd grown up – sitting on a wall, kicking her legs, waiting for him. The buzzing intensified and sounded vaguely like a dial-up modem or telex machine. She closed her eyes. She thought about the scene she had to teach from *Much Ado About Nothing* tomorrow and the sound subsided. Then she imagined, back on the wall, first seeing Elliott's approach, his rucksack on one shoulder, his awkward gait. The buzzing again, the buzzing of a guitar being plugged in.

Breathing fast, she googled *Does electricity respond to your emotions?* Most of the articles were about the physics and chemistry of emotional reactions. People also asked *How do you release suppressed emotions?* and *Can you die from sadness?* She tried googling *No, really, can electricity respond to your emotions?* but got the same results. She closed her eyes again and imagined the way seventeen-year-old Elliott would look at her when he saw her, something pained in his expression: *You;* how he walked faster, broke into a run to reach her, placed one hand on either side of her knees on the wall and waited for her to fall into his arms.

It was buzzing so loudly that she pulled out the jacklead of her toy-sized speakers and cut it dead.

'So stupid,' she said, out loud, and googled *No but really though* and learned that *During conversation, after using an anecdote to explain a viewpoint, one might use the phrase really though to further emphasise the broader point they are trying to make.* She emptied the peppermint tea into the sink and poured herself an inch of whiskey from the bottle she'd bought Steven two years ago.

19

This is how it starts. Checking in. Is it non-uniform day? No, that's next Thursday. God I can't keep track.

> — How are you getting around the 'no squash' thing?
> — Oh my god, right?
> — Can't believe they banned squash. Squash is one of the few pleasures in life.
> — If I give Matty water he just doesn't drink it. He comes home with a full bottle of water and severe dehydration. So I've bought opaque drink bottles.
> — Ooh. That's smart.
> — I *am* smart.

And from there it didn't feel like too much of a reach to start sharing the occasional existential crisis.

> — Do you ever feel like there's something just … inherently humiliating about this?
> — About what?
> — About being a parent.

— Hahahaha! Elliott, hush.
— I don't mean … I don't mean what it does to
    your life, the uncivilising, the shit scrubbing. It's
    something deeper.
— You become this sort of abject, obsolete thing,
    like a giant old VHS player or something.
— Yeah!

That night it occurred to Emily that she could write to
Elliott whenever she wanted, whenever she felt remotely
bored or restless.

— Hey you.

and then wait until the little 'sent' symbol turned to 'seen'
and for the pulsating ellipses of Elliott's imminent reply to
appear, which was usually within a minute.

— I was beginning to think you were avoiding me.
— Oh yeah, I just love being alone with my
    thoughts.
— You've tried audiobooks? Podcasts?
— Are you trying to get rid of me, Elliott?
— No, it's just we completely eradicated that years
    ago. Nobody ever has to be alone with their
    thoughts for a single minute ever again.
— I completely lost it twice at work today. Like
    vein in the side of the head pulsing stuff.
— With *drama* students?
— No. I have to teach some GCSE English.
    Macbeth. Year 10 middle set. I hate them.

— Ugh.

— Uggggh.

— I could never do what you do.

— You'd be fine.

— No, they'd destroy me. I'd sooner join the army.

— You will do no such thing.

— What do you do, when a whole class is fucking annoying?

— They just drag each other down.

— I *mean* that about the army. If you're going to be broken and rebuilt in the image of a murderous psychopath you might as well keep fit while you're doing it.

— There's this boy who tries to keep a low profile and he's perfectly bright and sweet and of course they just give him hell.

— Oh that was *me*!

— Hahahaha! Lil' Elliott.

— I'd have had a *big* crush on you.

— Hahaha

— I'd have come up with all sorts of reasons to talk to you after class.

— I think Arthur has a slight fever. Again. He's hot and he won't stop kicking me.

— Aww.

— I mean that's pretty much every night.

— Poor Arthur. Poor Emily.

— Your kids don't seem to get sick at all.

— Oh they get sick.

— No they don't. Plague pit over here. You should quarantine us.

— Immune system is just a lottery.
— That's not true either. You eat healthy. Your kids sleep all night. You probably run marathons and don't even tell anyone about it. You're like an ... optimised family.
— Haaaaa!
— Dictatorships would use you in propaganda.
— I don't know how you got this impression of us.

This would go on until the messages tagged 23:59 and earlier were accompanied by little 'yesterday's. Some nights she'd message him – Hey you, and he wouldn't respond at all and in the morning she'd find an apology sent at 2 a.m. saying that he'd been working or he'd fallen asleep or the kids were up late, but she thought it more likely that he'd been spending time with Alathea, because *duh*. So the excuse was really an acknowledgement on Elliott's part that it would be absurd for Emily to have to tell him that she wasn't jealous – which she wasn't, or at least it would be so unreasonable of her that she wouldn't have believed herself if she was. Best to short-circuit that whole mess with a simple lie. It seemed worth acknowledging, nonetheless.

— The thing is, I think I fancy both of you. And it has to be both of you. You make one another more attractive.

she wrote to him.

— That's nice.
— Does that make me pansexual?

113

There was a pause before Elliott responded.

— You're probably looking in the wrong place if that's what you're after.
— That's a shame. It could have worked out really well. What do you want from me, Elliott, really?
— I don't understand the question.
— Are you attracted to women who seem sad because you think you can make them happy?
— Oh my god, Emily.
— I don't think I'm really any more unhappy or lonely than anyone else. I think I'm just unhappy and lonely enough.

After ten minutes Emily messaged Elliott to ask if he was asleep and he didn't respond until the morning, apologising for falling asleep. When they saw each other at the school gates or walked Dimitry and Arthur to sleep together or spent the afternoon at one another's houses they never made any reference to the ever-extending litany of messages that had passed between them; it was as if they were four different people, two who were just language and who would exchange any information without shame or self-editing, and two restricted in that regard by the realisation that the other was an actual physical being, shy around each other, more careful. If there was anything to say, Emily felt that she might talk about it as if it were a boxset or a radio drama: how about those two bozos – what were they on about last night, eh?

— Do you know that Lacan quote, 'To love is to give what you don't have'?

— Yeah … I mean I just looked it up, so yeah.

— What do you think of it?

— You love someone if they … seem to be a better version of yourself?

— Hahaha no.

— If they seem to have something you lack?

— No. Do you think this is like the way people used to keep really detailed diaries?

— What? Us?

— Yeah – I'm thinking it's like that. You expect a diary to be read at some point and this way it's like: Instant audience of one.

— I'm your audience?

— One person who tells me I'm brilliant and funny.

— You're brilliant and funny.

— Even if it's not true.

— It is true.

— I could get very accustomed to it.

— I think you can see it however it helps you to see it.

— I'm asking how *you* see it.

…

— You still there?
— Yeah. Sorry. Minor child-based drama.
— Tell me about it.
— Was that rhetorical?

20

She took Matty's hand to cross the road and he didn't let go when they reached the pavement. He carried on holding her hand all the way to school, and Emily felt a swell of affection for this stern little soul she had somehow been entrusted with. Her heart felt like a startled bird which had just flown into a window. Little heart shivering on a windowsill.

'I love you,' she said, and held his hand tighter.

After a while he told her that Ibrahim hadn't been at school yesterday.

'Oh dear,' said Emily. 'Poor Ibrahim. Do you know what's wrong?'

'We were talking about horror characters and I think he got too scared,' said Matty.

'What are horror characters?' said Emily.

'They're really bad,' said Matty.

'Right,' said Emily. 'But what are they? Where are you seeing them?'

'They're just characters in things,' said Matty. 'I don't really want to talk about it.'

'Okay,' said Emily. 'That's okay.'

* * *

When she got back to her house she noticed a small white van parked outside Elliott and Alathea's, *Maid4U* printed on the side in big blue cursive. She could hear the sound of a vacuum cleaner from across the road. It felt funny. Emily took a job cleaning rooms in halls throughout her three years at university – it was convenient if sometimes disgusting part-time work, and never took place in the halls she lived in herself. It was nice to imagine Domestic Services were sensitive to that potential embarrassment, but it was more likely just a coincidence that she'd never been assigned to service her own room while her room-mate lay in bed reading *The Iliad*. None of the students she encountered knew she was also a student and it made her feel like a spy. The point was, it occurred to her as she unlocked her door and kicked the muddy children's shoes out of the way, that fifteen years later she wasn't the kind of person who would ever consider employing a cleaner, even if she could afford to; it just didn't sit right. Even if it was another thing Criterion Gardens offered as a cheap monthly subscription. She was the cleaner and not the cleaned, and that was that.

Steven was covering another speech-therapist's caseload, but he had a morning's flexitime to catch up on paperwork and had already dropped Arthur at nursery. She made him a cup of tea and put it beside him on the IKEA desk in the corner of the bedroom. She leaned in the doorframe. He looked up from his laptop.

'Thanks, Emily.'

'How's your mum doing?'

'Same as ever,' said Steven. 'Confused and agitated. I took her the Choco Leibniz.'

'The official cookie of the Enlightenment.'

'Thanks for getting them.'

'Ain't no thing.'

She waited for him to look at her. She thought about saying it was the first time they'd been alone in the house together for a while and if the paperwork was going okay maybe he'd like to make out for a little bit? Even if it was just until the tea cooled to a drinkable temperature. He didn't look up. It was unfair of her anyway. Life was heavy for him. She felt for him. What was she expecting?

For him to do some research into How to Reconnect with Your Long-Term Partner?

A friendly punch on the shoulder. Anything.

— Let's come up with some doomed love stories.
— You think that's going to help?
— We'll just improvise them.
— Okay. We're in a cult.
— Yeah. Good. A cult which … stipulates
  non-exclusive relationships.
— Like we both, first and foremost have to satisfy
  the sexual desires of the cult leader?
— Sure. We're both really committed to it.
— We live in these little … permanent tents.
— We have to raise the leader's many children.
— But secretly we're crazy about each other.
— We're plotting … to elope?
— No. Bloodless coup. We're both pretty well
  thought of in the cult.
— And the leader is getting increasingly ugly and
  authoritarian.
— Everyone's noticed.
— We'll run the place differently.
— Just have to gradually gather support from our
  … fellow cultists.
— But …

— It's been going pretty well, but the leader's horrible PA is onto us. And he's just filling his head with poison.
— Oh, I hate when someone's head gets filled with poison.
— But also that's okay: we get excommunicated and we'll finally have what we want.
— Will we, though? Won't we feel sad outside the cult?
— Emily, don't introduce *doubt* to a fantasy.

…

…

— Nother one: we're related to an organised crime … family.
— Oh, I've always felt *so lucky* that I'm not part of an organised crime family.
— And there's a feud.
— Of course there's a feud. Your father did over a lorry of rare electric guitars.
— Yes – and *your* father was supposed to get some of the action but he didn't and it's just turned into a whole awful thing. Lot of hurt feelings.
— He's all: you fucked me! you fucked me over on the electric guitars.
— I never thought my own flesh and blood would fuck me over on the electric guitars.
— We're cousins in this story?

— No. Ew. By marriage, sure. Cousins-in-law.
— I'm just trying to make it impossible.
— No, what makes it impossible is we're both on different sides in the whole electric guitar feud. Someone's already been severely beaten up.
— Yeah – your brother-in-law is in hospital, fighting for his life.
— The poor bastard. And there needs to be recompense for this. It's not even about the electric guitars anymore.
— And we've always tried to stay peripheral to the whole organised crime family thing.
— But at the same time, the proceeds pay for our kids' private schools.
— Uh huh, so we're implicated whether we like it or not.
— We have to reap what we sowed.
— I'm going to end up tied to a chair in this story, Emily.
— You are, but I'll rescue you.

…

…

— God it's late.
— Don't go. I'm just warming up. Okay: Something high-concept with parallel universes and time-travel.
— Oh good.

— We have all these different lives in different eras
and we meet and we're crazy about each other
but there's always something which means we
can't be together.
— You gonna fill in any of the details here.
— Nah, can't be bothered. Plus we'd probably
mostly just have toothache. There are lives where
we never even *meet*, but maybe we have, like
… a weird dream about each other.
— Oh my god, I genuinely, for real, had this dream
when I was eight and it's stayed with me forever:
it was at the edge of a desert and I had this
chipped metal cup in my hand, and I was an
adult even though I was eight years old and
there was a woman next to me and she turned
to look me right in the eye and I realised, at that
moment in the dream, that I was completely in
love with her and then I woke up and I was
devastated.
— Woah.
— I could barely speak at school the next day. And
obviously I couldn't tell anyone what was wrong
because it was ridiculous.
— Hahahaha oh god l'il Elliott surrounded by other
eight year olds who couldn't begin to
understand his pain. You kill me.
— So maybe that was you.
— Yes! Me! Yes. I came to you in a dream to ruin
your childhood!
— It's 2am.
— Ohhh dear.

— We're going to gradually kill each other with sleep deprivation.
— Yes do it yes.

21

'I'm getting used to your regime,' Elliott said. 'Some mornings I expect to see you and I don't and I'm crestfallen. Crestfallen.'

'Yeah, likewise,' said Emily, frowning at him. 'Where were you yesterday?'

'Department meeting. Funding panel. What does Matty do on the days you're working?'

'He goes to the before-and-after-school club over the road.'

Elliott whistled. 'Makes for a long day.'

'Yeah, Matty has the most punishing schedule of any of us,' she said.

'Shall I make a scene in a café again?'

'Ha,' said Emily. 'I actually … I really don't like coffee houses. They remind me of being depressed.'

'Oof,' said Elliott. 'I'll remember. Why do they make you depressed?'

'I had to kill a lot of time on maternity leave,' said Emily. 'I felt sort of … erased as a human being.' She cleared her throat. 'Actually, Elliott, I was really sick.'

'You were?'

'Like psychotic-episode sick. Post-partum. But it *really*

dragged on. Some days I feel like … I worry it might come back and just destroy everything. I'd understand if you …' She looked at the ground.

'What the fuck are you talking about, Emily? You'd understand if I didn't want to be your friend?'

'I don't know.'

'Because of my zero–tolerance mental–health policy?'

'Ha. I don't know. You maybe don't want a high–maintenance friend. That might not be what you're in the market for.'

'Go on, play right into my saviour complex. So this is, like, the big chains?' said Elliott.

'The what? *What* big chains?'

'Coffee,' said Elliott. 'Because I know some very good independent coffee houses.'

'No, the chains and the indies,' said Emily. 'All of them. That quality of being overstimulated and bored at the same time.'

'Oh, no, I get that,' said Elliott.

'Sitting in very comfortable chairs and talking but feeling essentially absent,' said Emily.

Your conversation sedated by low lighting and muted wall prints. Your baby climbing on your lap or sleeping, the buggy in the way. In the way. A permanent sense of being in the way. The oversized classic biscuits – the giant Jammy Dodgers and Bourbon Creams – which seemed to mock her, seemed to say you are a giant baby. A vague, nebulous sense of guilt at spending too much money on coffee, of eating too many sweets; of drinking something vast and saccharine which you don't even really want and realise after a couple of sips that you had no real need for, to be full but eating anyway, of overindulging in something which is supposed to be a treat. A nebulous sense of unease as if every café were a waiting room; that sense of waiting, of doing nothing, because wasn't it exactly what you did at an airport or a train station when the flight or the train was delayed or cancelled? And here you were voluntarily taking that experience for no reason at all. And the difference was that you weren't waiting for something, for your conveyance to the next place, but if you felt for it, put the antennae out, it was there, that same sense of frustration, delay, the difference being that it was *never* going to be fulfilled or ameliorated, never satisfied no matter how many three-pound flat whites you tried to douse it with. You would never actually alight, because you would never actually go anywhere. The language on every interior and exterior seemed to fade and abstract before her eyes such that the bricks themselves seemed to separate, to float above one another and the plasterboards and poster prints of idealised plantations in black and white, or the overbearingly comical menus chalked on the walls. And who were all those people at 2 p.m. on a weekday, those well-dressed, healthy people of all ages who didn't seem to have anything better to do than her? What were their *jobs*? She felt as though she'd wandered backstage and rumbled some kind of enormous con, she often felt this as a prelude to slipping off the tracks: hardly anyone worked, money wasn't real, everyone is in an immaculately fitted Hell drinking cup after cup of coffee, taking more and more stimulants, made more acutely aware and more jittery in their acute awareness of themselves and their surroundings, but with nothing to solve, no place to channel the excess energy, nothing.

'Jesus,' said Elliott. 'Okay. I'd invite you to ours but Ally just painted the sitting room again and the fumes. Bad for the babies.'

'Come to ours, then,' said Emily.

It was the first time Elliott had been inside her house and she felt self-conscious. He and Alathea seemed capable of keeping a fashionable Sunday-colour-supplement lifestyle which their children had been trained out of disturbing. Her house felt like a junk pile in comparison. But when they arrived Elliott collapsed onto the sofa and undid his shoes and seemed as completely at home in her living room as he did everywhere else.

'This is lovely,' he said. 'It's a real home.'

'You mean it's cluttered and messy,' said Emily.

'Like a real home.'

Emily sat on the floor building Duplo staircases for Arthur and Dimitry who took turns smashing them to pieces and laughing when she pretended to cry. Sometimes they climbed on to the sofa and clambered over Elliott who turned them upside down and put them on the floor again.

'One of the stairs …' said Emily, 'I think it's about to give way, so watch out if you need to head up. I put a Moomin on it so you know which one to avoid.'

'You know they repair all the house stuff here?' said Elliott. 'Cheaply.'

'Yeah, I know.'

'But thoroughly. We pretty much had ours replaced bit by bit in the first year. Ship of Theseus.'

'Oh, I haven't even asked if you want coffee,' said Emily.

Elliott was staring at the collection of icons Emily had hung in the corner. He counted three icons of the Mother of God and the infant Christ in different styles. Two icons of Christ both holding one hand in a blessing and an open book in the other inscribed with Cyrillic letters. Several faded wooden icons of old men with long beards. An emaciated woman with sunburned skin and frizzy white hair walking through a desert. There were six others which depicted scenes Elliott didn't recognise. In the middle, a rough wooden cross with two extra horizontal struts.

'Ally mentioned the shrine,' he said.

'Shrine? Oh,' said Emily. 'I don't like the word shrine. I don't know why. The icons.'

'The icons,' said Elliott. 'Is that a thing?'

'A thing?'

'Like are you just into Byzantine art or are you a religious zealot?'

'The latter.'

'Oh, shit, sorry,' said Elliott.

'No, it's fine,' said Emily. 'I mean I *was*. I try to keep it quiet.'

'I suppose the Orthodox church is just about exotic enough to be acceptable,' said Elliott.

'The idea is that people are so impressed by my compassion and generosity that they ask me about it.'

'They ask you what the secret is.'

'Of the inner peace I exude.'

'And then you convert them.'

'Uh huh.' Emily clicked her fingers.

'I can't click my fingers,' said Elliott.

'You can't?'

'Weak bones. You're probably the only intelligent person I've ever met who believes in God.'

'What?'

'I mean usually I accept that someone believes in God the way I'd accept ... borderline illiteracy.'

'Hahaha.'

'Or, no, that's wrong. Someone who's big into cars. Something I have no interest in and which I consider stupid and damaging, but you know, whatever. Doesn't mean we can't be friends.'

'That's nice. You're so nice.' She punched him on the knee. 'Arthur, give that back.'

'And Steven?'

'What about Steven?'

'Is he a religious zealot too?'

'He converted.'

'Yeah,' said Elliott. 'That's the only way you convert someone – they have to be completely in love with you.'

'Ha.'

'So you pray? Do you mind me asking questions?'

'No,' said Emily. 'Of course not. I don't mind at all. My answers are all going to be terrible. You'd be better off reading a book about the Orthodox Church. I haven't been to church for ages because it's just ... with the kids, you know? They get bored, they make so much noise, you end up spending two hours outside and then you drive home feeling angry and disappointed.'

'I'm interested in you,' said Elliott.

'Yes, okay, I pray.'

'Do you pray for something to happen and then wait and see if it happens?'

'No. Mostly you just ask for mercy.'

'What's mercy?'

'You don't know what the word *mercy* means?'

'In this context.'

'You maybe pray that you're not going to be tested beyond your endurance.'

'Do you pray for healing?'

'Sometimes.'

'For yourself?'

'No … then you just sort of pray for strength.'

'But, like, if someone you loved was sick?'

'Sure.'

'Then you pray for them?'

'Yeah.'

'And what if it doesn't work? What if it gets worse and they die?'

'Well, we all do eventually, don't we?' said Emily.

'I mean it just seems so weird to me, thinking you're having a conversation with God.'

'No, that's … you can't have a conversation with God,' said Emily. 'That's insane.'

'So it's one-sided? When you talk to God?'

'I don't talk to God!' said Emily. 'Nobody talks to God. You pray, dummy.'

'When I've asked people about it before they kind of implied that they thought they talked to God,' said Elliott.

'It's sort of different in Orthodoxy,' said Emily. 'You don't just sit there going … You don't have a personal relationship with God. The prayers are basically written down and gradually you commit them to memory, and you light a candle and you say them out loud.'

'So it's by rote? Dimitry, no. Come here.'

'Do you think that means it's less … real? Because someone else wrote them? You're an academic. The prayers are very good – they're peer-reviewed. They're pretty much the final draft, you know? And at some point you maybe say the names of the people you want to pray for. You bring them to mind.'

'So it's more like magic?'

'Yes, Elliott,' said Emily. 'It's more like magic.'

'I really don't want to offend you,' said Elliott. 'Tell me to fuck off.'

'Babe, you can ask whatever you want,' said Emily, and felt very embarrassed that she'd accidentally called him babe and hoped he just thought it was something she did. Which it wasn't. 'It's a discipline,' she said. 'A lot of it is very practical. You keep a vegan fast during Lent. And before Nativity. In fact leading up to all the great feasts. And on Wednesdays and Fridays. Actually it's probably about two hundred days a year if you're doing it right, that you fast.'

'And you do that?'

'I'm not particularly observant. I try. I forget. You might describe me as lapsed.'

'Okay,' said Elliott. 'Do you hate gay people?'

'What? No!'

'But you think they're going to Hell?'

'This is some Christian Union shit,' said Emily. 'Plenty of saints were gay, probably.'

'But not practising?'

'I don't see that as any of my business,' said Emily.

'It's just I saw this thing on the news a while ago, and it was in Russia and there were some thugs going out to beat up people in a Gay Pride march in Moscow and they had banners with icons on them and there were priests blessing them before they went out gay bashing.'

'Russia is pretty messed up,' said Emily.

'So that's just a Russian thing?'

'I don't know.'

'This is upsetting you.'

'No.'

'I mean can you pick and choose, though?' said Elliott. 'Can you be a Christian and just not believe in the stuff you think it gets wrong? I thought you kind of had to accept the whole … thing, otherwise what is it?'

'If it's without reason, then it's completely meaningless,' said Emily.

'But faith is beyond reason, right?'

'You think I'm a hypocrite because I'm not homophobic?'

'I'm wondering how you square it.'

'I don't know,' said Emily. 'I guess I pray for the homo-phobic. Elliott, I'm probably the worst person you could talk to about the Orthodox Church. If my priest knew you were asking me about it right now, he'd probably scream.'

'I'm done,' said Elliott. 'I'm sorry. I'm just curious.'

She barely noticed that Arthur and Dimitry had become temporarily transfixed on the staircase and tower she was building out of multicoloured Duplo. And Arthur said, 'Higher,' and handed her another piece.

— You busy, pal?

— Noo. I was reading.

— Oh I just *love* reading, don't you?

— Hahahahaha. Yes, Emily I also just love reading.

— Just escaping to a world of pure imagination

— Yeah fuck off, Wonka

— What are you reading? Something reeeeeeal snart I'll bet.

— Snart?

— Uh huh snart.

— You drunk, Emily?

— Little bit. ANSWER ME.

— Nothing snart at all. I was reading an article about a distant planet made of solid diamond

— Ooh, pretty. Is that real?

— Yeah '55 cancri e'

— The girl's best planet

— If you want to look it up

— No you can just tell me about it – men love that, right?

— We do. Try to look interested. So it's a planet made of diamond, just a big old spherical diamond. I mean that's not exactly true but it's boring to go into detail. But here's the thing: if there was some way of capturing it, which of course there isn't because it's really, really far away and it's a planet, but *if* we could just grab it and tow it over here and then mine the hell out of it

— We'd have so many diamonds! Such diamonds much wow
— Yeah! But *then* diamonds wouldn't be worth shit anymore.
— Oof.
— It'd be like, whatever, here's some sand.
— Is that a metaphor for something, Elliott?
— No.
— Because I don't like metaphors.
— Yes you do.
— I don't like metaphors or matadors.
— You love metaphors.
— Hate matadors, though. I'm starting to drop my phone on my face Elliott.
— Flights of angels, sweetness.

22

Emily could feel her mood going into a tailspin, unpicking every small pleasure, negating anything to which she might plausibly have to look forward, revealing the happenstance of every achievement and the vanity and narcissism behind her every act of kindness. It felt like solving an equation, a stubborn one she had been working on for years; all of the numbers clicked into place and revealed the endlessly disappointing truth; fractal disappointment – there is no end and no beginning to your sordid motivations, your underlying weakness and cruelty. Lord have mercy on your worthless and unworthy servant, save me and have mercy on me. *Oh boy*. I could message him, right now, and he'd probably respond and he'd probably take as much time out of his day as it took to calm me down, he'd probably drop everything just to make me feel better. And why? What is he getting out of this?

She excused herself while the class were working on ten minutes of close textual analysis, went into a student bathroom and splashed cold water on her face in the mirror, then rubbed her face with a wad of dark green paper towels.

Back in the sixth-form classroom she gave them another two minutes to write and then told them they would read the soliloquies aloud until the end of the lesson.

'How weary, stale flat and unprofitable seem to me all the uses of this world—'

'Jenny,' said Emily, 'That's beautifully clear, but I'm going to stop you and share some advice I received from a director fifteen years ago. I'm going to ask you to read the lines again, but this time as if you're trying very hard not to laugh.'

23

The Arts and Humanities building looked like half a giant paracetamol. Once inside, Elliott's journey to the Fine Art corridor was hindered by eleven over-weighted sets of double doors. By the last you'd get a sore shoulder if you hadn't alternated right to left. But worst was if you fell in line behind a couple of other people and they had to hold every single fire door for you. Or you'd alternate, holding the doors for one another, going through first then holding the next set, over and over again, moved to make some cheap comment about it, to say thank you every time, with increasing graciousness, or just be silent — a heavy, ironic silence, and over the years any approach had become very, very tired and only marginally better than perishing in a fire. The best tactic was to take an interest in one of the notice boards after the first door, perhaps take a poster for the Student Staff Committee down and put it back up again, cutting the quick of your index finger on a drawing pin, and then continuing once the corridor seemed clear. But usually it was unavoidable. Someone else would appear — a colleague from another department hunting for a working photocopier, a small collective of students, and

138

the stupid process would begin again with up to ten doors to negotiate still remaining.

When he reached Fine Art, its title stencilled in cursive above the eleventh set of doors, he found the entrance pinned open and plastic sheeting covering the floors. A fine dust filled the air and the intermittent sound of a drill. Donna, the head of department, was behind her desk. Elliott hadn't seen her since she returned from medical leave a fortnight ago, and hadn't responded to any of her messages since the one that had upset Alathea. She was wearing a dark floral headscarf, which gave him a twinge of guilt.

'Mm, hi,' she said, her voice muffled by a white surgical mask. She removed it. 'Sorry. Asbestos. Not that it really matters. What are you doing in?'

'I work here,' said Elliott.

'Oh shit, the committee, of course.' Donna stuck out her tongue and mimed being dead. 'Forgot that was today.'

'I was going to take a nap in my office first.'

'Well you can't,' said Donna. 'You didn't get the email?'

'What email?'

'The emails.'

She told him the offices were being dismantled and converted into a hot-desk room where academics could reserve workspaces as and when required. They did a survey and it turned out that lecturers in the Art department used their individual offices an average of twelve hours a week between them.

'What about my books?'

'I'll get someone to scan them all and you can use the hard copies to make an installation piece in the foyer.'

'Ha.'

'Hot-desking,' said Donna. 'I think the last time I heard that phrase was the late nineties.'

'Yeah, it was big around New Labour, I think.'

Donna took the detachable eraser out of the end of her pencil, put it back in again and then adjusted her headscarf.

'But hot-desking is coming, Elliott,' she said. 'Whether we like it or not, a mere twenty-five years behind schedule. I had your things packed. I made sure your kids' pictures were double-wrapped in gossamer.'

'That's sweet of you.'

'And your photo of your wife. Or did that come with the frame?'

'What if we need to see students confidentially?' said Elliott.

'They're pretty resilient,' said Donna. 'And if anything comes up you can refer them to counselling.'

'I'm supposed to be seeing Billy today.'

'Oh, god, well, there's nowhere. Cancel, and we'll just go to the bar after the meeting.'

'I've quit drinking.'

'Piss off.' She tapped a few keys. 'No, we're absolutely at capacity today. There's an Ancient History lecture happening in a stairwell. Oh, there's one thing ...' She picked up her phone and started dialling. 'There's an aisle in the student mini-supermarket which is almost never used.'

'You want me to meet Billy in the Spar?'

'I know Brian – he's the manager – he'll be fine. It's ringing. He always takes ages. Just carry a couple of chairs over.'

'To the Spar,' said Elliott.

'Brian's a total babe. The cleaning stuff aisle – it's all ridiculously marked up. If students are going to buy bleach at all they're not going to spend £3.99 on it. I don't buy bleach – I just have the bathroom refitted every few years.'

'I'm going to have a tutorial in the detergent aisle of the Spar,' said Elliott.

'Billy's whole project is about consumerism,' said Donna. 'Field trip. No, I'm joking – look, I'm emailing Billy now.' She put down the phone and read as she typed. '*Dear Billy, Dr Broughton has explosive diarrhoea and will need to reschedule for the following week. We sincerely apologise for his poor choices. Yours, Donna.*'

'Thanks,' said Elliott. 'How's it going with the … remission and everything?'

'You tilt your head to the left when you're trying to be concerned,' said Donna. 'It's cute.'

'I *am* concerned.'

She hissed. She always hissed instead of laughing. Last year he had found himself unconsciously copying her.

Throughout the meeting Elliott drew star shapes and Venn diagrams on the minutes of the previous meeting, then got involved in creating increasingly complicated arrangements of geometric cubes. He thought about long car journeys in his childhood and how he would sit in the back seat staring out of the window playing blinking games with the signs and posts and telegraph poles: blinking between each one, as if taking a photograph or planting something in every gap. If he missed one, he had to reset the count. Blinking at exactly the right moment for over an hour. How he still felt like that, motivated to create something with no function by some force which felt altogether blank and meaningless. At some point someone was sure to notice that there was an eight-year-old boy in the meeting and politely escort him from the campus.

In the staff bar Donna bought them two tall pints of yellow beer. They sat on high stools and watched a fly repeatedly throw itself against a tall window.

'What's eating you, Elliott?' she said. 'You haven't filled in the promotion paperwork – the deadline was two weeks ago.'

'I decided I don't really want it,' said Elliott.

'No,' said Donna, 'but you have to.'

'It's just not something I'm very interested in,' said Elliott. 'Progression.'

'Well then we need to think about why that is,' said Donna. 'About why you're not very interested in yourself. The articles are fine but that's not why we hired you.'

'No, no, I know, I'm coasting,' said Elliott.

'Is this about me?'

'You?'

'When I got sick, it was an opportunity to rethink a few things, it gave me some perspective.'

'Right.'

'Haha!' said Donna. 'I was being facetious, it was nothing of the sort. Everything was exactly the same but I was sick as well. It was awful!'

'Ha,' said Elliott, 'no, right, I bet.'

'That it coincided with us breaking things off ...'

'Breaking what off?'

'Well, exactly,' said Donna. 'I can take a hint. But I'd understand if you still felt weird.'

'I don't feel at all weird about you,' said Elliott. 'I like you very much.'

'You're not scared of me?'

'Scared of you?' said Elliott, panicking.

'Okay,' said Donna, 'well it was good to clear the air. What's holding you back, then?'

'When I come up with something …' said Elliott, sitting back in the chair he'd been hunched forward in.

'Like the gun silencers?'

'Yeah, or whatever. I can work it all the way through to completion in my head, from the first page of the first notebook to the gallery opening to some kind of award ceremony.'

'An award would really help,' said Donna.

'And I feel nothing. A little self-disgust, maybe. All I have left in me is saying nice things about other people's work.'

'Yes, you're good at that,' said Donna.

'I'm a flatterer,' said Elliott. 'I belong in the eighth ring of hell.'

'Okay,' said Donna.

'But if I have to make something to keep my job here then I will.'

'Unfortunately, it's *my* job to get the best out of you,' said Donna.

'I feel like anything I have to offer is surplus to requirements,' said Elliott. 'Or taking up space someone more deserving could use.'

'You know that's not the … I mean you're occupying that space now, regardless of your feelings on the subject,' said Donna. 'So unless you're going to quit on principle—'

'And do what?'

'*Exactly*. What do you say to your students when they come to you like this?'

'That I feel the same, but that they shouldn't because their work is worthwhile and sincere and dangerous,' said Elliott. 'It feels weird getting a pep talk from someone recovering from chemo.'

'Yes, it's more than a little tactless of you,' said Donna. 'So the thing is you're on their side.'

'Which is my job.'

'But even if it wasn't. You treat everyone like that. Makes you nice to have around. Despite my limited capacity for compassion I'm almost starting to worry about you.'

'You really shouldn't.'

'So if you want to do something to make a woman who almost died happy …'

'Always.'

'Fill in the fucking promotions paperwork and then churn out a completely soulless project if you have to, but do *something*.'

'Okay.'

'Okay? It's your round.'

'One more,' said Elliott.

He went to the bar. When he returned Donna put her phone away and took a sip from the fresh pint then one from the old pint.

'God, Elliott, I really missed talking to you,' she said. 'But now I can't for the life of me remember why.'

— Emmmmily.
— Hey. 11:30pm. You're late.
— Oh, thank god.
— What's up, pretty?
— Nothing. Vague sense of dread I wanted to share with you. What's plaguing you today?
— I don't know. My classroom assistant is kind of a dick. You?
— I wrote Dead Michael instead of Dear Michael to a colleague on compassionate leave.
— Eesh.
— It autocorrected.
— You know, the things you really fret about, the things you lose sleep over, probably nobody thinks about at all.
— That's potentially true.
— The things you think you've done to people, the let-downs, the hurt feelings, the humiliations: nothing. Never enters anyone's mind.
— Yeah.
— Whereas the *actual* things people dislike about you

— Hahahahahhaha
— The reasons there are people putting hexes on you as we speak – you probably don't even remember them.
— That's a comforting thought, Emily.

24

For a while it felt like something easy to sequester, to separate from their actual lives like a dream from reality, and if
the edges bled sometimes, well, so did dreams. Because that's
the thing, Elliott supposed, even if you don't have much to
complain about, all bonding is trauma-bonding. Technology
is a fire and if you gather round a fire, you're going to tell of
your struggles. And for some reason he wanted to draw that
out of Emily. He would be sitting, at 10 p.m., grading a pile
of formative assignments with his phone balanced on his
knee when it would occur to him that Emily might need
some reassurance, which is to say that he might need some
attention, and he'd send her a message.

— How are you?
— I'm sad.
— Why are you sad?
— I don't know.
— Poor Emily.
— Poor me. At least I have my emotional support
  terrier.

...

— Me?!
— Hahahaha yeah you.
— A *terrier*?
— What do you see yourself as, dogwise?
— Not a terrier.
— A big manly dog?
— Fuck off.
— St Bernard?

And day by day, message by message, they meshed their lives together in a way that would have been impossible without the capacity to constantly communicate your innermost thoughts via the smallest physical gesture.

— When I was at university nobody even had a phone.
— How did people used to be emotionally unfaithful?
— Elliott.
— They'd actually have to *speak* to one another and they'd probably think better of it.
— That's not what this is to you, right?
— No. It's just nice to have someone to talk to.
— Yeah! I think so.
— I mean … If I don't hear from you for a few hours I kind of … wither.
— Jesus. You need to meet more people, Elliott.
— I meet plenty, Emily.
— Because if *this* is stimulating.
— Hahahaha

Within weeks they developed shorthands and running jokes and references; they took turns being the needy one. *I'm sorry, I'm sorry I'll leave you alone now. I'm going to teach so you'll be free of me for literally hours.*

— I wonder how generic this is. I wonder if everyone's messages are more or less the same.
— Oh yeah, I'm very much standard issue.
— You're very much not.
— You're not even speaking to Emily. This is an AI.
— Tell Emily she's wonderful.
— File not found.
— Hahaha
— Whatcha doin?
— I, Emily, am washing the eco-car.
— Hahahahahahahaha!
— With a J-cloth.
— You're so masterful. I'll leave you to it.
— No, I'm done.
— You're not getting your phone all dirty?
— I don't mind if I get my phone dirty.
— Elliott.
— Speaking.
— With your job …
— Uh huh?
— Do you ever just think, oh, I *hate* this?
— Oh for sure, that's part of having a job, isn't it?
— Whatever it is. Surrounded by books: god, I hate books. God, I hate cooking, I hate my chef's apron. God, I hate operating on people's hearts, I hate hearts.

— I hate mines.

— Factories, ugh.

— God, I hate racing formula one cars. Fucking look at them.

— God, I hate my parishioners

— And God.

— Him too.

— I hate maths.

— God, I hate music.

— Yeah! It works for everything.

— Why can't I be literally anything else?

— That's what most people are thinking most of the time, ah reckin.

— Some people seem to really love what they do, though.

— Nah, that's all a front.

She looked up from her phone to see Alathea extracting Dimitri from his buggy, parked next to hers at the entrance to the playground. She held up her hand and smiled. Emily quickly closed WhatsApp and stuffed the phone in her pocket, aware that it might look like the actions of someone desperately trying to cover up what they were doing, which, in fact, it was.

'Don't let me distract you.'

'Oh, hey,' said Emily. 'We had the same idea.'

'Just trying to dispose of an hour.'

'How was the meeting I abandoned you at the other day?'

'Oh, pointless,' said Alathea. 'David is so *nice* and so completely ineffectual. I tried to bring up the charter, like the original vision the estate was based on and he said it sounded like social eugenics, which I told him I didn't appreciate.'

'Ouch,' said Emily.

'So I had to reverse-ferret and say that in *that* case I thought a proportion of Criterion Gardens ought to be social and council housing. Make this the only place in the country that *isn't* a social eugenics project. So now I have to lead a research group to look into it.'

'Oh, well good for you,' said Emily.

'Meh,' said Alathea. 'What's new in your world?'

'Nothing. I'm one of life's great constants,' said Emily.

'That's what's so good about you,' said Alathea.

25

Elliott hadn't responded to her messages the previous night, so Emily googled the fragment of a poem Magda had given her and read about Bob Tickner (d. 2012) and his career for a couple of hours.

Arthur dragged her along on his reins but she managed to direct him towards Magda's house. Magda was outside in her long green coat and gardening gloves, tending to a long narrow wooden planter made of recycled doors. She looked up as Emily approached.

'You don't usually walk by this way.'

'What are you planting?'

'Hibiscus,' said Magda. 'I like things which require very little attention.'

'Oh, you're going to *love* me, then. I looked up your husband,' said Emily. 'I have an advanced Wikipedia addiction when I can't sleep. Eleven books. It's impressive.'

'Well,' said Magda. 'If you keep writing them they tend to mount up.'

'Do you still go by Tickner?'

'I do,' said Magda.

'It also mentioned Criterion Gardens.'

Magda stopped digging and looked up.

'Yes?'

'It said his last collection ...'

'*The Private Experience and the Public World*,' said Magda. 'I can give you a copy.'

'You helped to set up Criterion Gardens? You and Bob, I mean?'

'I tend not to talk about it,' said Magda. 'He came from money. We'd both lived communally before we met and we wanted to make a difference. This place was derelict – a disaster.'

'A little ghost town. I don't mean to be nosy,' said Emily, 'I'm just interested.'

'No, no,' said Magda. 'It's quite all right. The original vision was a lot more selective. We were creating a vibrant community.'

'Selective?'

'I mean that literally. We chose people based on vocation and also their character.'

'*Character*?' said Emily.

'You can try to make something beautiful, Emily,' said Magda, 'but it will inevitably get gobbled up and regurgitated as something unrecognisable. Especially if it was working. Think of ... what do they call it? Airbnb. It was supposed to be for real people to briefly sublet each other's homes and it was so successful it's now overrun with slumlords posing as hoteliers.'

'Oh yeah!' said Emily. 'Or Etsy – that used to be for artisans selling the lovely things they've made. Look at it now and it's just vulgar trinkets mass-produced in slave conditions so they can still call it 'hand-made' and name their sweatshop factory in the Philippines *Tablecloths by Emily*.'

'But it still masquerades as what it was. So there's not even any space for the people who originally wanted or needed it. And those responsible don't even have to see themselves as directly involved.'

'And that's what happened here?' said Emily. 'I mean it still seems quite nice.'

'This was years ago,' said Magda, tending to the hibiscus again. 'Bob's health was deteriorating anyway. I quietly stepped down. So now it's more or less just where I live.'

'More or less?'

'I take a vague interest. In who comes and goes. There's still something of a screening process. And a waiting list, as I'm sure you know.'

'I didn't. We were pretty much straight in.'

'Good. It's working, then. I like to think—'

'I think you *have* made something good,' said Emily.

'I'm an idealist. I like to think it might still be possible … I'm glad you're here, anyway, Emily.'

'Well that's flattering,' said Emily. 'Although I have no idea what you see in me.'

26

The next evening Emily and Steven were waiting for the second load of laundry to finish and the first load to dry on the radiators and Emily wondered, while settling territorial disputes between her sons' rival Brio train franchises, whether they'd need to extend the kitchen to fit in a tumble dryer. This made Steven close his eyes and lean back on the sofa. Then he took out his phone and started comparing reviews of compact tumble driers.

They were disturbed by a loud and urgent knock. Steven locked his phone, got to his feet and answered the front door. Alathea was wearing a grey woollen dress and a pink scarf and she leaned in their doorway as if she was about to be photographed for a mail order clothing catalogue.

'I'm going to take your wife for a drink,' she said.

'Oh, right,' said Steven.

'If that's okay with you.'

'Um, if she—'

'We'll make it up to you. Do you have any hobbies and interests?'

'Ally?' Emily called from the living room. 'We do *not* bite, Arthur.'

'Pub,' said Alathea. 'Now.'

Emily extracted herself and went to stand beside Steven.

'We have, like, three loads of laundry and it's not drying because it's raining and it's too hot to have the heating on,' she said.

'I'm sure Steven can manage that,' said Alathea, looking Steven in the eye. 'When did you last have a night off?'

'Ally, I really can't,' said Emily. 'I'm still co-sleeping with Arthur.'

'Steven, do you mind, really?' said Alathea. 'Just tell me to fuck off and I'll go to the pub by myself.'

'No,' he said. He looked at Emily. 'Go. If he doesn't settle, we'll just watch *Peppa Pig* for four hours.'

Emily looked Alathea up and down. Since they'd met Alathea had reminded her of someone, but she couldn't quite identify who it was until one night, scrolling the news on her phone, she realised that it was Asma al-Assad, the First Lady of Syria.

'Can I get changed?' she said.

'Oh, my god, we're just going to a pub, don't be silly. And the taxi's waiting.'

They got into the middle row of the people carrier and Emily apologised for keeping the driver waiting. Alathea slapped her on the knee.

'Where to?' he said.

'Oh, I don't know,' said Alathea. 'I feel like a proper pub – a really dead pub in the middle of nowhere – do you know one?'

The driver said he could take them out of town.

'Well, we're already out of town,' said Alathea. 'But yes, further out.'

They had already passed two worn out looking buildings which promised Sky Sports and hot food and which Alathea dismissed as too horrible before they came to an old floodlit stone building called The Half Moon with a dauby oil-paint sign of a half-moon against an orange sky.

'Oh, this one's perfect,' she said, 'stop anywhere here – keep the change.'

The place was almost deserted but for a corner table of four clearly underage emo kids drinking snakebite and black and playing *Magic: The Gathering* in silence. The barman was wearing an orange button-down shirt tucked into black trousers. His apron, exactly the same shade of black, looked like a knee-length skirt.

'Hi,' he said, blushing. 'Sorry, I'll be with you in a moment. I'm just—'

He disappeared through the back door with a plastic crate of glasses.

'Yeah,' they heard him say. 'Yeah, no, I'm just serving some customers.'

He was young – it was probably a holiday job and he was probably, to go by his floppy hair and posh accent, from a good university.

'I don't know what to drink. Wine?' said Emily.

'Oh, yeah, pub wine,' said Alathea. 'Purple or yellow?'

'Purple,' said Emily.

The barman came back, wiping cobwebs off his hands onto his apron.

'What can I—'

'A bottle of red and two glasses,' said Alathea.

'We have a Cabernet Sauvignon or a Pinot Noir or—'

'Oh, god, like it matters,' said Alathea. 'Just close your eyes and grab one.'

'The house red is—'

'That will be perfect,' said Alathea. 'Do you want one for yourself?'

'Oh, I—'

'I'm leaving my card behind the bar. Knock yourself out.'

'I'll have half a Carling. Thank you.'

He began screwing a waiter's friend into a bottle of red with a purple foil top. Half her life ago, when Emily worked in a hotel, she misheard the owner identify that type of corkscrew as a *whaler's friend* and ever since she'd imagined someone using it to pull a cork out of a whale's blowhole. She hated being the quiet one, but Alathea had a way with people which didn't include her. The cork popped out with a surprised *boh* and the barman started picking off bits of foil.

'Does anyone ever come in here? You must get bored.'

'I have' – he looked down and raised his eyes to look at her – 'great inner resources.'

'Ha! What's your name?'

'Sam.'

'Okay, Sam,' said Alathea. 'Emily and I will be back for more wine soon, so make sure you're concentrating.'

'He's pretty,' said Alathea as they dragged out their chairs in an alcove around the corner.

'Ally, he's what, eighteen?'

'And quiet and modest – big-dick energy.'

'Oh my god, Ally.'

'You can tell.'

'You're the worst.'

'It's a look – it's hard to define.'

'You're all the popular girls at school who would never talk to me.'

'Aw.'

'And here you are, twenty years later, exactly the same.'

'Did you hate school, Emily?'

'Every day since is like a gift. Did you love school, Alathea?'

'Oh, every minute. One long highlights reel. But, I mean …'

'Yeah, I know.'

'My parents were very wealthy.'

'Sure.'

'I mean not to say that everyone was …'

'No, I mean, of course not.'

'I mean, one girl killed herself.'

'Christ.'

'And some people could be really horrible.'

'I don't doubt it.'

'Having access to more expensive drugs doesn't necessarily mean you're having a better time.'

'But in your case.'

'Oh, just the best time. God, sweetheart, why did you become a teacher? Drink your wine.'

'I don't know.' Emily obediently took a sip. It tasted like bark chips and balsamic vinegar. She took another. 'Maybe

I wanted to rescue kids having as shitty a time as I did. I think good teachers … They love teaching. They like their subject well enough, but mostly they love teaching.'

'And you love drama?'

'I love plays.'

'You don't love teaching?'

'What is teaching, really?' said Emily. 'Nobody ever learns anything. I had a violin teacher once and all he did was get me to play the violin over and over again and I was terrible, I just stayed completely terrible.'

'Oh, babe.'

'But I don't … I don't know. I'm thinking of quitting teaching.'

'You're unfulfilled?'

'I'm doing two days a week. It covers the childcare. I mean what's the point? If I quit, the boys get to have their mum around all the time. Their mummy. God, the word mummy kills me. It makes me want to cry.'

'Drink.'

'How does it work, with your job?'

'It's great, actually. I just reduced my client list, so I feel like I'm doing a much better job with all of them. The thing about being a therapist, though' – Alathea topped up her glass – 'is that everybody talks to you like you're their therapist.'

'Ha, yeah, I bet,' said Emily.

'They can't help it. As soon as they find out what you do. They just spill everything.'

Emily took a small sip of her sour wine and looked across to the dark window. A crescent moon was visible in the top right panel.

'You seem to balance everything so effortlessly,' she said.

'Ha! Hardly.' Alathea's eyes widened.

'I mean my head just feels full, of the boys. I just feel like I'm getting stupider and stupider,' said Emily. 'Do you ever feel that?'

'Oh, we're going straight into this?' said Alathea.

'I wanted to make something beautiful. And I—'

'Are you?' Alathea stared at her. 'Are you doing this deliberately?'

'No. A little.'

'You're hysterical, Emily.'

'Get your notebook. I just feel like I'm doing such a terrible fucking job of my job and such a terrible fucking job as a mother. One is just … compromised by the other, and that's all I get to choose. Which to compromise.'

'Drink. Please.'

Emily drank. Alathea topped up her glass.

'Just tell me you feel that way too and we can move on,' said Emily.

'Have you thought about talking to someone?'

'I had a little counselling when things were really bad,' said Emily. She started turning the wedding band on her finger.

'Everyone should be in therapy,' said Alathea. 'I mean I would say that, right? But it's something really worth considering.'

Alathea, it struck her, would have just the right amount of pain, would show, on occasion, just the perfect level of weakness, a homeopathic dose of self-doubt. To fit in? Not to come across as too intimidating? But this would pertain to groups and ultimately, she wasn't going to insult Emily's intelligence by pretending she was struggling when she clearly wasn't.

'I used to talk to Father Daniel,' said Emily, finally. 'And he's fairly depressive, so …'

'Your priest?'

'Do therapists …? I always got the sense that therapists were kind of anti-religion.'

'Oh, not at all.'

'Trace all your guilt and neuroses back to your religious upbringing.'

'Well,' said Alathea. 'Some, maybe.'

'Some guilt?'

'Some therapists. It's a little bigoted, though, isn't it? I try to keep an open mind.'

'How do you therapise someone who believes in the ultimate denial of the self? What would you say to an anchorite? A Buddhist?'

'Oh, one of my clients is Buddhist,' said Alathea. She pronounced it boo-dist. 'I think. He's probably a bit of a dilettante. Nice guy, though.'

'Anyway, I suppose in the Orthodox church confession is really more a kind of counselling,' said Emily. 'It's not like the little booths in Catholicism. You don't get given penance. Honestly, the way I used to feel when I left a service, the … peace. I mean that's a whole other thing; the kids were so fucking noisy in church I was spending most of every Sunday outside with them picking up little wedding sequins, stopping them eating acorns. Eventually I just stopped insisting that we go.'

'That'll change,' said Alathea, kindly.

'I know.'

'Honestly, you'll look back on these years—'

'I'll wish they were babies again, I know.'

'Oh no,' said Alathea. 'I didn't mean *that*. I have friends with the most charming teenage children. You change with them. It's very English to see all the joy and meaning in your life as utterly fleeting. Partly because the English repeat the shittiest things everyone else says. Number of comments I get about Tomasz's red hair. And they don't even mean it. They're just saying it because other people say it. Never occurs to them that I might be offended by them criticising my son's appearance.'

'People are silly.'

'But the worst is the … constant low thrum of negativity.'

'Don't be sad because it ended. Be sad because it's *going to end*, ruin it by being sad and then be sad because it ended.'

'Yeah, exactly,' said Alathea. 'Except I don't think the English are sad, per se. It's not that noble. They're just pathologically incapable of enjoying anything.'

'You *are* English, aren't you?' said Emily.

'Oh yeah,' said Alathea, 'but it's worth trying to act like almost *any* other nationality. Have you travelled much? Everyone else is just so, so great! They have a … correct attitude to life. The French, the Dutch, the Germans, the Norwegians, Canadians, the Chinese. I had the most incredible month in Nigeria.'

'You don't need to list every country, Ally,' said Emily.

'No, but I could,' said Alathea. 'Jesus. We suck.' She pointed at the far wall outside their booth. Dark brown flock wallpaper, peeling at the edges, fraying so as to give the impression of mould. 'That's us. That wallpaper. We're a hangover. I hope someone nukes us.'

Emily finished her glass and Alathea tried to refill it but the bottle was almost empty. She rose to her feet instantly and headed back to the bar where the barman was rearranging the whiskeys. Emily heard her say, 'Hi, Sammy,' affectionately, but didn't catch the rest of the exchange.

'Classics and ancient history,' she said when she got back to the table. 'I knew it. That or theology.' She refilled Emily's glass.

'This is really going to my head,' said Emily. 'I haven't been drinking very much recently – I should probably slow down.'

'Emily, babe, you need to do this regularly,' said Alathea. 'You need to release the pressure or the whole factory explodes. We'll make this a monthly date, okay?'

After the second bottle she noticed the barman wiping the tables around them – it was almost midnight.

'Oh we're the only ones here,' she said. 'I'm so sorry.'

'No, no, it's nothing,' he said. 'Don't rush.'

'He's an angel,' said Alathea, and sipped her wine. 'Sam, darling, I have no signal – can you radio for a cab from here? We live about ten miles away or we'd visit you more often.'

When Emily opened the front door she found Steven sitting cross-legged on the doormat with Arthur in his lap.

'Oh no,' said Emily. 'I'm so sorry.'

'Mummy,' said Arthur. She picked him up and held him to her neck.

'I love you.' She felt woozy.

'He wouldn't stay in bed,' said Steven. 'Every time I took him up he'd get into bed with me and then say "Where's Mummy?" And then he'd climb back down the stairs and start knocking on the inside of the door.'

'Oh my god.'

'Did you have a good drink?'

'Yeah, it was great. Is Matty okay?'

'He's fine. He's asleep. Okay. I've got an early start, so I'll head up.'

'I really appreciate it, Steven,' said Emily.

'It's nothing,' said Steven.

— Bat signal.
— Bat signal. You exhausted, Elliott?
— I'm worn out and nobody's asleep yet.
— Okay. I'm gonna give you some peace.
— Plz don't.
— Tell me something.
— I'm flat, Emily.
— Boooo.
— This is mostly what I'm like. You get an unrealistic idea of me because I'm generally very eager to impress you.
— Oh wait, I have something: so I've been watching a lot of YouTube videos about narcissism.
— We've talked about self-diagnosis, Emily.
— Just a coupla narcissists
— Out to have some fun
— Hahahahhaha
— Why am I in your life, Elliott?
— You moved here.
— I'm an interloper. I don't understand why I feel so close to you. It's not right to feel so close to someone I've only just met.

— Do you think things happen for a reason? I mean you must do, Emily – you're a Christian.
— Ugh. Why would that follow??
— You believe in an ordered universe created by God and in humanity as the … apex of that creation – you believe that everything matters, every life, every decision, every thought.
— Why are you telling me what I believe?
— So it would follow
— You asshole
— Hahaha I *am* an asshole; it would follow that you think this is happening for a reason too.

27

Elliott was in the living room marking essays on the impact of technology on contemporary abstract art. He heard Tomasz approach the kitchen, where Alathea was washing up.

'This isn't what I asked for,' said Tomasz, accusingly.

'What isn't?' said Alathea. 'You asked for plain toast.'

'I asked for bread on toast.'

'What,' said Alathea, 'do you mean by bread on toast?'

'A piece of *toast* with a piece of *bread* on top.'

'Bread on toast,' said Alathea.

'Not in squares,' said Tomasz. 'Triangles.'

'Oh for goodness' sake,' said Alathea.

Two minutes later Tomasz entered the room and sat next to him with his yellow plastic plate.

'Hi, Daddy.'

'Did you say thank you to your mother?'

Tomasz said nothing and took a bite of one of his triangles of bread on toast.

'Tomasz,' said Elliott. 'Go back and say thank you.'

'What does *thank you* mean?'

'Oh, come on, Tomasz. It means you're grateful. It's an expression of gratitude.'

'What is gratitude?'

'When we're grateful it's because someone has done something or said something which helped us or made us happy. So we say thank you.'

'But what does it *mean*?'

'Saying thank you lets someone know that you appreciate them.'

'But what does *that* mean, appreciate?'

'That we're grateful,' said Elliott. 'Your mother does a lot of things for you because she loves you.'

'I *know*.'

'You know,' said Elliott. 'And it's good to say thank you so that she knows you know.'

'Because she doesn't know?'

'No,' said Elliott. 'She knows.'

'So why do I need to say it? Why does anyone need to say *thank you*? Isn't it better to just do something nice for them back?'

'In exchange?' said Elliott. 'No. *Thank you* doesn't mean you're going to do something because of the nice thing someone did for you. They didn't do it because they wanted something from you.'

'But you say *thank you* in shops,' said Tomasz. 'Yesterday you said *thank you* eight times in a shop.'

'That's true. It's polite.'

'But in the shop,' said Tomasz, 'they wanted your money and you wanted their things, but you still said *thank you*.'

'Because in a shop,' said Elliott, 'you have to make an extra effort to treat one another like human beings.'

'That's why they have big signs which say *thank you*?'

'That's more to make you *feel* like you're a human being. As an organisation, as a business, the shop just wants your money and they don't want you to give it to anyone else.'

'Hmm.'

'Which we're free to do. And they know that.'

'That's why I don't say *thank you* to Mummy,' said Tomasz. 'I want her to be free.'

'But it's different when you're talking to a person. Then it's important to say *thank you*. We're the thankful animals. Actually,' said Elliott, 'I had a friend who never said *thank you* to anyone. Once I helped him move house, in my car. We drove back and forth across town from his old place to his new place, completely filling the car and unloading it each time. We did eight trips in total. It took all day. And he didn't say *thank you*.'

'Did that make you cross?'

'No,' said Elliott. 'Not really.'

Alathea appeared in the doorway. 'We're out of oat milk.'

'Oh.'

'Would you?'

As well as allotment produce, Exquisite Crops carried a range of alternative dairy. He crossed the estate drawing deeply on his electric cigarette – a rhubarb-and-custard flavour he wasn't enjoying – and saw Magda coming towards him with her dog. Usually, if crossing her path was unavoidable, he'd have nodded grimly or blanked her quizzical smile. But that afternoon he found he was profoundly tired of the situation. Tired of thinking about it, and tired of it being one of the things that upset Alathea and made

her, in his opinion, colder and less affectionate more generally. Besides which, as Alathea once told him, he was
extremely conflict-averse and unaccustomed to situations
he hadn't pre-emptively deflected or charmed his way out
of by being nice or apologetic or both before he even had
to take a position. Maybe he should just take a position.

'Magda,' he said, when she was close enough.

'Oh,' said Magda.

'I'm sorry ... to bother you.' It was starting to rain –
good – keep it brief. 'There's a certain tension,' said Elliott,
'and I don't think it really needs to be the case anymore.'

'Really?' said Magda. 'Well good, there needn't be any
tension as far as I'm concerned.'

'We don't need to be friends or anything, but we can be
friendly to each other at least?' He put a hand down
towards the dog, which shuffled back behind his owner.

'I know who you are,' said Magda, matter of factly.

'Do you?' said Elliott.

'I've always thought it's rather unfair,' she said, 'that we
can judge people who over-eat based on their appearance,
whereas a man could spend the entirety of his free time
pleasuring himself to internet pornography and nobody
would really be any the wiser.'

'Yes, I've often thought that, too,' said Elliott. 'Poor old
gluttons get a raw deal.'

'In reality, of course, everything makes its mark on us; it's
only that most people don't realise what they're looking at.'

'It's raining,' said Elliott. 'But as long as we can agree to
basic courtesy, I'd be more than happy.'

'And people talk about seeing the best in others as if
that's a rare quality; as if the laziest, most oblivious way to

live isn't to do *just* that.' Elliott smiled at this in a manner he hoped conveyed vague amusement. 'And I think it's rather tempting to live as if nobody would ever doubt our essential decency.'

'I'll be off then,' he said. 'Have a good evening, Magda. If you could just be nice to Alathea if you see her.'

'It's rare for anyone to say *I don't approve of what you're doing*. So we're not accustomed to hearing it. We really will let one another get away with anything. But some things …'

'Goodbye, Magda. I'm getting wet and I need to get oat milk.'

'One only discovers what people will really put up with once it's too late. You're excused,' said Magda.

Lying on his futon in the dark Elliott waited until Tomasz's breathing regulated. Then he took out his single head-phone and switched off a YouTube Let's Play of *Shadow of the Beast 3* on the Amiga 500. A strange habit, to seek some kind of solace in the things he'd wasted his time on when he was eleven. He rolled onto his side and messaged Emily.

— How you?
— Is that an abbreviation you're going to use now? You're going to take out the 'are'?
— How. You?
— Tired. Sad. Starved of attention.
— Oh Emily.
— No, I'm fine. How you?
— Yeah.

— Yeah? I sometimes think, what if we had American gun laws, like if we had a cabinet of guns in the house?

I love her, Elliott said to the ceiling.

— Ruh roh.
— Scoob. The number of times I'd have calmly excused myself, wandered up to the attic, BLAM. I mean how doesn't that happen?
— It does. In America. Every day.
— Oh god. Sorry. It's probably not something to joke about is it?
— What's your favourite suicidal ideation?

wrote Elliott.

— My what?
— Like when you remember something humiliating or something which casts you in a bad light or some violent and horrible thought and you start to think maybe you're just completely awful, just a garbage person. The best way to shake it off, I always find, is to imagine your total bodily destruction.
— Oh, no shit, you do that too?
— For me it's a giant egg-slicer with 8 diamond-sharp blades. One fluid motion and I'm cut into ribbons.
— Ohhh.
— At least 8 ribbons.

— Okay. I tend to picture myself getting crushed.
— That's good too.
— In a big machine.
— Yeah, that works. Well, good night, Emily.
— Hahahaha. Good. Night.

— Can't sleep.

— Me neither, Elliott.

— Tell me another one.

— Hmm. Walk out into the snow, just keep walking.

— Yeah.

— Because for some reason I'm somewhere snowy. You?

— Sometimes when I really need to distract myself from my own awfulness, I have to make it more elaborate.

— Like what?

— Like just spontaneously combusting or tripping into a piranha pool doesn't cut it.

— I'm not sure I like where this is heading.

— So my latest one is: I'm driving, on a motorway, late at night, and there's a diversion.

— Uh huh.

— They've closed maybe three junctions. It's going to add hours to my journey. So I just drive right through the traffic cones and scatter them. The maintenance vehicles are blaring their horns, guys are gesticulating. I know they're probably going to call the police, but I just keep driving, faster and faster.

— In one of the little electric cars?

— I'm in a horrible, shiny prestige car.

— Nice.

— Gouts of toxic fumes. I've taken a handful of these weird red capsules and I don't even know what they are, but I'm feeling sleepy. Up ahead I can see that the overpass has collapsed.

— Ooooh.

— I'm not concerned about other motorists because the roads are all closed anyway.

— This is good.

— So I just put my foot down.

— You could do a whole show about this, about ideation. Raising awareness. People love having their awarenesses raised.

28

Emily felt something crunch under her sock. Despite her instructions, Matty had eaten a bowl of cereal on the bed and strewn them all over the floor. She didn't mind, really – everyone did that: *I know you told me not to do this, and I agreed, but I have every confidence that I can do it without the repercussions you've predicted so that you'll never even find out I went against you.* It was the most consistent element in human behaviour.

But what if they got mice? Feeling the pressure on her spine she crouched to gather the stray Coco Pops into a pile. On her knees she could see that someone had drawn something just above the skirting board in the corner. It was a clumsy pencil heart, drawn in one stroke, with *StE* written vertically within it. At first she read it as *Ste* or Saint something – a school? Who does that? – but perhaps the *t* was more likely a + between the initials *S* and *E*. Had this been a teenager's room? She breathed in as if trying to detect something. She licked her thumb and rubbed at the heart so that it smudged. This was not a good way of cleaning a wall. She would have to get some kind of spray. Arthur drew on the walls whenever he could and her mother suggested water and vinegar.

* * *

The next day Emily stopped Arthur from getting dragged under the roundabout and saw Magda walking through the park alone.

'Magda,' she said. 'Where's your dog?'

'Oh, sleeping,' said Magda. 'He has a tumour. I dare say he'll be dead by the end of the year.'

'Oh I'm so sorry,' said Emily. 'Poor little thing.'

Magda looked at her. 'You *are* sorry, aren't you?' she said. 'How sweet.'

'I'm like a Disney princess,' said Emily.

'But I need to keep my joints moving even if he doesn't. Keeping a close eye on your little one?'

'Yes,' said Emily. 'Then lying awake at night thinking about all the ways he could have died during the day.'

'Sounds wearing.'

'Magda,' said Emily. 'Funny question … The house was already vacant when we were shown around; did you know the previous owners at all? Were you still involved in being *selective*?'

'Oh, not really,' said Magda, frowning. 'By sight, I suppose. Young couple. She was rather pretty – they both were. Actors, I believe.'

'Sure.'

'Nobody famous. Oh no, I remember – they were both called Sam, that was rather funny – Samuel and Samantha. They didn't stay very long. In fact the young man left first in a rental van. One doesn't like to pry.'

'He left her?'

'Oh I haven't the faintest – the act of leaving doesn't necessarily imply who's leaving whom. She didn't look happy, I suppose, in the way she carried herself after that.

She was gone within a matter of months and then your family moved in. I suppose you could ask Alathea – they seemed to be on friendly terms. Why are you interested?'

'And Elliott and Alathea have been there for … I'm sorry, I'm treating you like some kind of tourist board.'

'Ha,' said Magda. 'And the only local amenities are *people*. Those two have lived there for … two years? No, perhaps it's more like three now.'

'You don't like him, do you?'

'I don't allot much of my time to thinking about him at all.'

'But you don't.'

'You should ignore me,' said Magda. 'I don't really know him.'

'I think with good neighbours that's ideal,' said Emily. 'Anything more than a nod should be strictly optional.'

'Hmm, how very English,' said Magda. 'Practically Scandinavian. I'm not a naturally curious or meddlesome person, Emily, and I hate people who talk about "people watching" as if they're some kind of separate species, but I get very bored and I can't help but observe. And he's shifty.'

'I think he's sort of … openly shifty,' said Emily. 'He's very upfront about being shifty.'

'Well, yes, if you rate style over substance,' said Magda. 'You could certainly just talk to Alathea or Elliott – As I said, I think they knew each other.'

'I don't know why it's even bothering me,' said Emily. 'And that's just such a weird thing to start asking someone about, isn't it? What were your old neighbours like? What happened to them? They'd think I was mad.'

'But you don't mind asking *me* about it,' said Magda. 'Because you think I'm mad.'

'No, you just put me at ease somehow,' said Emily.

'How peculiar,' said Magda. 'I dare say most people tend to find me quite abrasive.'

29

'Oh, look at you,' said Alathea, taking off her coat. 'Scratching at the door.'

'The boys have eaten,' said Elliott, doing up his coat. 'You're later than usual.'

'Traffic,' said Alathea.

'That's a drag. Well, I'm expected.'

'Sure – run.'

Elliott went to Marketa and Stefan's house once a month to play a board game. Sometimes Anton would join them, but sometimes he was doing Anton stuff and didn't show up, which enraged Stefan if he had planned a game that required more than three players.

As he crossed the green to number 171 he noticed some shaved patches of ground and supposed they were putting in benches. The committee were always looking for ways to make the communal spaces feel more communal. But it struck him as odd to choose to sit in public just outside your house and eat a sandwich. On a plate? And then walk back a hundred yards to your house to wash it up? Weird.

For Elliott board games created a closed system wherein victory or defeat was immaterial; the point was distraction via the illusion of complete agency; something Alathea had told him he clearly felt was missing in the rest of his life. The game should be deep enough that you could temporarily lose yourself in it, but not so complex that you were only thinking about how difficult it was. He wasn't terribly interested in orcs or dragons, but neither had he enjoyed Stefan's recent choice – a strategy game about trainee firefighters, which he found too bleak and technical. Too many charred corpses and ruined lives.

Stefan was more of a connoisseur. Their monthly meeting should, he averred, be more than just a gaming group – it should be an appreciation of the form and its history. The previous month he had printed and laminated a board game the CIA used to train agents in the 1960s which had only been made available via a Freedom of Information request.

But tonight Stefan had got hold of a copy of an out-of-print game called *Academia* which involved each player running a rival university and competing for admissions numbers, staff, research grants, international reputation, facilities and land acquisition, which ultimately translated into victory points. You had to maintain various decks and trees of cards, purchasing new commodities from a central pool, while building hexagonal campus and departmental territories on the same, small board in the middle of the table. Stefan had also bought two add-on packs, *Outreach* and *Star Professors*, which only complicated things further. If you neglected any individual category there were sanctions which could undermine your entire system.

Marketa worried that the game would be something of a busman's holiday for Elliott.

'It's just the *theme*, Elliott,' said Stefan. 'You can imagine you're colonising distant planets or besieging medieval castles. The point is it's a beautifully executed mechanic – it's deck-building, it's worker-placement, it's a viciously tight trading game and, ultimately, it's war, but it's so well integrated you barely notice the discrete dynamics.'

'The theme *matters* to Elliott,' said Marketa, lowering her eyes at him indulgently. 'He's an artist.'

'Look at the little wooden lecturers, then,' said Stefan. 'Aren't they lovely?'

After two and a half hours Elliott was on his fifth craft beer and had two staff-trees and a satellite campus over which he couldn't maintain oversight – he just added random cards to its deck and hoped for the best. Admissions were through the roof but he was failing to keep up with Marketa and Stefan's grant proposals and he was fairly drunk.

He felt his phone vibrate in his pocket. He took it out to make sure it wasn't Alathea telling him the boys were awake and screaming, but it was Emily.

— Whatcha doing, Elliott?
— Game night.
— Game night?
— I play inscrutable European board games with Marketa and Stefan.
— Haaaaa hahaha! Nerd.
— I know I know.
— Does that mean you're going to neglect me?
— I'm afraid so.
— To save the world?

— Quite the opposite.

— I can't believe I'm infatuated with a nerd.

'Elliott, stop texting,' said Stefan. 'Bad manners.'

'God,' said Elliott. 'I know, sorry.'

He put the phone back in his jeans and ignored the next three vibrations. Stefan was right, of course. As with anything, if one participant was distracted, it ruined the whole vibe – a little doubtful voice entered everyone else's head; what are we *doing* here? It broke the spell.

It was his turn to take a Press card for the table – which could be positive or negative and set one of the agendas for the next round. He revealed a story about labour exploitation and zero-hours contracts and realised that he was going to have to close his satellite campus.

'Fuck,' he said.

'You're telling me,' said Stefan, folding an entire branch of his employee tree. 'Couldn't have come at a worse time.'

They played in silence for ten minutes, exchanging cards with the central pool and with each other, wordlessly by now, swapping wooden pieces and scowling in concentration. They had entered the period of the evening which Stefan called the bubble – nobody was trying to be amusing anymore, no side quips or real-world anecdotes inspired by the events of the game; nobody was breaking the fourth wall at all. They were invested, and tired and grimly determined to see it through.

'Marketa is being very quiet,' said Stefan.

'Marketa,' said Marketa, 'has carefully maintained a good relationship with her union.'

'Cynically,' said Stefan. 'And against the spirit of the age.'

'I cannot run an institution which pontificates on ethics and economic philosophy but doesn't pay a living wage.'

'Yes, well, some of us were about to cure cancer,' said Stefan. 'But laugh it up. Throw a big vegan picnic.'

'Guys,' said Elliott, laying out eleven black cards embossed with tiny writing in front of him. 'I think I just won.'

'What?' said Stefan. 'The hell you have.'

Marketa and Stefan stood up and moved around the table to lean over Elliott's shoulders.

'That one professor I bought in round three,' said Elliott.

'Oh my god,' said Marketa, sounding genuinely downcast.

'Her bid came through.'

'With a monograph on animal imagery in the works of D. H. Lawrence,' said Stefan, spitefully.

'It's put me on twelve victory points.'

'It fucking has, as well,' said Marketa.

'Fuck you, Elliott,' said Stefan.

'It's your domain so I guess we prostrate ourselves before you,' said Marketa.

'The theme is irrelevant,' said Stefan.

'I wasn't really concentrating,' said Elliott.

'Fuck you,' said Stefan.

Walking back to his house Elliott took out his phone again and found four messages from Emily spaced roughly fifteen minutes apart.

— I can be your board game. You have to keep me happy at all times by saying nice things to me from the Nice Things pile.
— This is obviously one of those times during which you are not to be disturbed. Good to know.
— I hate you.
— I don't hate you. I'm sorry I said I hated you.

— Okay, I have a new one:

— New what?

— Suicidal ideation: I imagine giants playing football with me.

— You what?

— I'm the ball. I was never big into sci-fi or fantasy, really, but

— It's unavoidable.

— Or football. It's *all* unavoidable. Yeah. So this is a really detailed one: the stadium is massive, obviously, like scaled up from human to giant-sized – the crowd of giants are in stalls that tower above me like cliff faces. The smell of … sulphur and tar, flaming torches at the corner posts as tall as trees. Little goblin selling enormous hot dogs one at a time. Staggering under the weight of a single hot dog. The two teams are limbering up, groaning like aeroplanes. Clods of grass the size of haystacks flying through the air. And I'm just crouching in terror in the middle of the pitch.

— Ooooh

— On the centre spot. And then the whistle goes and it's loud enough to burst my eardrums, so from then on the roar of the crowd is strangely muted.

— Yes yes yes

— And the centre-forward

— Do the teams have names?

— No. Not yet. The centre forward punts me halfway down the opposition's territory.

— Does it hurt?

— Exquisitely. The landing is worse. I think I break my collarbone and my leg. And then there's a bad sliding tackle and I end up in the crowd who pass me around for a bit and then chuck me back onto the sidelines – I catch the back of my head on a massive railing.

— Ow

— But then it's a throw-in, obviously, and I'm back on the pitch again. Whump! Mostly I have to try to stay in the foetal position – that's my job – but it's not easy – I kind of unravel whenever I'm kicked. The contact of the giant boots, the pain. And I just focus on that, being kicked through the air like a ball until eventually

— Uh huh?

— I don't know – shot on goal that finally snaps my neck.

— Eeesh.

— Or a pile-on which I suffocate under. Or the striker giant kicks me so hard I just burst into pieces. Limbs and organs everywhere.

— Human Ball.
— Foot Human. They have a little goblin who runs onto the pitch to clean up the remains then they bring out the next human.

...

— Which is just me again.
— Okay, I'm sad now, Elliott.
— Don't be – it's part of my mental hygiene regimen.
— Please don't fantasise about being kicked to pieces by giants.

30

Emily was never sure why she laughed so much in correspondence with Elliott, or at least typographically represented it. It seemed to have less to do with whether something was especially funny and more mutual validation. You're funny. Everything you say is funny. Sometimes Emily's phone would be low on storage and she would have to clear the cache – or archive it because she didn't want to delete it – and be presented with the fact that they had exchanged 8,402 messages within a fortnight.

— I think this is getting out of hand.
— What is?
— Us.
— I don't know what you mean.
— Elliott.
— There's an 'us'?
— Insofar as I have never exchanged so many words with another human being in my life, yes, there's an us.
— Okay.

Okay? Irritated, Emily locked her phone and put it by the cereal boxes. She tried to find the knife she liked to use for dicing onions but it wasn't in the drawer or the new dishwasher or with the dirty plates so she said *For fuck's sake* out loud and then she picked her phone up again.

— What does that mean? 'Okay'?
— You're in a really bad mood with me.
— No, you're just being obtuse.
— Emily, if you're saying you think we should stop talking
— Of course I'm not saying that.
— So what do you mean by out of hand?
— When I'm not writing to you I'm waiting to hear from you. I'm already conditioned to salivate at the sound of the message alert.
— You too, huh.
— Even when you're being a dick like you are now.
— Especially then?
— And even when I'm being a moody bitch.
— You're not being a moody bitch. I'm trying to help Tomasz make a collage.
— Of course you are. That's lovely. What of?
— I think it's supposed to express ennui.
— Advanced.
— Maybe that's all collages. Emily, I get it. I'm sorry. Do you want to just shelve this for a bit? See if we can break the pattern.
— I don't know.
— A week?
— Yes, okay, a week.

— I mean only if you *want* to.

— Because you're fine with it all?

— I didn't say that.

— You're fine either way?

— No. I'm fucked either way.

— Okay, as long as you're in pain too.

— That's the nicest thing

— Hahahaha

— anyone has ever said to me.

— So we'll be civil to each other in person and just stop messaging?

— If that's what you want, Emily. Whatever you need.

— Ugh. Whatever I need.

— A week then?

— Yeah speak to you in a week I hate you.

When the lasagne was in the oven Emily changed Arthur's nappy, told Matty that he could have another film after dinner and asked him to pick up the Lego. She heard the message alert on her phone while she was gathering plastic plates and beakers from the living room. Once she'd dumped them in the sink and dried her hands, she picked up her phone, saw that the text was from her mother and burst into tears.

When Steven returned from work Emily had determined to be as nice to him as possible, but she'd also drunk three glasses of red wine and had a slight headache. He hung up his jacket and fumbled in the pockets for his phone and she wondered, if she didn't say it first, whether he would even say hello. He looked like a sun-damaged print of a man and kept rubbing his face. When the boys ran to him and grabbed him around the knees and shouted 'Daddy!' she tried to smile, even if she couldn't work out quite what the big deal was aside from scarcity.

'The cold tap won't stop running,' she said to him, knowing it would upset him. 'The bathroom sink. It's just trickling constantly.'

'Ugh. I'll try to get a washer tomorrow – it's an easy job.'

'Steven, can we just sign up to the repair service now? If I promise to cancel my ballet and life drawing and Japanese-cooking classes?'

'Your what?'

'I was joking. Can we?'

'Yeah, I suppose,' said Steven. 'It just seems …'

'Because otherwise I feel like we're waiting for the place to literally collapse,' said Emily. 'I'll sign us up then?'

At the table Matty said that the lasagne tasted funny and Emily said not to be ridiculous and that it was his favourite.

'It doesn't usually taste like this.'

'Matthew,' said Steven. 'Eat.'

'No, it's fine,' said Emily. 'We'll just cross it off the vanishingly small list of things he likes.'

'I'm sorry,' said Matty.

'Don't be,' said Emily. 'Do you want some … dry bread or something?'

After dinner Emily put Arthur in front of the television so she could vacuum up the parmesan. Then she carried him upstairs, babbling in her ear, to put her phone on her bedside table and put a book on top of it. Steven loaded the dishwasher and Emily said, 'Shall we do something?'

'Like what?' he said, rearranging the oily salad bowl on the rack so it rattled.

'I don't know. The weather looks okay – we could drive somewhere?'

'Where?'

'I don't *know*.'

She put a hand on his shoulder and he didn't react.

'Somewhere pretty?'

Steven said that there wasn't really time – the boys needed to be in bed and he had a stressful day tomorrow.

'How *was* your day?'

'Oh, the usual,' said Steven.

'Are you still,' said Emily – it felt like such a physical effort to even speak – 'are you still dealing with Carol's workload?'

'That's temporary,' said Steven. 'It's not just me.'

'Okay,' said Emily, quietly. 'Sounds rough.'

'It's all right.'

'I'll take Arthur again tonight. It's not working, and you need to sleep too.'

'That would actually be great,' said Steven.

At 11 p.m. Emily was propped up in bed with Arthur sleeping on her chest. If she removed him, however gently, he would wake up instantly, so it was better to stay completely still under his weight and grab whatever moments of unconsciousness she could. Only she couldn't because she was furious and crying softly. She almost pulled an arm muscle trying to reach her phone.

— Please don't be angry with me.

she messaged Elliott. And then, when he hadn't replied by 11:40, she messaged:

— Elliott?

And then she screamed silently at the ceiling for a while because it seemed very clear that he was deliberately torturing her. And then she wrote:

— I don't want to stop talking to you. I don't
   want to not write to you for a week. I don't
   want to *ever* not write to you and I'm sorry
   and I'm frightened and I've been crying for two
   hours.

And Arthur stirred slightly and she rearranged him on her chest and whispered *it's okay it's okay* and stroked his head until he stopped squirming. Then she cried again and wondered if it were really possible to cry yourself to sleep or if that was just a meaningless thing people said because everything people said was meaningless because people were so stupid. God, everything was just so hateful and stupid. But at thirty-two minutes past one her phone lit up and she grabbed it and Elliott had written:

— I'm sorry, beautiful, I fell asleep.

and she felt like she could breathe again.

— Oh *HI* Elliott

— Are you okay?

— *twirls hair nonchalantly* I'm just great. Did I
reply too quickly? Did that come across as
desperate?

— Emily.

— Should I have left it a couple of minutes?

— I'm here.

— You're there.

— I've got up. I'm standing at the window. I can see
your house. Ugh. That sounds creepy.

— Hahahaha no it's nice.

— You want to call off the … calling off?

— Am I scaring you, Elliott? Am I being too
intense?

— You're not scaring me. You're not being too
intense.

— Is part of you thinking, oh god, what have I
done?

— No, Emily.

— Little part of you thinking, fuck, I've managed to
get a mad woman obsessed with me I wonder
how much it would cost to have her killed

— Hahahahha Jesus, Emily.

— Thousands, for the record.

— Probably more than a loft conversion.

— Uh huh and just as inconvenient.

— I felt sad too.

— Did you?

— Yes, Emily, I felt really really sad and I was
worried that I was being pathetic.

— Well it's nice to be able to give you a benchmark.
— Pathetic Index.

Emily reread their messages and wrote:

— Don't call me beautiful.
— You are beautiful.
— I'm not. I missed you. Real rough … evening.
— I'm so sorry.
— You have nothing to apologise for.
— I love you.
— Elliott, for fuck's sake.
— I do though. That's that.
— I love you too.
— It's terrible.
— It's the absolute worst. I wish I'd never met you. What about Alathea?
— We have our moments, Emily. I don't really love her, not like … I didn't realise that until I met you and remembered what love was supposed to feel like.
— Oh *god*
— We don't have sex. That's not been … And that's not … I just think that's completely over as far as she's concerned
— Elliott you don't need to talk about this.
— It's relevant. Promise me something.
— Elliott, anything, tell me what you want from me, tell me what to do.
— Whatever happens
— Yes

— Remember that right now I felt like I was in
your arms
— Okay
— And nothing was wrong
— Nothing
— It's all going to be okay.
— I'm sorry. I'm so sorry.

31

Elliott made an effort to set off on time and got Dimitry strapped into his buggy while Tomasz was still eating his toast.

'Other foot!' he said crossly, but changed shoes while Tomasz retracted his leg and replaced it with the other. 'No, now it's the ... Tomasz, I'm sorry. I'm being impatient.'

As they left the house he saw Emily setting off with Matty and Arthur.

'Emily!'

'Oh,' she turned around. 'Hi Elliott.'

Matty and Tomasz walked ahead. Occasionally one of them would break into a run and the other wouldn't try to catch up, leaving a gathering space between them. It vexed him a little that the boys weren't getting on better – ideally, they'd be demanding to see one another all the time and he could say, *We-ell*, okay.

'It's a pretty morning.'

'Isn't it?'

'Can we just pretend,' Emily said quietly, 'that that was a bad dream?'

'That what was?'

'Good. I'm so sorry. I don't know what's wrong with me.'

'There's nothing wrong with you,' said Elliott. 'Did you sleep?'

Emily looked him in the eye. 'Yes. Because I felt like you were holding me. Oh god, Elliott. We have to put it away. We shouldn't even be talking about it out loud.'

'Yeah.'

'Someone could just see us from across the road and know that we were discussing matters of great urgency.'

'No, that's true, something else,' said Elliott, feeling suddenly quite light-headed.

There was something … Wait …

Elliott looked straight ahead and called for Tomasz, but his voice sounded uncertain. His pace had slowed such that Emily soon found herself several paces ahead and turned back to face him.

'Are you okay?'

'Yeah,' Elliott smiled, but then he pitched forward as if falling through an unsecured pane of glass. It was such a fluid motion that Emily thought he was performing some kind of pratfall, and laughed, before she realised that he'd hit his forehead hard on the pavement and wasn't getting to his feet.

'Jesus!' said Emily. 'Matthew! Tomasz! Come back!'

Emily crouched by Elliott's side. His eyes were closed and he was convulsing and quietly growling. She put her hands under his head. His hair was drenched with sweat. A lump was forming on his forehead. She knelt on the ground and tried to drag his head into her lap. His neck was still jerking slightly.

'Fucking hell, Elliott,' she said. 'Boys, come back *now*!'

Matthew and Tomasz approached timidly.

'Daddy?'

'Tomasz,' said Emily. 'Has your daddy ever fallen over like this before?'

'No,' said Tomasz and started to cry.

'Darling, it's okay, he's going to be okay – he just fainted. Come here.'

'Why did he fall?' said Matty.

'It's going to be okay,' said Emily.

She took out her phone and was about to dial 999 when Elliott opened his eyes.

'Oh,' he said. 'It's you.'

'Elliott.'

'What's going on?'

'You fainted.'

'I was having a dream.'

'Elliott, you've hit your head.'

'Is it the morning? Tomasz, what are you doing here?'

Tomasz had buried his head in his father's chest, sobbing.

'I'll call Alathea,' said Emily.

'No, no,' said Elliott, trying to get to his feet. 'Oh, wait a minute.'

'Elliott,' said Emily. 'Don't get up. Do you … do you have epilepsy? Have you passed out like that before?'

'No,' said Elliott. 'I don't think so.'

She stroked his forehead. 'Don't try to stand for a minute. Matty, can you give me your water bottle?'

Matty proudly handed it over.

'You hit your head hard,' said Emily. 'I think we should take you to hospital as a precaution.'

'Ally,' said Elliott. 'I don't need to go to hospital for a bump on the head. You look so beautiful.'

'It's Emily,' said Emily.

'I know,' said Elliott. 'You look so beautiful.'

'Hush. I think I'm going to call an ambulance.'

'Please,' said Elliott. 'Don't.'

Emily held the water bottle to his mouth and he sipped it.

'I'll be fine in no time,' he said. 'Let's get the kids to school.'

He sat up and held his head in his hands.

'No,' said Emily, standing and brushing herself down. 'We're going to double back and take you home and you're going to take a painkiller and lie down. I'll take the boys to school and then we're going to take you to the doctor or something.'

She helped him to his feet and he immediately had to brace himself against number 144's garden fence.

'God, Elliott, you scared me.'

'Sorry. Ally, what you were saying last night—'

'I'm not Alathea.'

'Stupid of me.'

'You haven't fainted before?'

'Not in years,' Elliott muttered. 'Emily. Sorry. We used to make ourselves faint deliberately in school, in Craft Design Technology, we were supposed to sweep the sawdust off the tables but instead of using the brushes we'd blow it and it would make you really light-headed and if you … I'm babbling.'

'Can you walk? Can you take my arm?'

'You can't push two buggies, Emily,' said Elliott. 'I'm fine – I can lean on it.'

'Where are we *going*?' said Matty.

'We're going to take Tomasz's daddy back home and then I'll take you both to school.'

'I want to stay with Daddy,' said Tomasz.

'Tomasz,' said Elliott. 'It's fine – we'll all walk to school.'

Emily said that she really wanted Elliott to lie down, but he took Tomasz's hand and started pushing Dimitry's buggy.

'Elliott,' she said, and followed. 'Come on, Matty.'

'That was weird,' said Matty.

Once the boys had entered the school Emily heard Elliott on his phone.

'No, don't do that, I'm absolutely fine. She shouldn't have texted you.' He looked at Emily. 'You shouldn't have texted her.'

'I was worried!'

'I'll see you later … I love you too.' He put his phone back in his pocket and tentatively touched the lump on his forehead. 'Okay,' he said to Emily. 'I have to write some shit for tomorrow. Thanks for—'

'Elliott, I'm worried about you.'

'That's sweet,' said Elliott. 'But unnecessary.'

'Promise me you'll lie down? And if you feel weird call me *straight away*. Actually, no, I'm just going to come round and check on you every hour.'

'Honestly,' said Elliott.

'I will be so furious if you die in your sleep,' said Emily.

* * *

She messaged him at midnight.

— Baby, are you okay? Tell me you're okay.
— Haaa, Emily, I feel completely fine, stop fretting. I'm sorry I passed out.
— Is your head okay?
— Bit achy.
— Meep.
— I'm just playing for sympathy.
— I'm going to keep writing to you and I'm going to be absolutely sparkling company because if you fall asleep you might die.
— You can keep writing to me.

Emily was halfway through typing a message asking Elliott about a new exhibition which had opened in the city museum when a message arrived from Alathea.

— Emily babe, thanks for looking after my stupid husband.

She froze and shuffled up in bed.

— Oh that's fine!

she wrote back.

— I didn't do anything. I tried to make him see a doctor.
— I've given him arnica. I asked him if he'd had anything for breakfast and he said he wasn't

hungry. So he fainted. It's honestly like having three children.
— God. He's okay now?
— Yeah haha he's glued to his phone as usual.

Fuck.

— Well that's a good sign. He's as bad as Steven.
— Like I said, three children.

• • •

— Are there times when you wish I'd just leave you alone?
— No, Emily.
— Are there times when I annoy you?
— No, Emily.
— Am I annoying you now?
— Yes.
— Hahahaha. Good. You're so fucking polite it's hard to know. Did you ever read about ELIZA?
— I did not.
— It was in the 60s. Early AI. Fake therapist. I forget the name of the programmer.
— I just looked it up. Joseph Weizenbaum.
— ELIZA was programmed to respond in the way a therapist would. ELIZA asks you what your problem is and you type something in and ELIZA responds. It asks a follow-up question or sympathises or just says it understands. When Weizenbaum tested it on his administrator he let her use it for a few minutes and then asked her what she thought and she just waved him off

irritably and carried on talking to ELIZA for over an hour.

— What does that tell us?

— Maybe that nobody was listening to women?

— Oh my god there's an actual ELIZA you can talk to online!

— If you start talking to it instead of me I swear to god elliott

— Okay okay

— What I was asking, I guess, is is there a part of you that wishes I'd just vanish?

— At this point I think you're fairly integrated into my life.

— Oh is that so?

— So if you *did* annoy me I'd just accept it because I love you.

— Hahahahaha.

— We're basically married.

— Is it … sometimes is talking to me something you do because you're BORED?

— I don't get bored. Do you ever get bored? I get restless, sure.

— Where otherwise, if you weren't talking to me, you'd be trawling eBay or reading conspiracy theories or looking at porn?

— All good wholesome activities, Emily.

— I'm kind of like Candy Crush for you, right?

— You are not. Stop it.

— And you're hooked because the endorphin reward is a little micro-dose of affection [screws up nose endearingly].

— Sometimes I wonder if you're talking about yourself when you ask me things like this. Do I annoy *you* sometimes?
— Oh god no. I fucking adore you. I'm in awe of you.
— Hahahaha jesus why?

32

There were days when everything felt so arbitrary her life took on the quality of detritus rather than construction. And other days where life felt like an intricate flow-chart, but one she had processed through without giving a great deal of thought to the decisions and forking paths which would go on to define her, the forces which had washed her up here.

She microwaved her second cup of coffee, meaning to sit outside her house with it again. It was exactly things like this, as much as anything else, which made her faith so hard to maintain. Letting her cup of coffee go cold and choosing to microwave it rather than making a fresh pot; the fact that this decision had been eternally preordained, could be traced back to the development of the microwave oven based on radar technology from the Second World War and everything which had happened to her since birth which had made her the kind of person who didn't think she deserved a fresh pot of coffee, respectively, all coming to a point in this immediate moment which had never existed before and would never exist again. Was it possible, when everything felt so indescribably small and irrelevant, that she was really suspended on a wire over a ravine? That part of the eternal, internal struggle was to find any meaning in the present moment at all?

This feeling of deadness, this dead time, would be, she supposed, the ideal opportunity to take a prayer book, to stand in front of the icons Steven had put up for her and recite something long and laborious. Make me grateful. Make me realise, during this specific dull and empty hour to which my entire life has been building, that I'm being held up by angels. But it was like physical exercise; she'd just as soon not. Nobody had even asked her about her faith before Elliott had the other day and his asking had stirred things up, that was all. Usually it hung around the back of her mind like a neglected houseplant.

She went out to the common green, sat on the ground and balanced her coffee cup on a clump of grass.

The fact remained that Steven had been willing to change his life for her, and quite drastically. It felt increasingly necessary for her to look back, as if the strength of a long-term relationship depended primarily on nostalgia and the collective ability to sustain it. She had asked him, early in their courtship, if he was an atheist.

'Not especially,' he'd told her.

'That's good,' said Emily.

'Why?'

'Most people are.'

'Are you a Christian?' said Steven.

'I'm an Orthodox Christian.'

'Oh,' said Steven. 'Greek? Russian?'

'No.'

'Is there an English Orthodox church?'

'No,' said Emily. 'Not exactly. Well, there is, but it's a bit weird. I don't think it's in communion with the actual Orthodox church. I go to a Romanian place.'

'Okay,' said Steven. 'Do you speak Romanian?'

'No. I mean, I can say Lord have mercy in Romanian. It sounds like *Dom DeLuise*. The priest is fluent in English, actually.'

'I don't really know anything about the Orthodox church,' said Steven. 'Why are you Orthodox? Your family?'

'No. Actually they don't like it and they think I'm crazy. I started going when I was nineteen. I took a module in Russian literature. I was trying to write an essay on *The Brothers Karamazov* and *The Idiot* and all of the papers I was reading talked about how central Dostoevsky's faith is to his writing. And I thought, well, I should check that out. Is this boring?'

'No.'

'So I went to an evening service in a Russian Orthodox church. The choir were singing the Rachmaninoff vespers and the priest had this incredible bass voice. I just cried and cried and cried.'

'Oh,' said Steven.

'I'd never felt anything like it.'

'Right.'

'And then the more I read about it, the more it just felt right, like I'd actually found something true, you know? It's a journey. Is this really off-putting?'

'No, not at all.'

'It's important to me.'

'Sure,' said Steven.

'I actually do believe in it.'

'Yeah.'

'Is that okay?'

'Why wouldn't it be?'

'You don't think it's insane?'

'I think if I'm serious about you, and about this, which I am,' said Steven, 'then you should expect me to be supportive.'

'Babe, that just sounds like you're following some kind of guide to being a good boyfriend.'

'Oh,' said Steven. 'Well I don't think it's insane.'

She gave him a battered Pelican copy of Timothy Ware's *The Orthodox Church* and he read it at night – she'd lie on her side next to him, watching him read and occasionally he'd put his hand on her waist, which she liked. He finished it in a week and said it was very interesting.

'If you want to think about it in practical terms,' said Emily, 'and actually a lot of this stuff is basically very practical, it's about how we'd bring up our children.'

'Okay.'

'That's sort of what you'd be committing to,' said Emily. 'I mean that's exactly what you'd be committing to.'

'Right,' said Steven. 'Well, that's fine. I think it's good for children to experience some structure and culture.'

'Okay. Because the prevailing opinion,' said Emily, 'is that raising your children in any religious tradition is a form of child abuse.'

'Is it?'

'Ask almost anyone.'

'Well that's stupid,' said Steven. 'People who think that are stupid.'

'In the Orthodox church your babies get baptised pretty much straight away. There's no Age of Reason. They don't get to make up their minds when they're … twelve or something.'

'Sure.'

'Because it's not a lifestyle choice, it's the ultimate meaning of the universe. Why would you leave your children to make up their own minds about that? I'm sorry, I sound crazy.'

'No, I hear you.'

She'd told him he was very sweet.

'I'm not,' he said.

'It worries me. I mean would you convert to *any* religion for my sake?'

Steven thought about it. 'Maybe not *anything* anything,' he said. 'If you were in a cult or something. But then I probably wouldn't even have met you.'

'I'd have been too busy with the cult.'

'If you want me to say I'm not doing this primarily for you, I can't say that,' said Steven. 'Because that obviously wouldn't be true.'

'"Converting",' said Emily.

'But I can tell you I'm not just going through the motions.'

'Well, it's lucky you found the right motions,' said Emily, and tickled him. He didn't respond, so she rolled on top of him and kissed him.

'I love you,' she said.

* * *

The next Sunday Emily took Steven to the Church of the Holy Prophet Elias, an old almshouse crowded with its congregation. Steven stood, sweating, throughout the two-hour service, but whenever she checked his face for signs of anger or boredom he seemed to be deep in concentration and afterwards, once she had taken communion and stood next to him again, he squeezed her hand.

'Is it okay?' she said. 'You don't hate it, do you?'

Steven said that he found it very calming. That it was like meditation.

'And all the standing?'

He told her that he liked the standing because it was difficult and made it feel like you were actually achieving something.

'I know the singing can be a bit atonal,' said Emily. 'And Father Daniel takes some getting used to.'

He told her that he liked the singing because it was rough round the edges, and that he liked Father Daniel because he was grumpy, and also because of his beard.

'Oh, he's super grumpy,' said Emily. 'But I think if you're genuinely going to try to love people a lot of things are going to make you fairly cross. I think being a priest is really draining. I remember once, after a long service leading up to Pascha, he was sitting against a wall and he looked like Darth Vader in *The Empire Strikes Back* after Luke's almost killed him and he takes his mask off. Just pale and completely thwarted. Except with a beard.'

'Except with a beard.'

'You're not just saying you like it for me?' She put her arm around him.

'When you made me watch that four-hour film with subtitles about a man being sad in space,' said Steven, 'and when you asked me what I thought of it, I said I thought it was boring.'

'Right.'

'I wouldn't pretend to like something for you even if it would be easier if I did.'

'That's what I like about you,' said Emily. 'I was worried that a church service might feel a bit like four hours of being sad in space. I'm not expecting some kind of epiphany – I just want to make sure you really want this.'

'It was beautiful,' said Steven.

After a month she lingered in the church with Steven after the rest of the congregation had left and Father Daniel was clearing up. Once he noticed her, he looked up.

'Coffee is in the hall,' he said.

'Father?'

'Yes?'

'This is my fiancé.'

'Ohh boy,' said Father Daniel.

'He wants to be received.'

Father Daniel sighed, put down his large green flask and brushed his hands on his vestment. He walked over, looked Steven up and down.

'Do you actually want to become Orthodox or do you just want to marry this one?' he said.

'He's very serious,' said Emily.

'Emily,' said Father Daniel. He peered at Steven. 'Well?'

'I don't know if I can answer that,' said Steven.

'Hmm,' said the Priest. He looked at Emily. 'He'll do,' he said.

Emily looked around the little chapel and tried to see it from Steven's perspective, every space on the walls covered by a small wooden icon of a saint. The Byzantines' particular obsession with the warp and weft of cloth. The smell of myrrh.

'Do many people convert for …'

'For sex?' said the Priest. 'Yes, in fact sometimes I have to barricade the door against the tide of young men desperate to become Orthodox.'

'Ha ha,' said Emily.

'Look,' said Father Daniel, 'whatever your motivation, the fact is you'd soon get bored and tired and stop turning up if your heart wasn't really in it. Anyway, none of us is married in heaven – Christ tells us that.'

'Oh, that seems sad,' said Emily.

'To read the saints,' said Father Daniel, 'we're lucky if we even recognise anyone in the next life.'

'Oh, Father,' said Emily. 'Ignore him,' she said to Steven.

'I'll give you some books.'

'Oh, I've given him books,' said Emily, brightly.

'You'll be a catechumen for a year – that's how it works, and it's best to get to know the seasons of the church and to really make up your mind one way or another. About two thirds of the way through every liturgy either me or the deacon will chant, let all catechumens depart, let none of the catechumens remain, but you can ignore that. We're fairly progressive.'

'Mm,' said Emily, 'the thing is, we sort of wanted to get

married this summer. Is there a way of fast-tracking the whole catechumen thing?'

Father Daniel growled.

Matty was four and Arthur was six months old when they decided they needed to find a way of buying a house. It was either that or face moving the kids to a different school on the whim of whichever landlord controlled their fate at the time. They'd moved six times in the last decade, losing a couple of grand in damage deposits and rent in advance each time, and they were sore about it, and also broke. Criterion Gardens had come up during a long, nocturnal web search, Matty temporarily asleep on her lap. Emily read the terms and conditions of the tiny deposit the estate was asking for several times to herself in disbelief before taking it to Steven.

The first few years of parenthood had been painful. It was three months before Emily was diagnosed with post-partum psychosis – a term which still made her feel sick, but at least gave some sense to the mirror world she'd fallen into on the day after they returned from the Women's Hospital. Aside from the physical exhaustion she had felt deeply confused about everything. She'd arrange daily visits from everyone she knew then call them off at the last minute, unable to talk to anyone. Whenever her mother called she did her best to sound buoyant and when her parents called in to meet Matty she hugged them and went to bed and her mother said that of course she needed to rest.

People would walk past the house and she'd *hear* them muttering about her. That stupid woman. Doesn't know what she's doing. They should make people take exams before they have babies. *Having a baby* doesn't make you a mother – you have to earn that.

One evening Steven got back from work to find her sitting on the living-room floor, staring at the wall. Matty was swaddled in a white muslin cloth and lying on a sofa cushion in the middle of the room, writhing like a chrysalis and screaming.

'Angry little burrito,' said Steven.

'Look at his face,' said Emily.

Steven picked Matty up and inspected him. 'He just looks like Matty,' he said, and turned, bouncing gently on his heels. 'Shhhh.'

Emily felt this as a rebuke, the turn. 'Look at his face properly,' she said, coldly.

'I can't see what I'm supposed to be looking for,' said Steven, loosening the swaddle. 'Tell me.'

'It's not him,' said Emily. 'That's not our son.'

'What?' said Steven, smiling. 'Oh, no this is him all right – I'd know that scrunched-up screaming face from a hundred miles away, wouldn't I?'

He kissed Matty on the nose. She wasn't sure how Steven could be so stupid.

'Please put him down.'

'I was trying,' said Steven, evenly, 'to give you a break.'

'I know what you're trying to do,' she said and walked out of the room.

For some reason Steven just put up with it – as if he thought her behaviour was par for the course; neither of them had heard of the condition, they didn't raise any alarms and, on the day of the home visit, Emily played the part of an obnoxiously high-functioning new parent then yelled at him after the nurse left for sounding less than enthusiastic to her every question. When he suggested the next day that she might need to see a doctor to talk about how she was feeling, she reacted so violently – assuming he planned to have her locked up and take Matty away from her – that he didn't mention it again.

After a while the *psychosis*, the *psychotic episode*, ugh, seemed to have burned itself out and she just felt worthless and depressed, which she suspected Steven found significantly easier to deal with.

'You're not worthless. You're wonderful. You're an amazing mother.'

'How can you love me?' she'd say to him. 'I'm nothing.'

He'd hug her and hush her the way he hushed the baby.

For the next two years, despite his protestations, Steven seemed increasingly exasperated with her. After she agreed to see a doctor various checks and measures had to be put in place, sedatives (which made her feel more worthless), a mood diary (rate the day on a scale of one to ten), fortnightly check-ups (how are we doing today then?) a lot of sleep (which made her feel guilty). She took Matty to Baby Massage or Baby Sensory or one of a number of mother and baby groups with boxes of donated toys and a wooden slide and a crash mat in the middle. Absolutely everyone seemed to be thriving. Some of the mothers were sitting on school chairs, drinking coffee while their toddlers played or their babies gurgled independently and smiled at each other. What the hell was she getting so wrong? Matty would scream and wail and scream until she found a quiet, dingy corner to breastfeed him, but he struggled to latch on and spent most of the feed screaming, and the other mothers would look at her with pity and disgust so she'd leave before coffee and walk Matty around and around in the buggy for hours while he screamed and wailed and screamed until she picked him up and she'd either try to feed him again, shivering on a bench, or he'd fall asleep on her shoulder while she pushed the heavy buggy with one hand, struggling to keep it on the pavement all the way home. If she tried to put him back in the buggy he started screaming again. Every day.

When it was dark, Steven would get back from work, lie on the sofa and put his hands over his eyes. There'd been funding cuts and his speech-therapy caseload had increased dramatically. She felt for him, but he gave her almost no opportunity to express it. And she felt that she shouldn't complain. Steven helped a lot at night. Emily told him early on that if she didn't get some sleep she might consider walking in front of a bus. So he walked up and down the hallway, carrying Matty, later Arthur, humming every song he knew until they fell asleep, which sometimes took hours, sometimes took the whole night and he, Steven, would set off for work looking like an extra from a zombie film. And hating her, she was fairly certain.

Before the kids were born they had tried to save most of one of their salaries every month as a down payment, which seemed to be the done thing. They were at an age where their friends – Emily's friends; Steven didn't really keep in touch with his – were starting to buy houses and wondering aloud why she and Steven hadn't yet. Annie, for instance, lived in a semi-detached with a kitchen you could have played five-a-side football in, and a nursery for the child she wasn't even pregnant with yet, which Annie had already painted with long grass and jungle animals. Annie regarded Emily as profligate, silly, entirely responsible for her status as a renter. You need to choose, really, she would tell Emily, between eating out and going on holiday and owning a house – you have to make those kinds of sacrifices. But then it emerged that Annie's parents had given her and her husband thirty-five thousand pounds as a deposit, so Annie could fuck off.

She finished her reheated coffee. It had made her feel anxious and dry-mouthed. The empty cup fitted into a perfectly round hole by her side. The holes for the new saplings had been punched into the common green like a perforation line, as if the estate could be torn down the centre, dividing one row of houses from the other.

She felt a hand on her shoulder and turned, half expecting to see Elliott, but it was Steven. He looked concerned.

'Emily?' he said. 'What are you doing out here on the ground?'

'I was taking the air,' she said. 'Finishing my coffee. The door closed behind me.'

'You don't feel self-conscious just sitting in the middle of the estate?'

'Should I?'

'No,' said Steven. 'As long as you're okay.'

— I read something about emotional affairs and it's kind of bummed me out.
— You know what I do when that happens? I don't read it.
— *You*? Really?
— No, you're right, I have no impulse control. If something's hurting me I get a whole bundle of it. I spent two hours reading about limerence last night.
— When you could have been talking to ME, Emily, your Limerent Object?
— You were asleep. What was the article about – what was it? Emotional affairs?
— Oh it was on mumsnet or something
— Good source.
— This woman posted about being infatuated with another man and they'd stopped talking and she felt completely devastated and could anyone relate to that? and then everyone just tore her to pieces. It was like the giants playing football.
— I don't think discussion forums are good places to go fishing for compassion.

— Funny, really, to live at a time where so much is written down. People go on about surveillance culture when we're all just doing it to ourselves – we give away absolutely everything.

— There've always been problem pages, Emily.

— No, but then it was random and very occasionally you'd read something and think oh god that's ME! But soon you'd be using the page to wrap up a broken glass, you know?

— That's true.

— So the binmen didn't cut themselves because we didn't recycle anything. And now there's just this constant, overwhelming archive of *everything*. Every mistake you could make someone else has already been there and recorded all the repercussions.

— Doesn't seem to actually stop anyone though.

— What does Ally do when you're talking to me?

— Works, sleeps, parents.

— Do you two spend any time together at all?

— Oh we have moments. We're essentially strangers to each other now. But maybe once a month. Sofa dates.

— Hmm. That's cute.

— Is it?

— You're very cute together.

— We drink wine on the sofa and watch extremely violent films.

— Ridiculously cute couple.

— Are you passively aggressively repeating yourself, Emily?

— Cute cute cute cute. I'm not. I love Alathea. I'm just as jealous of you getting to be with her. Are you jealous of Steven?
— I've never been especially jealous or possessive.
— Ohhh yeah because you're not human I keep forgetting.

33

When Elliott got home from giving a two-hour lecture on the use of text in installation art he arrived to the smell of coffee. His forehead still felt tender, but the swelling was already going down, which Alathea ascribed to the arnica. Six pieces of clarinet were strewn across the living-room floor.

'Hey,' he said.

'Sorry,' Alathea called from the kitchen. 'They found it.'

Elliott picked up the clarinet's mouthpiece and flicked the reed.

'It's not like you ever play it, right?'

'No, that's true,' said Elliott. 'I didn't know I still had it.'

'It's funny what amuses them,' said Alathea.

The espresso machine sounded like a light aircraft.

Elliott gathered up the parts and the case which was open in the corner by the television. He stroked the furry lining. He messaged Emily.

— I found my clarinet.
— You play the *clarinet*?
— I mean the children found it. I think it's dead now.

— Goddammit, Elliott. Play it for me sometime?

— Hahahaha no.

— Pleeeease.

— It's embarrassingly important to me that I come across well to you and I would shatter that in one honk.

— I'd love it anyway.

His energy boosted by the exchange, Elliott gathered up some used plastic plates, put the stray Duplo bricks back in the box and carefully put the clarinet away piece by piece. He took the case up to Tomasz's room and found a space at the back of the wardrobe. It felt strange, handling the clarinet again, like a past self, a past consciousness, pressing urgently against his own, like two panes of glass.

The clarinet had, at one point, been the most useful weapon in his arsenal. A stutterer with no natural talent for ball sports, Elliott had a vaguely unpleasant time at secondary school, relying on the occasional impulsive social kindness of more-popular boys and grateful for whatever he could get. His mother described him as painfully self-conscious, but the truth was Elliott was barely aware of himself at all. He wanted to be erased, or replaced by a small recording device, a little black box sitting in his classroom chair, taking it in. Because, he could see in retrospect, he was constantly frightened: nobody was bullying him, but it seemed quite likely that they might – and bullying looked absolutely horrible. When he tried to offer anything in conversation with his peers it was met by a short, concerned silence before everyone moved on, and it seemed wise not to push this any further.

His solution, after two years of isolation, was to learn to play the clarinet and to learn it adequately enough to join the school orchestra. His parents were pleased that he had found an extracurricular interest, even one for which he had little natural aptitude. He would spend hours in his room sounding as though he were patiently training a belligerent goose which at least, they felt, demonstrated his love of the instrument and commitment to mastering it. But for Elliott the clarinet was simply a means to an end. If you went to a large comprehensive school you had to be *something*, and it might as well be clarinet boy. And the clarinet was compact and convenient enough to carry with you at all times, even if it wasn't one of the two days a week when he had a half-hour lesson with three other woodwind students. Having the clarinet case with him *explained* him in a way that everyone could more or less accept.

He made auditions the following year and became one of four clarinettists. In the relatively small sub-culture of the school orchestra he felt safer and less permanently cowed. Some of this self-possession seeped into his life outside the practice room. His fellow musicians would say *hey* to him on the path between lessons and he felt, for the first time, that he belonged in the school or had some stake in matters. Twice a year the orchestra would go on residential trips to towns in the next county. On his second trip, after the final concert, the brass and woodwind sections pooled the money their parents had given them for food (the entire weekend had been catered) and escaped to a provincial nightclub with very lax doormen. The place was fire-risk busy, spread out over six small rooms – it appeared to have been converted out of a family home – and played drum and bass. At one point the second clarinettist said it was shit and asked him what kind of drum and bass he was into, and Elliott had to say that he wasn't familiar with the sub-categories, and she said, Yeah, just not this though, right?

The bar was tiny, and Elliott took three-quarters of an hour to get served before Simon (cello, prodigious) took his money and said he'd get the drinks for the rest of the night.

He was pressed into a corner having failed, for the second time, to find a place in the gents quiet enough to urinate when a trombonist called Lindsey approached him purposefully.

'Elliott,' she said. 'Why've you got two drinks?'

Lindsey's family had moved to the area from London for some reason, so she had the kind of accent most of them were affecting to have.

'Simon's,' said Elliott, holding up the gin and tonic. 'He went to the toilet.'

'People have probably told you,' Lindsey said, 'that you're too nice. Is that true?'

'I'm not nice.'

'What?'

'People have said that,' said Elliott.

'What?'

'*People have said that*,' he shouted, nodding emphatically.

'When people say you're too nice, what they mean is,' she spilled some of her Jack Daniels and Coke and brushed it off her dress, 'what they mean is they feel …' She jabbed him in the chest. 'What they mean is they can't be bothered to be nice back.'

'Right,' said Elliott.

'So you just carry on being nice, is what I'm telling you. Don't listen to them.' She leaned close to him so that he could smell the booze on her breath and a perfume that seemed to be mostly vanilla essence. 'Don't be ashamed of who you are,' she said.

'That's really kind.'

'What?'

'*I said that's really kind.*'

'You just fucking remember it,' said Lindsey.

By the time he was seventeen, Elliott was skinny but had big hands and big feet. Like a puppy. If he'd been a girl people wouldn't have even commented on her *handsome features* – they'd just have said she was pretty. A couple of times a year he went to visit his uncle in London and spent the days riding around on the Tube and skulking in Rough Trade records. He had been to London on school trips, but the freedom, when he was there alone, was too much for him to cope with – he found himself going round in circles or walking aimlessly for miles or getting lunch in a terrible café when there were innumerable far-nicer options.

One evening his uncle was busy so his wife, Maria, interrupted his clarinet practice to tell him that he worked too hard and that she would take him out for dinner. Maria was very high up in recruitment and Elliott was in awe of her. She took him to Pizza Express – he had never been to a restaurant other than a service station or a pub with a climbing frame, so the large, brightly lit room with table-cloths and candles felt like something from a film.

As they were getting out of the taxi, he closed the door too suddenly when Maria's hand was still on the handle. It cracked one of her immaculate, darkly lacquered nails. She drew back, showing her teeth, and said it was fine, but he could see it wasn't – it was both painful and inconvenient and it was his fault – she just wanted him to stop apologising. In that moment he realised that he was a burdensome child whom Maria was looking after as a favour and the shame of it almost made him cry. She was over it by the time they took their seats.

'I've been meaning,' she said, 'to talk to you.'

'Oh?'

'Because I don't think anyone's really talked to you before.'

'Oh, plenty of people talk to me,' said Elliott, 'I'm fine.'

'No,' said Maria, 'don't be so literal, that's not you. I've known your uncle for twenty years. You come from a family of gentle, considerate people and that's all to the good, but it means they probably don't give you very much advice because they don't want to impose. They might ask you, if you were balancing on the edge of a cliff, whether you thought it was such a good idea.'

'I think they …' said Elliott, but then he wasn't sure of either what he wanted to say or what Maria expected him to say. It felt odd hearing anyone pass judgment on his family and he wondered if that wasn't because she was right and he was unaccustomed to anyone he knew passing judgment at all.

'Have you not, so far, been allowed to do more or less exactly as you please?'

Elliott looked at the red wine in his glass. 'Yeah,' he said. 'That's probably fair.'

'You do like women, don't you?' said Maria. He had ordered a pizza with an egg on it, she had ordered something with pine nuts and green side salads for both of them, which struck Elliott as classy and extravagant.

'Uh, yeah,' he said.

'I didn't like to assume.'

'I don't know,' said Elliott. 'I'm not sure where you place yourself on the Kinsey scale if you've not had any experiences one way or the other.'

'Kinsey scale,' said Maria, impressed.

'But I think I'm pretty much straight.'

'Are you seeing anyone?'

'Ha,' said Elliott. 'No.'

'Some women, Elliott, are not going to be interested in you at all.'

'No, god, of course,' said Elliott. 'I mean why would they be?'

Maria topped up his wineglass. 'You'll be irrelevant to them,' she said. 'As if you're a different species. But there are going to be other people' – she sipped her wine – 'who you *really* do it for.' He laughed, then coughed and covered his mouth.

'You don't believe me.'

'I mean I suppose that's the same for everyone, isn't it?' said Elliott.

'Mm,' said Maria. 'No. Not at all. And I'm telling you this because it's actually quite important.'

Elliott laughed again. He wasn't sure if it was a genuine laugh, but he made sure it sounded genuine.

'It's dangerous. What you've got is dangerous.'

'Why?'

'Because when you finally realise it, it's going to be such a novelty …'

'But what have I got?'

'I'm going to have to use words,' said Maria. 'How disappointing. For a start, and this isn't the *half* of it, people go on and on about confidence being attractive, but they don't really know what confidence *is*, or they confuse it with brashness. Your parents raised you to think everyone is wonderful, but I have to tell you something, Elliott.'

'What do you have to tell me?'

'Almost everyone is stupid.'

'I really disagree,' said Elliott. 'There are different kinds of intelligence.'

'No,' said Maria. 'No, no, no. There's one kind, and most people don't have it. At any rate, people vastly underrate vulnerability, or they confuse humility with it.'

'I'm vulnerable?'

'Disarmingly so,' said Maria. 'I know plenty of men, Elliott, some of them are even self-aware. This isn't about picking people up in bars, it's about who's still thinking about you months after they met you. You're charming and attractive and you don't act as though you're aware of it – you're all, Who, *me*? about it – and that's going to really screw with people's heads.'

'I don't really see myself that way,' said Elliott.

'Precisely,' said Maria.

'Or at any rate I'm not doing it deliberately, it's not calculated.'

'Even worse,' said Maria. 'There are people who are going to want to … I don't know. Look after you. Mother you. Even men. They're fairly simple. They're too stupid to see you're perfectly capable of looking after yourself. It'll work up to a point then they'll come to resent the fact that you don't actually need them.'

'But why would they think I needed them in the first place?'

'People are going to have all *kinds* of ideas about you and do you know why?'

'No.'

'Because you're very good at making someone feel as though they're the only one who sees you for who you really are.'

'Who am I, really?'

'That's not relevant. You make people feel as though the way they, specifically, see you, is exactly the way you are. It's a very roundabout way of making people feel special,' said Maria, lining up her cutlery and lighting a cigarette. 'But Jesus, if it isn't one of the most intoxicating.' She offered him her packet of Marlboro Lights.

'Thank you.'

'Practise on me,' said Maria. 'Imagine you're breaking up with me. No, that's not right. Imagine we're in the school cafeteria and you're explaining to me why you don't want to go out with me.'

He took too deep a drag on the cigarette and tried not to cough. He put it in the notch of the Pizza Express ashtray.

'We're really just friends,' he said.

'But I want us to be more than friends.'

'Really?'

'I can't believe it's taken you so long to realise how I feel about you.'

'I …'

'I thought I was being so obvious.'

'You weren't.'

'I mean I thought you were really into me, but then I noticed you're just nice to everyone. You could be into the caretaker for all it told me.'

'I really like you too,' said Elliott.

'I'm in love with you.' She took his hand across the table. 'Do you think we could … Could we just try it?'

Elliott stared at her. 'Okay, yeah,' he said.

'Elliott,' said Maria. 'Ten years later we'll be married with three children and you'll be sitting alone in our garden at 2 a.m. with a cigarette wondering why you didn't have the strength of character to tell me to go away.'

'Mm.'

'You see the problem? I'm not trying to talk you up here,' said Maria. 'I'm not trying to give you a big head. Part of the issue is that you're extremely passive.'

'That's true,' said Elliott.

'You'd be so shocked if someone showed an interest in you, you'd join a fucking … doomsday cult for them.'

'I think I could really thrive in a cult,' said Elliott.

'So, three things. One: you need to be really, really selective. Decide very carefully who you're going to waste your time on. Two: people like you tend to make very bad marriages. You just marry whoever bullies you into it. Don't do that.'

'I'll try not to let anyone bully me into marrying them.'

'The third one is important because it's definitely not the way you see yourself. I said it was dangerous, and it is, because you're not going to change. You'll carry on being Who, *me*? when someone's interested in you even if it becomes a pattern, even if you can see yourself doing it. Partly you'll do it because you're addicted to the attention, and partly you'll do it for the lonely little boy who nobody ever talked to and … and there'll be a kind of anger somewhere in there. About that. And there could come a point—' Maria paused and looked into the middle distance for a moment. 'I don't know. I've had too much to drink today, Elliott.'

'There could come a point?' said Elliott.

'When you hurt someone, several people, yourself included, beyond any hope of repair, and you won't have the first notion of the repercussions until they arrive, and you'll unleash hell and you'll look around and say, Who, *me*?'

'Wow,' said Elliott.

'Now, if somebody had tried to pull this on me when I was seventeen I'd have given them a real dressing down. And you just take it.'

'Meh.'

'Take this,' she said, removing a small enamel brooch of a barn owl from her lapel. Elliott, buzzed on half a bottle of red wine called Lacryma Christi, solemnly attached it to his jacket.

'You don't need to *wear* it,' said Maria. 'Just keep it so that you remember. Blu-tack it to your wall or something.'

* * *

235

At this point the contingent of the orchestra who had gone to the club, solidified by the month's detention they'd received for absconding from a school trip, had found one of the four pubs in town that were happy to serve under-age drinkers. On Friday nights Elliott told his parents he was going to a friend's house, but eventually he dropped the ruse and told them he was going to the King's Head. Nobody had enough money to drink very much anyway, more than a tenner at any given time, except maybe Neil who spent it all on weed which he was incredibly stingy with. They would congregate at a redbrick banana-shaped planter up the road from school and walk to the high street together. Everyone smoked. Pubs were smoke saunas. Everyone's clothes stank all the time, and the pub was the only place where that didn't matter.

One night he said something to Tara, who played the oboe. He couldn't remember what it was, but it made her shoulder-barge him off the pavement just as a souped-up Ford Fiesta was roaring by. He laughed and caught up with her and deliberately walked into her so that she stumbled into the wall, laughing.

'I could have killed you,' she said. 'Sorry.'

Tara, the daughter of a local vicar, had a kind of *Swallows and Amazons* vibe – you wanted to row into a lake with her and fight pirates. That night he found that he was frequently sitting next to her and, when he wasn't, she would look at him and pat the seat next to her. They talked about going to university. She laughed at everything he said and, at one point, after reflecting that it was so weird that all *this* was almost over, she leaned her head on his shoulder. She was going to take a gap year.

'But not, like, missionary work or anything,' said Tara, whose father's vocation had always been something of a burden. 'I'm volunteering at a Buddhist monastery in Nepal.'

'That's amazing,' said Elliott. 'Your dad's okay with it?'

'He's very much an All Roads Lead to God type of vicar,' said Tara. 'Which sucks – I'd prefer it if he was scandalised.'

Later, swimmy from three pints of cider, lager and black-currant – a drink they called Diesel – and having success-fully urinated in the cubicle of the delightfully quiet and dingy gents, Elliott leaned against a fruit machine and watched the coloured lights go through their sequence. Lindsey looked at him from the bar and frowned. She walked up to him with her tall glass of rum and Coke and pressed a few buttons on the machine.

'So are you and Tara …' she said.

'What?'

'I just didn't realise, that's all,' said Lindsey.

'Didn't realise what?'

'You're kind of all over each other.'

'I think she's just very tactile,' said Elliott. 'Tara is a very tactile person. Why do you ask?'

'Why do I ask,' said Lindsey. 'I thought I'd made it pretty clear.'

'Made what pretty clear?' said Elliott.

'Do I have to go around with a sandwich board or something?' said Lindsey. 'Nice owl brooch, by the way. Is it your mum's?'

'My aunt's.'

'Well, it suits you,' said Lindsey. 'You don't really give a fuck what anyone else thinks about you, do you?'

Elliott wasn't sure he ever thought about anything *other* than what people thought about him, but in the time it took for him to consider telling Lindsey this she had kissed him, hard on the lips.

34

'And that owl brooch,' said Emily, 'is now a lifestyle and dating guru with a million YouTube subscribers.'

'I actually don't know when I lost the owl brooch,' said Elliott. 'It turned into a real owl and flew away.'

'Oh, poor Elliott,' said Emily, making a mental note to look up owl brooches on Etsy, 'you lost your talisman.' Arthur accepted a spoonful of Bolognese, the spaghetti cut into inch-long pieces. 'He seems to eat better in your house,' she said.

'That's good. Do you ever think this is just a shared delusion?'

'What, me? You?'

'Whole thing.'

'Of course I've thought about that.'

'Or like, grass is greener,' said Elliott.

'Greener where you water it,' said Emily. 'Fortune cookie.'

'Yes, exactly, so we should stop watering it.'

'Don't want to. Want to nurse an inappropriate, life-ruining crush on you forever.'

'So even if it was …' said Elliott. 'What worries me, about me, I mean, is *what if I just tend to ruin everything anyway*? What if we'd met, years ago, and we were together and we had to deal with normal everyday stuff?'

'I *want* normal everyday stuff with you,' said Emily. 'All we talk about is normal everyday stuff and I love it. Did you go to the doctor?'

'Ally made me.'

'You didn't *tell* me?'

'Nothing to tell. I just fainted. I got a brochure about the importance of eating breakfast.'

'It's nice that she made you go,' said Emily. 'Nice that you have two women who care so much about you.'

He frowned at her.

'Sorry.'

'Don't apologise,' he said. 'I'm sorry.'

They were silent for a while and then he said, 'I mean what happens? What happens with something long-term where you're not idealising each other.'

'Do you think we're idealising each other?'

'I don't know.'

'Because I feel more like you're the only person who's ever understood me.'

'Yeah, that's … Me too. And that's what people say when they're delusional: they say things like *I feel like I've always known you*.'

'I *do* feel like I've always known you.'

'Which means we remind each other of something.'

'Like what?'

'Something buried.'

'Oh something *bad*, you mean?' said Emily.

'How did you meet Steven?' he asked her. 'Were you childhood sweethearts?'

'No.'

As he knew, Emily told him, Steven was a speech therapist and the first time she saw him he was giving a speech at an INSET day she was contractually obliged to attend. She was on her Newly Qualified Teacher year, one of two hundred in the lecture theatre, and in the second to last row, but even from that distance she was struck by his poise, as if unaware he was in front of so many people, carefully attaching his lapel mic and smiling at the technician. He was wearing a white button-down shirt and black jeans and he was handsome, if a little thuggish; he looked like he went to the gym or boxed or something, but his voice, when he started his lecture, was gentle, sincere – possibly Mancunian, but she couldn't say for sure.

Steven talked about the social model and the medical model and, unlike the other speakers, he talked fluently and naturally rather than reading from his PowerPoint slides. He showed statistics and diagrams of the tongue, of the ear, of brain activity. There was nothing funny or cynical about him – he didn't try to win anyone over, but spoke quite movingly about his own speech impediment growing up, about being written off, about his clients and their families. The number of kids held back or thought of as *thick*, unacademic. He gave them some simple, practical tips on how to work with students who were struggling. It was rousing. The room applauded spontaneously when he thanked them for listening and he nodded, switched the projector off and quickly left the room.

During the lunchbreak she scanned the room, saw him at the Klix machine and walked straight over. He was doing something with two cups, transferring powders and liquids between them.

'Sorry,' he said. 'I did some work in a prison and the inmates had this way of making a drinkable coffee out of one of these. Nearly done.'

'That was so, so good,' she said. 'I had to tell you.'

'Oh,' he said. 'I'm glad.'

'You're probably tired of hearing it. You're really brilliant. It was inspiring. It made me want to quit teaching and retrain as a speech therapist.'

'I wouldn't do that,' said Steven. 'We just do the basic maintenance so you can do the real work. What do you teach?'

'Drama.'

'Well there you go.' He looked at her lanyard. 'Emily.'

'Yes, sorry, Emily.' She shook his hand.

'Well, thanks for your kind words.' He picked up his plastic coffee cup by the lip and threw the mixing cup in the bin. 'I should go to the workshops.'

'Oh, me too. I hate workshops. Steven?' said Emily. 'Are you free after? There's a pub round the corner and I was probably going to get a drink. I mean workshops are deathly.'

Steven frowned, as if her sentence was hard to process.

'Okay, yeah,' he said. 'I need to visit my parents, but I could definitely manage a beer.'

'Yay! See you by that plant?'

Steven looked at the tall cheese plant by the revolving door.

'Sure. The plant.'

* * *

'This is a bit disingenuous of me, really,' she said, putting two dark pints of beer on the small table which Steven had wedged straight with train tickets. 'I've got a couple of boys in Year 10 and what you were saying about processing. I mean they're so bright, really, but they can't … It really chimed with me and I wanted to pick your brains.'

'Oh, that's fine.'

'Pick your brains. I hate that phrase. I never say it.'

'I'd be happy to.'

'I mean not now, obviously. Now we should just drink some beer.'

'I can give you my email.'

'That would be perfect. Do you do lots of these talks?'

'No, couple a year. Mostly to prove to myself that I can.'

'You're very good at it. What ages do you work with?'

'The lot. Primary and secondary,' said Steven. 'It's varied. It's good.'

'Do you have kids of your own?'

'Oh, god, no,' he said.

'Sorry. There's something kind of paternal about you. I'm no good at guessing ages.'

'I'm twenty-eight.'

'Oh dear,' said Emily. 'I'm twenty-three. The age difference is insurmountable.'

He looked confused.

'I get silly when I'm nervous,' said Emily, and sipped her beer.

'Why are you nervous?'

'I'm always nervous.'

'I find when I'm nervous – and this is usually what's bothering most of my clients, actually – it's about breathing. If you just take a breath in and count three and then exhale counting four and do that a few times, you really level out.'

'Oh, you're so lovely,' said Emily. 'I don't mean I get anxiety – it's just—'

'Try it.'

Emily took a deep breath.

'Then exhale for longer.'

She did so, and looked at him.

'Oh, that *is* good, actually,' she said.

'And if you visualise the air as, I don't know … As if the patterns in a Van Gogh painting were moving.'

Emily closed her eyes and breathed in and out. She did it four times.

'Hey there,' said Steven.

'Oh, sorry.'

'Thought I'd lost you.'

'Well now I'm very relaxed,' said Emily. 'And you've taken away my excuse for being silly.'

She excused herself and bought two more pints without asking.

'Oh shit, I forgot you had to go to your parents,' she said, approaching the table with the drinks. They were only halfway down their first pints.

'I thought you'd just gone to the bathroom,' he said.

'I'm not like a massive drinker or anything,' said Emily. 'I have a strict three-pint limit on a school night.'

'You shouldn't have bought the second round,' said Steven. 'Let me give you some money.'

'Agh – no,' said Emily, taking her seat. 'I'm not making you pay for a drink you don't even want.'

Steven downed the remainder of his first pint. 'This is a nice pub,' he said. 'My ex hated pubs.'

'How can you hate *pubs*?' said Emily.

'So for five years I don't think I set foot in one. I don't know – she was very *clean living*.'

'How awful,' said Emily. 'I'm so sorry that happened to you.'

'She'd get angry and say that all I cared about was my job, but really she meant I didn't care enough about triathlons.'

'Well it's an important job!' said Emily. 'I think it's sweet that it's all you care about.'

'The thing is I *did* care about triathlons,' said Steven, 'just not as much as she did. I suppose I always thought, why not just get really good at one thing instead of being pretty good at three – does that make sense?'

'What exactly *is* a triathlon?' said Emily.

'It's usually running, swimming and cycling,' said Steven.

'At the same time?'

'No.'

'No, of course.'

Steven, she ascertained over the second pint, seemed to be completely guileless and a little baffled by her, which she liked.

When they parted he gave her a light hug outside the pub and she kissed him on the cheek.

'Let's meet on a Friday next time,' she said.

'Oh right,' he said. 'You'd like to?'

'I'm going to *email* you,' she said.

* * *

Mostly, she was impressed that Steven seemed to lack a sense of humour. It was more than that. He seemed to have no interest in laughing or joining in with the laughter of others to support a consensus, and this struck her as remarkable strength of character. It made her three former boyfriends seem like flatterers and panderers, men with no real qualities.

On their second date they ate a pub lunch after walking in the hills and somebody smashed a plate and Steven didn't join in the applause – he didn't react at all. When she told him a fairly rambling story about the night she got one of her high heels completely stuck in a drain outside a club, he said, 'How did you get free?' with genuine concern.

'I had to pull my foot out and get down on my hands and knees and try to wrench it out of the grate, but the heel was completely stuck, as if it had fused with the drain cover. So they wouldn't let me in. I had to walk home with one shoe.'

'You didn't hurt your foot on the way back?'

'No I … Steven, this is really just an amusing story about me being hopeless. You don't need to ask things like that.'

'Oh,' he said, 'okay.'

'I am so, so tired of people being funny,' she said.

'Why's that?' said Steven.

'It's like, who are they trying to impress?'

'People use humour for a variety of reasons,' said Steven.

'It's like … people think life is a never-ending panel show. The way they try to outdo one another, to be more correct, to be more funny,' said Emily.

'I mean it's you, probably,' said Steven. 'If you're the one they're talking to, I suppose it follows that it's probably you they're trying to impress.'

'Steven,' said Emily.

She felt small next to him. Steven was broad, muscular and wore his hair close-cropped. He walked at a constant pace that Emily only ever attempted when she was trying not to miss a train or carrying takeaway food and very hungry. He was never short of breath. One day they ran into her friend Annie outside a Starbucks and Emily said This is Steven and Steven said Hi and Annie did the usual Annie thing of saying Ohhhh, I wondered why you weren't talking to me. Later Annie texted her.

— This is bizarre. I thought you liked skinny,
  floppy-haired poets.

And Emily, who was working on a lesson plan for *Bartholomew Fair*, a stupid play which she hated, replied that skinny, floppy-haired poets had got dull.

— I mean he's fit, don't get me wrong, wrote Annie.
  It was just, like … when Hannah went into local
  politics and we were all: Hannah?! It's just
  cognitive dissonance, that's all.
— I'm sure you'll get over it.
— It's nice. Why shouldn't you be with someone
  conventionally attractive?
— Yeah! Exactly – don't I deserve more than roll-
  ups and neurosis?

— You're probably too busy getting screwed
    senseless, but I'm meeting Lorna on Friday at
    the Spaghetti House.

And because it seemed to be what Annie wanted, Emily
didn't reply to the message or turn up at Spaghetti House
and enjoyed the thought of Annie telling Lorna about her
boyfriend and that she was probably too busy getting
screwed senseless.

Steven had a long scar on the back of his head which was
only visible if you mussed his short hair around a bit. She
found it when they were lying, post-coital, in her single
bed. Emily was thinking about a psychological-assessment
questionnaire she'd answered a few years ago, and that one
of the questions, right after 'Do you drink in order to get
drunk?' was 'Has sex ever really moved you to a different
place?' It struck her at the time, and whenever she thought
about it since – such as after sex – as an oddly phrased
question. It seemed to invite a negative, a raised eyebrow.
You're filling in this questionnaire, so we're going to
assume that it hasn't. But being 'moved to a different place'
was a strange thing to expect from sex, and a strange sort
of pressure to put on someone vulnerable enough to try to
self-diagnose their mental illness.

But it did, for her, was the thing: she always went somewhere else in her head. A barn in Hardy country; a backstage dressing room with illuminated mirrors. Sex seemed
to take place outside of ordinary time – the only equivalent feeling was during a liturgy: the total engagement of
the senses, the repetition. It was when she felt most herself

and most out of herself. At one. And as long as sex moved her to a different place Emily felt that she was probably okay.

Steven was drowsing, his face pressed to her breasts. She was moving her fingers in a circular motion on the back of his head when she felt the ridge and shuffled up a little to examine it.

'What's this?'

'What's what?' he murmured.

'How'd you get the scar? It's like … six inches long. Have you had brain surgery?'

He told her he was seventeen and walking to the news-agents round the corner from his parents' and some kids had beaten him with a bicycle chain.

'Oh my god,' said Emily. 'They mugged you?'

No, Steven told her. They were kids. They just wanted to whip him with a bicycle chain a few times and run off laughing. It wasn't anything much, he told her. He lost some blood. Someone called an ambulance. Twelve stitches.

'They could have killed you.'

'Nah.'

She stroked his head.

She muttered *fucking little cunts* and stroked his head until he fell asleep.

35

'So that's that,' said Emily. 'From then on it's more or less psychosis and clinical depression and taking each other for granted.'

She sat with her feet on Elliott's lap. Arthur and Dimitry were watching CBeebies and eating slices of cucumber. At one point it had felt like a relationship between four different people, Emily and Elliott and an Emily and Elliott made entirely of text. She wondered if he missed the textual Emily when he was talking to the flesh Emily. It would usually take her some time to work up the confidence to continue a conversation they'd been having via text the night before, but something had shifted. She moved her legs from his lap and said, 'Tell me about you and Alathea.'

'What do you want to know?'

'I feel like it might be good for me. If we can keep the focus on the two of you.'

Elliott told her that he rarely thought about the past.

'Really?' said Emily. 'It's all I think about.'

Unlike Emily, Elliott had little inclination to look backwards. But he'd read somewhere that projecting forwards into a notional future used exactly the same parts of the brain as recalling memories, so perhaps that wasn't strictly true – perhaps he was looking back all the time and thinking he was looking forwards. But he would rather live in a hologram of the future than a … zoetrope of the past. He told her that, like all men who were awkward children, awkward teenagers, awkward twenty-somethings, he found it difficult to believe it whenever someone was attracted to him. And he was aware, because at some point they would tell him as much, that this came across as charismatic and disarming modesty. He would protest that he was actually incredibly vain, but this would just confirm their impression.

The past held only sporadic charm for Elliott because – it seemed stupid not to admit it – he was less powerful then than he was now. In the past he was a joke, an underfed gadfly stubbornly pursuing his work, whose girlfriend bought him drinks when he could be convinced to go out, and whose ambitions as an artist were regarded increasingly, over several years, more with pity than envy. He wore the same bobbled Crombie whatever the weather and put up with their quiet derision. But for years now he had lived with a sense that things were really coming together. He was respected by his peers, his work sold, he held an enviable position at a university. And if his precise circumstances hadn't come together to form an especially coherent picture, and perhaps never would, they nonetheless retained the charm of eternal, postponed coalescence. The future felt bright.

'Ugh,' said Emily. 'How can you even live with that many clichés in your head? Like someone who hoards empty cereal boxes and junk mail.'

Perpetually bright, he told her. Like neon. He'd always been crazy about Alathea, had been crazy about her since he met her at the Venice Biennale – she was a publicist for Warshact-Benning, a corporate art consultancy (she was photocopying something in the press office and he told her it seemed like a terrible waste of her talents). But he hated her friends, who had dutifully fucked off out of the picture when she couldn't afford to go skiing with them anymore. Elliott abhorred skiing – it represented everything he was against, rich people falling down a mountain and calling it a sport.

Even before they had kids, Elliott and Alathea had sex rarely, every other month by his estimation. I mean at first you're all over each other all the time, right? Then it tapers off and …

'Did it *taper off* for you too?'

'No, but I think I have an unusually high sex drive.'

'So you're frustrated?'

'I didn't say that,' said Elliott. 'Who *is* it telling us how many times we ought to have sex anyway? What if they're wrong? What if *they* have an unusually high sex drive and they're setting the tone for everyone else, putting unnecessary pressure on people who'd rather do a crossword. Maybe normal people only like fucking on really special occasions.'

'If only,' said Emily. 'I read somewhere that if you have sex less than ten times a year that technically counts as a sexless marriage.'

'Well that's silly,' said Elliott. 'Even from the perspective of someone who'd happily have sex ten times a week. Having sex ten times a year isn't sexless.'

The thing was, near-abstinence seemed in keeping with his sense that things were only just starting, just beginning to turn in his favour. He lived in a perpetual state of desire for Alathea, waiting for her to respond to an arm across the shoulder, his hands on her waist, a brief kiss – and when she didn't react he'd think, *Maybe next time*. Maybe the secret to staying desperately in love with someone was to have that desperation seldom relieved or realised. He *was* desperate, he supposed. He hated men who saw sex as a need. It was important to him to be better than those men. There was no denying that it was a powerful urge, of course, and one that, for Alathea, seemed to arrive with similar ferocity only a couple of times a year.

'So do you and Alathea not have sex at all anymore?'

Elliott looked at her warily.

'You don't need to answer that. Sorry.'

'No, it's fine, it's just … I don't think that's massively unusual after kids,' he said. 'I think sex has become largely irrelevant to Alathea.'

'Really?'

'We don't want any more children, I don't think she ever particularly feels like it – I mean I can only infer that … If you're the only one who ever instigates any physical intimacy at all you begin to feel like you're pestering.'

'Hmm. I don't feel like I'm pestering Steven. I feel like I'm sending letters to the wrong address or something.'

'And even if … It's sort of depressing if you feel as though someone is only doing it to indulge you.'

'Yeah.'

'I mean actually feeling desired is a fairly important part of sex, isn't it? Central, even.'

'Have you talked about it?'

'What is there to talk about?'

'I'm hardly an example of candour,' said Emily. 'But I think it's generally quite a good idea to talk to someone if you're not happy.'

'But what's the end point? We're supposed to go to a couples counsellor to work on the fact that she doesn't want to have sex? Brainwash her into wanting me again … out of what? Guilt? A sense of duty. Gross.'

'And that's why you're looking elsewhere?'

'I'm not looking elsewhere.'

'Good.'

'I'm a grown-up. What does it matter, ultimately, what I want?'

'But what we're doing here …' said Emily.

'There are more important things than that.'

'But you want me?'

'I have never felt more attracted to anyone in my life,' said Elliott.

'Oh good. I want you too.'

'So we should probably stop seeing one another like this,' said Elliott. 'Because I'm mostly thinking about touching you.'

He put his hand on her knee.

'Yeah,' said Emily. 'That feels good. Little knee touch. Okay, I'm going to go.'

'Don't.'

'I'm absolutely going to go.'

'I'm sorry I put my hand on your knee.'

'That's completely fine,' said Emily. 'Come on, Arthur.'

36

— You sleeping?

— Nah.

— How are things?

— INSET day tomorrow.

— Oh yeah, I always forget those aren't days off for teachers.

— Haha. It's when they *train* us, Elliott. Latest updates on the county lines. How to work with your police contact. It's going to suck.

— Yeah?

— They're not a very good exam board so I'm just going for the pasta salad.

— Do they notice if you don't show up to these things?

— Ooh yeah. God knows how much they rinse the school for per attendee. Everything's a racket. It's why train tickets are so expensive.

— Because I don't … actually have anything at work tomorrow I can't cancel.

— What are you saying?

— That we're both potentially …

— Elliott.

— child-free/work-free. You could tell them your kids are unwell?

— *Elliott*

— Then you could come to London with me on research?

— I don't use the kids as an excuse – that's a big red line for me.

— I actually … This was probably a mistake, but I actually already booked you a ticket. You don't want to come?

— Are you kidding?

— Because you can just tell me you don't want to and I'd completely understand.

— It would make me very, very happy to go with you.

— So maybe you come down with gastric flu and meet me at the station at 9?

— That's good – an excuse should generally be something embarrassing.

She saw him standing by a sushi concession on the main concourse and broke into a run. When he saw her he looked shocked and then concerned – the way she imagined his expression would be when he watched a particularly heart-rending scene in a film – an expression which then resolved into a smile. He took her in his arms.

'I didn't think you'd make it,' he said.

'Oh, come on,' she murmured into his neck.

They took the first off-peak train to London, which was standing-room only. Elliott had booked seats and guiltily turfed out a middle-aged man with a backpack.

'Do you ever think, just *who are all these people*?' he whispered.

'Who are *we*?' said Emily.

'Educators!' said Elliott. 'We're at work! People are generally supposed to have jobs, right? Whenever you take an off-peak train it just seems to give the lie to that. All the stuff they told us at school. And you look around and it's like the majority of people just bought a bunch of properties when they were cheap and live off their tenants.'

Emily felt excited as the train pulled away, like a child on a ride at a theme park – was that the last time she'd had that sensation? She sipped from a paper coffee cup and held Elliott's hand under the seat tray. Then she leaned her head on his shoulder and closed her eyes.

'Do you know I've never done this in my life?' she said.

'What, exactly?' said Elliott.

'I never played truant – even when I was at school. I never so much as pulled a sickie.'

'You were a good girl.'

'I was a *very* good girl.'

'Yeah,' said Elliott. 'Me too. I was well-behaved to the point of pathology.'

'You're a terrible influence on me, Elliott,' she said. 'Do you have specific things you need to do today?'

'No.'

'Pure ruse,' said Emily.

'I just like to remember that London exists sometimes. Like bathing.'

Then she closed her eyes again until Elliott said, 'We're here.'

'We can't be,' said Emily. 'That felt like about five minutes.'

They went straight to the bar outside the station. Emily sat at a tall table and Elliott bought them two pints of American beer.

'Not too early?' he said.

'No,' said Emily. 'If I concentrate on drinking I'll stop worrying about what the hell I think I'm doing.'

'I always find that works *wonders*,' said Elliott, taking a large gulp. 'It's really, really good to be with you.'

'You,' said Emily. 'Oh my god. I feel happy and it's like when the feeling comes back in a numb leg.'

'When you've been sitting like a pretzel.'

'I always sit like a pretzel.'

'Terrible at sitting in a chair.'

After two more pints Elliott helped her down from the stool and they linked arms as they walked purposefully down the street.

'If you're a little drunk before noon you feel invincible,' said Elliott.

'You look at all the sober people and think, *Ha!*' said Emily. 'You poor fools.'

'You poor fool!' said Elliott to an approaching man in a navy blue suit whose eyes widened as he quickened his pace to get away from them.

'Elliott!'

They caught the Tube to the Tate Modern and Elliott took her hand and led her up a couple of escalators until they stood in front of Christian Schad's *Agosta, the Pigeon-Chested Man, and Rasha, the Black Dove.*

'I don't know why, but I always have to see this,' said Elliott. 'I'm not even into the New Objectivity.'

'Ha! Are you *not*?'

'Although if you think of what else was going on in the twenties ...'

'It was like Protest Realism,' said Emily.

'It was like, hey, guys, there's stuff going on you can't capture with cubes.'

Agosta's bone structure reminded Emily of the obsession with the warp and weft of cloth in a Byzantine icon, his upside down ribcage like a twisted chicken-wire fence.

'And it's not ...' Elliott drifted off.

'It's not what?' said Emily.

'It's not like some heavy-handed reversal, like *these side show freaks are people too!* It's not some crass attempt at ennobling ...'

'Even though it's kind of a throne,' said Emily.

'I just really like their faces. They're not defiant or confrontational, they just look dignified. That's not really it, though.'

'Do you still paint, Elliott?' said Emily. 'You're more installation-y now, aren't you?'

'No, I paint,' said Elliott. 'I've just never been able to commit to anything. Do you want to eat pizza and get smashed?'

'I'd *love* to.'

Emily took a sip of her red wine and a smaller sip of her overpowered negroni then rolled up her last slice of pizza and ate it in two bites.

'Ugh. *So* good,' she said. 'You take me to the best places.'

'Pizza and darkness,' said Elliott.

She scanned the basement room – dark furnishings around the central kiln. It was packed and she felt pleasantly anonymous. She felt him staring at her.

'You know when there's a lull?' she said.

'A lull?'

'Between us.'

'There are lulls? I hadn't noticed.'

'You *know* there are lulls.'

'I figured you were just giving me some time to look at you.'

'When there are lulls I get scared that you think I'm boring.'

'Hahaha!'

'Because *deep* down I think I *am* quite boring.'

'I'm not even going to dignify that with a refutation.'

'And for some reason you find me attractive.'

'Good bone structure.'

'So you're willing to overlook my being *boring.*'

'I'm terrified of being boring,' said Elliott. 'It's one of my big underlying fears. It's why I wear so much leopard-skin.'

'I'd wondered.'

'Someone … who was it? I think it was Julian Clary who said the nicest thing about a stable relationship is that you can have a good, long silence between the two of you without it being awkward. I'm paraphrasing.'

'That's sweet.'

'But on the other hand I quite enjoy feeling insecure around you.'

'I'm getting very drunk,' said Emily. 'This place is so lovely.'

She leaned against him and tried to think nothing, tried to give him a non-awkward silence if that was what he wanted. She looked up at him and he tilted his head towards her and she thought about trying to kiss him and then very briefly did until he pulled away.

'So is work okay, Elliott?' she said.

'Oh, don't,' he said. 'It just feels very arbitrary. I don't really know what any of it means or why I'm doing it. Sometimes I get to talk to a student in office hours who's really unhappy and I listen to them and try to be sympathetic – that's the closest I get to feeling useful.'

'They probably really look up to you.'

'God no,' said Elliott. 'They absolutely don't, which is good. Anything that makes you feel important is a great evil. To you and everyone else.'

'Is that so?'

'I don't know,' said Elliott. 'I've seen it turn people into real arseholes, anyway.'

'Theoretically?' said Emily. 'The fact that you can't make anything at the moment, what do you think that is?'

'Beats me,' said Elliott. 'Mid-life crisis?'

'That you can't take yourself seriously? That you see yourself as, essentially, not a serious concern? There must have been a time when you believed quite strongly that what you were doing had value.'

'It's always been fairly centrally bound up with *shame*,' said Elliott. 'Shame before value.'

'Your inability to articulate what you desire?'

'I feel real, right now, and it's such a novelty.'

'What is it,' said Emily, 'about thinking you're in love with someone, that you can just sit together and marvel over it, as if you're gathered around a … a—'

'Precious objet d'art?'

'Camp fire. You can just sit there staring at it – can you believe you feel the same way as I do? Can you *believe* that?'

'So it creates a third thing,' said Elliott.

'It's such a surprise to be so pleased to see someone. I think that every time I see you.'

'Emily.'

'We can talk about something else. I'm saying that I'm in my thirties but I haven't felt this way about anyone before and I don't know what to do about it.'

Then it was as if something passed over them, although the restaurant had no windows, a fluctuation in the lighting, something leaving or arriving, she wasn't sure.

'Shall we move on?' said Elliott. 'I know a place that does martinis with *onions* in them.'

'Ooh. Yeah – can we split this?'

'I paid.'

'Elliott.'

'I'm still living off the reserve of a couple of consolation prizes from five years ago – it's nothing.'

'It's *not* nothing. I don't want you to pay for everything.'

'I forced you to come to London so I could hog your attention for a whole day,' said Elliott. 'It's the least I can do.'

'You're sweet.'

When they staggered out of the basement bar Emily said, 'Oh my god it's still daytime.'

'It's barely *lunchtime*,' said Elliott. 'More art or more booze?'

Emily slept on the train home and woke up blearily with a pounding headache to Elliott stroking her hair and saying her name.

'Oh *god*,' she said. 'I've wasted over an hour unconscious I could have spent with you.'

'You slept on me,' said Elliott. 'It was lovely.'

She held his hand again as they alighted on platform 2.

Elliott said it was probably best that they didn't arrive back at Criterion Gardens together. He would get her a cab and stay at the station for half an hour checking some emails. Emily asked if he was sure and told him the duplicity made her feel sad. He said it was probably best to embrace the sadness. She had that daytime drunk out-of-place feeling, like being very over- or underdressed and convinced everyone was judging her for it. She found it hard to maintain a conversation with the taxi driver and, when he pulled up outside her house, realised she didn't have any cash.

'Could you wait here a second, I'm so sorry,' she told him.

She fumbled in her bag for her keys then hammered on the front door. Steven opened it, holding Arthur on his shoulder.

'Oh,' he said.

'Steven, darling, I'm so sorry – there was free wine at the INSET day and I think I got carried away. Hi baby!' she picked Matty up and kissed him. 'I need money,' she added. 'For the taxi.'

'That's fine,' said Steven. 'I'm glad you had a chance to let off some steam.'

— New one: personal drone strike.
— Oh, that's genius. It could just be an app on your phone!
— 79p.
— No, free, but with ads.
— You can pay 4.99 to get rid of the ads.
— You don't even need to put in coordinates, it just tracks you.
— It knows *exactly* where you are. So the app is literally just one button.
— You press it and within minutes AKAKAKAKAKAKAKAKAKAKAK!
— I love you.
— I love you.

37

Aware, after promising her mother, that she'd neither had nor made an opportunity to talk to Steven in any serious capacity, Emily considered the possibility that he might entertain a text conversation with her. Should he take to it, that might be a way of keeping in regular contact, might break the spell of quite how alive and full of light she felt whenever Elliott wrote to her. She tried to think of a reason to message Steven.

— Babe I feel really stressed and worn out – can we just get a takeaway tonight?
— Sure okay x
— It might give us some more time together. How's your day going?
— Fine thanks x

Bah. She went back to loading the washing machine. The fitting for the exit pipe was loose from the wall and Steven had attached a clothes peg to the tubing as a temporary fix. She felt a passing irritation that they'd committed themselves to this paper house, that they were trying to make something permanent out of something which felt so stubbornly flimsy. But whatever. It was fine. Stop complaining. So many people had real and awful problems.

Once the machine was on, and promising to take upwards of three hours to wash the school uniforms and shirts and underwear, she brought up the Criterion Gardens directory on her phone – she could finally write a little profile for her and Steven, try to find a flattering photo where she still looked enough like herself so that it wasn't obvious she'd chosen the most flattering photo. She pressed the 'Edit Your House Profile' button and found that the entry for number 22 was blank except for a leftover photograph of the previous owner, Samantha Edwards, yet to be deleted by the system, probably in breach of data-protection laws. It was a black and white portrait which Emily recognised as a Spotlight headshot. Samantha was an actor, she remembered. Her dark hair a little windblown, an eyebrow slightly raised, a half-smile. The face of someone who could bring any given character to life: beautiful eighteenth-century ingenue, defeated matriarch, corrupt politician. She saved the image to her phone before hitting delete. Then held her phone at arm's length and took a selfie in which she looked grey and concerned.

She deleted it and messaged Elliott.

— I'm bored.

She opened *Restaurant Fever: Cooking Dash* on her phone to wait for his response, which came after two minutes spent flipping imaginary burgers.

— Hey. I'm half-asleep in a meeting. You okay?

— Oh, don't let me bother you.

— No, no, everyone has their phones out. You just have to look up and nod occasionally. Code we've agreed on.

— Good manners.

— Yes. Ever-shifting margins of good manners. I'm sorry you're bored.

— Nah I'm just whining. Can I ask you something?

— Of course

— Did you know the couple in the house before we moved in?

— Sure – the Sams. They were both called Sam. They were great. It's best not to get too attached to people here, they move on.

— That's why you've been so cool and distant with me.

— Haha exactly. Why do you ask?

— This probably isn't the time.

— No it's fine – they were a lovely couple. She babysat a couple of times, actually.

— Oh – you were close?

— I wouldn't say close, just friendly. They were fun. Then they separated or he left or something and I guess she couldn't afford the place by herself. But it all worked out for the best.

— In what way?

— I'd never have met YOU otherwise.

— Dawwww

— Ah the mysteries of the universe

— She have a crush on you?

There was a pause of about thirty seconds before he replied.

— I very much doubt it.
— Okay.
— Why do you ask?
— I'm just interested. I mean actually I just saw a photo of her and she's hot.
— We got on.
— Hm. Sure.
— And I like people.
— You like attractive interesting people
— Who doesn't? so we talked a lot, I guess
— This is probably really silly. I started thinking, maybe you just start things like this ...
— Things like what?
— Like me!
— You're a 'thing'?
— And by extension that I could be just ... anyone.
— Emily, I have to talk about plagiarism now. You're beautiful. We can talk about this later if it's bugging you.
— No, oh honestly, no, it's nothing.

38

'Can you say things from the future?' said Tomasz.

'Can you what, darling?'

'Can you say things', said Tomasz, carefully, 'from the future.'

'Can I personally?'

'No. Can anyone?'

'I'm not sure I understand what you mean,' said Elliott.

'Ugh,' said Tomasz, exasperated.

'Give me your bag. Don't drag it along the ground.'

'I think you can say things that are from the future and things that are from the past,' said Tomasz.

'Do you mean as in different tenses?' said Elliott. 'As in *we went to the shops* or *we will go to the shops.*'

'No,' said Tomasz. 'I mean, what if before you saw someone you said "Hi!" and then when you see them, you've already said hi.'

'But why would you do that?'

'Hi Mummy,' said Tomasz.

Elliott looked up, expecting to see Alathea, but she wasn't there.

'That was from the future,' said Tomasz.

* * *

That evening while the boys were eating their yoghurts he went to fetch a clean shirt for the morning and found Alathea standing in front of his framed print of Eric Gill's *Amnon* on the bedroom wall.

'I'd forgotten that was even in here,' said Elliott. 'You look very smart.'

'I'm going out for a bit.'

'Oh?'

'Couple of hours. I've never really liked this being in our room. I don't think I'm willing to separate the art from the artist anymore.'

'No,' said Elliott. 'For sure. You still see this as *our* room?'

Alathea put her hands on the side of the frame and unhooked the print from its nail.

Elliott, caught off guard, reached for a pot of face cream on the dressing table. It was in a heavy white pearlescent jar.

'Ooh,' she said. 'That moisturiser was developed by an aerospace physicist and it's probably worth seven times your print.'

He unscrewed the lid and dropped it on the floor.

'It's made of thousands of pearls.'

'Tell me what's wrong. Where are you going?'

'You think I'm stupid,' said Alathea.

'No.'

'It wasn't a question. Do you think you can just change the rules as you go along?'

'What am I doing?'

'Is it different this time, Elliott?'

'Is what different?'

'Oh my *god*, you're impossible.'

Alathea undid the catches on the back of the frame.

Elliott swabbed as much of the face cream out of the jar as he could, as if it was hummus on a Pringle. Alathea's breathing was fast and shallow as she started wrenching the frame apart. She pulled the wooden parts off and threw the glass on the bed and then started to tear the image itself, staring at him.

Elliott looked to the wall, then the window, then the bed, then he shrugged and threw the palmful of goo at Alathea, as if casting a spell.

She tore *Amnon* into six pieces then she ran to him, grabbed him by the waist and kissed him.

'You've basically ruined my top as well as …' she said. 'Kiss me. Properly.'

39

Boundaries, Emily said to herself. Remember what's at stake. Remember you can't do anything. Remember a meaningful life pivots on what you choose not to do as much as what you do. And sometimes maybe you have to fight yourself for that.

But without planning or talking about it, she would take Arthur to Elliot's after the school run every Tuesday, when their days off aligned with Alathea's work. Once the boys were asleep for a nap that ran to anything up to three hours they'd go to Elliott's study in the barely converted attic and he'd tap away at his computer and she'd read or do school admin.

'You two,' Alathea would say, giving Emily the side-eye when she got back from work to find her and Elliott sitting on the sofa, Matty and Tomasz playing on their phones on the floor. 'Thick as thieves.'

'She calls you my girlfriend,' said Elliott.

'That's sweet.'

'Yeah, I mean,' said Elliott.

'Yeah, it's also really depressing and makes me feel very bad,' said Emily.

'I don't know,' said Elliott. 'I think you can joke about something over and over again and then it happens. Ally gets a kick out of being jealous and it's kind of key to our whole … thing, but she also has this genuine paranoia that I'm having an affair or that I've had an affair. It's kind of the only thing she shows any vulnerability over so that's … key to our whole thing too.'

'Your whole thing,' said Emily. 'It's funny – sometimes I suppose I infer that your marriage is dead, sometimes that you're kind of … semi-detached and other times it feels like it's something vibrant and intriguing.'

'Oh, god,' said Elliott. 'You know I'm trying not to be just a textbook bastard, complaining about my partner.'

'Pardner,' said Emily.

'I mean I could tell you literally anything – I could tell you that once the front door's closed she keeps me locked in the attic and doesn't let me see the children, that we maintain a façade of—'

'You're feeling got at,' said Emily. 'I didn't mean that you should get your story straight, I was just saying.'

'Of course, yeah, I'm sorry.'

'And now you're desperate to stop talking to me.'

'I'm not.'

'Because I questioned something.'

'Emily!'

'Sorry. That's not fair. I don't even know what I'm pushing for.'

'I think Alathea and I have a fairly standard contorted relationship, you know, the way two trees grow around each other.'

'Accommodatingly.'

'Until they're just one ugly hybrid freak tree.'

'That's love.'

'We threaten to break each other's things.'

'You what?'

'If we have a row it usually concludes with breaking one or more valuable possessions. It's actually quite expensive.'

'That's …'

'But it feels like a kind of intimacy.'

'Twisted.'

'Everyone has their little rituals, right?'

'I mean, I suppose, sort of. Like what sort of things do you break?'

'It's more about the threat,' said Elliott. 'It has to be something literally valuable and also of great sentimental value.'

'Wow.'

'It acts as a kind of lightning rod for the contempt which would otherwise … strike all over the place.'

'Okay,' said Emily. 'You're a hybrid tree getting struck by lightning. I'm glad we cleared that up. It's sweet and funny that she calls me your girlfriend, but of course she trusts me completely, because what kind of human garbage would … Actually, that's something I was meaning to ask you,' said Emily. '*Have* you had an affair?'

'God, no,' said Elliott.

'Colleague you end up working late with? Grad student?'

'I wouldn't countenance it.'

'The former owner of my house? Because, you know, you're very attentive and you're a flirt.'

'That's just another way of being needy and insecure,' said Elliott.

'And it doesn't really seem like *you*, but I don't know.'

'You don't?'

'Because part of what makes you attractive is that you're a moral and decent person.'

'Real Catch-22,' said Elliott.

'So if … hypothetically if we somehow ended up together would we actually be able to trust each other? After we'd smashed that decency to pieces? Move our blended family to another city, another estate – like, what do you think, we'd take one kid each and force Alathea and Steven into a marriage of convenience?'

Elliott laughed nervously.

'Marriage of vengeance,' said Emily.

'Marriage of proving a point.'

'There are worse. So we've moved with Tomasz and Arthur or Matty and Dimitry, all the paperwork and the therapy bills are settled, nobody killed themselves even though it was touch and go for a bit. We lock eyes over the table on the first day in our new home – what do you say to me?'

'Hey you.'

'Hey. And we carry on – we've got the same jobs in new places. Things are good. You still love Alathea and some-times you miss her intensely, but then you fuck me and forget about it. That stops after a while, we get used to each other.'

'Ha, Emily, stop it.'

'How long before you found another Emily?'

'And just followed my heart.'

'*The heart wants what it wants*,' said Emily, in the low, theatrically masculine voice she usually used when she was making fun of Steven.

'And I'd be like …'

'You'd be like *sow-wy*, *Emily* and head off to … Italy with the little … skank.'

'Teach English as a foreign language.'

'Get lazy with birth control.'

'Raise some bilingual babies.'

'Chronic back pain. Then you'd leave *her* for a woman ten years younger.'

'Ah,' said Elliott. 'That's the life.'

The reasons for having an affair had always been entirely opaque to Emily. Firstly: who has the time? But mostly it seemed like something middle-aged estate agents did at hotel conferences, drunk on complimentary Pinot Grigio. It was an old-people thing. You sat through the evening keynote, found someone else as cynical and loveless and passably attractive as you by the rhombus of half-filled glasses and clumsily fumbled with them until 2 a.m. before staggering back, alone, to your identical en-suite on the next floor to throw up the salad bar. When you got home you immediately told your partner everything, crying hysterically and begging for forgiveness and they said no, and then you went to prison or something. I mean, wasn't it illegal? Anyway, it was a sad, dull, disastrous thing which adults did, and even in her thirties with a husband and two children of her own, she still felt sort of like a child. The point was – Emily stirred a second sugar into her instant coffee and stared at the buggy where Arthur had been asleep for just under twenty minutes (his right foot kicked twice) – the point was, she had always thought, re. affairs: why would anyone ever want to have one? Look at these people! Gross. And so it was a shock to find herself surrounded by other couples in their mid-thirties, all of them distractingly attractive. Had they been there all along?

'But it's like my aunt was saying,' said Elliott.

'Your beloved aunt.'

'My beloved aunt, yes, her point was—'

'That you're pretty.'

'Her point was, if someone finding you attractive is a *novelty* to you, then that remains quite a dangerous thing forever.'

Emily laughed and said, 'I think it's just called growing up, Elliott.'

'I think it's maybe the exact opposite.'

Quite how she had ended up lying across him on the futon in his study – who had made the decision that this was how they would sit – she wasn't sure. The boys were asleep in their buggies. One moment Elliott had been sitting there answering an email on his phone, the next she felt herself leaning against him and, when he didn't shift over, murmuring that she was exhausted and lying across his lap with her book, but doing so in such a way that he *could* have shifted over if he really wanted to.

'I think I'm just going to nap here.'

'That's fine.'

'Is it work stuff?'

'Oh,' said Elliott, 'my job is 88 per cent emails.'

'Poor Elliott. They should give you an assistant to do things like that so you can get on with being brilliant.'

'What are you reading?'

'*The Disinherited Mind* – you got it for me, remember?'

'Oh yeah.'

Elliott had started gently stroking her waist where her top had ridden up. In that moment it felt like the best and worst thing which had ever happened to her. She was drowsy, but every time she breathed in it felt somewhere between pleasure and pain, as if she'd just finished a long crying jag.

'When I was … thirteen I think?' she said.

'Mm?'

'There was this guy at my parents' church and he must have been in his early thirties. So younger than I am now, oh my god. But all adults seem impossibly sophisticated when you're a teenager, don't they?

'Your parents' church?' said Elliott. 'You told me they thought you were weird for believing in God.'

'Oh, we went to church in this villagey way,' said Emily. 'I wasn't supposed to take it seriously. But bless you for noticing that.'

'I keep detailed notes about you.'

'So this guy, he was married and they had two little girls. I can't remember any of their names but I can visualise them – they were a really good-looking couple. They were both very tall. And he rode a motorbike so he was always in leathers. Big, black Honda. I don't know why I remember the brand. But anyway, he had an accident, on the bike, a bad one. Serious brain injury.'

'That's awful,' said Elliott, distantly.

'Oh, Elliott,' said Emily. 'I'm not telling you this to make you feel sympathy for some complete strangers.'

'That's what all stories are for, aren't they?'

'No! They're to illustrate a point about the teller. When I tell you a story it's to make me look good or because I'm troubled and confused about something or just to feel less alone, usually all the above. It has nothing to do with sympathy for the people in the story. They're just my props.'

'What happened to the motorbike guy?'

'Pretty much everyone with a motorbike is eventually going to have a serious accident, aren't they?'

'I don't know the statistics. I think motorcyclists are actually quite safety-conscious.'

'But anyway, it was a bad brain injury and he was in a coma and I suppose he needed some sort of operation, I don't know. But when he came round he had actual full-blown soap-opera amnesia. He'd lost like … ten years.'

'Wow.'

'He still remembered his childhood, remembered being a teenager. He didn't have … what's the word, the short-term thing. He could live a perfectly functional life day to day. And it wasn't like his mental age was reduced to that of a sixteen-year-old, either – he was still an adult man, still himself, basically. But the last decade was just wiped out. He had no recollection of his wife or his daughters whatsoever.'

'Fuck.'

'Fuck, right? Their courtship, their marriage, the fact that they were in love, that they knew each other at all. The birth of his daughters, every single day they'd spent together. He woke up from his coma and found three expectant strangers around his bed.'

'But if … How could he still be himself without his experiences?'

'I don't know. He just still seemed like a thirty-year-old man is what I'm saying.'

'Christians marry young,' said Elliott.

'Uh huh – sex thing.'

'Did you see them, after the accident?'

'Yeah. At least once. I think they left the area. It was awful. I mean, as far as I know they stayed together. But she was devastated, obviously, and his daughters were probably too young to know exactly what was going on. And my memory of it's vague because it was a long time ago. But I just have this image of his face and he looked *haunted*.'

'I suppose one *would* look haunted.'

'There was nothing physically different – he wasn't visibly injured, you know? But he looked completely … His whole bearing. He looked exactly like someone who couldn't remember the last fifteen years of his life. Every moment just thinking … *What?*'

'What did you say the point of the story was again?'

'I just say whatever comes into my head when I'm with you. But, like, Elliott, you know when you totally declutter and clean a room?'

'No.'

'And once it's done you can't believe you were putting up with it. That you'd come to accept three mugs with … *spores* in them, just utter disarray of papers and toys and … that you'd grown so accustomed to … squalor. Before you did something about it.'

'I think I can dimly recall that feeling.'

'That if you went to someone else's room and it was like that, you'd be a bit disgusted. Or if you were suddenly plonked down into your own life with no context and you were faced with how you'd been living …'

'Oh, I see where this is going.'

'I don't. I'm free-associating. You think I'm saying it's like what we come to accept from each other?'

Elliott stopped stroking her waist and put his arms around her.

'Is this okay?'

'Uh huh.'

'Are you sure?'

'Yeah,' said Emily and closed her eyes.

He held her for a few minutes until they heard Dimitry, and shortly after Arthur, fussing in their buggies.

'Oh, there they are.'

He let go of her and she stood, smoothing her top down.

'I'm sorry,' said Elliott.

She shook her head.

— Austen era: You're a misunderstood …

— Pastor?

— Plantation owner.

— I don't want to be a plantation owner.

— You're either a plantation owner or you're ministering to them, Elliott, it's much of a muchness.

— Feels more doomed if I'm a pastor.

— Yeah, I guess. I'm betrothed to a plantation owner but he's kind of a dick.

— But you have an excuse to come and see me because I'm the pastor.

— Oh but it's so painful to see you.

— And I have to make house calls. You're teaching your little sisters to play the piano. I sit awkwardly with a sherry. There's nowhere to put it so I can't applaud. Your eyes when you smile at them. Kills me.

— Maybe we should go more Henry James … We plot to very subtly suggest to my fiancée that he takes his own life.

— How do we do that?

— Just gentle undermining. Takes absolutely aeons.
— Ends badly.
— For all of us.
— Cut to present day. Big, mature conversation about what's happened and what everyone wants to do about it.
— Ha!
— Hahahaha.

40

— I want to see you again. I'm greedy. I want to go to London with you once a week minimum.
— Okay. It's important that we don't get greedy.
— Right.
— That's when you start steering too close to the edge, you know? There are plenty of nice bars in town, for example.
— That's true.
— Do you have an old friend you haven't seen in a while?
— Oh yeah that's literally all I have.
— Good.
— I'm a *mother*, Elliott.
— Hahahah. So you start seeing one of them again, maybe once a month. I deal with my end. We go drinking.
— Yaaaaay.
— I just got a profound twinge of guilt.
— Don't feel guilty. You're doing me a huge favour.
— Hmm.
— You're probably saving both our families.

The first time they snuck out they didn't reach the town centre until gone nine, both in separate Ubers, and Elliott suggested they start with cocktails to make up for lost time. As they were walking between one bar and another they passed a group of five women, spray-tanned, big hair, tiny dresses. Their perfumes combined into one bafflingly complex super-perfume. They were laughing. She looked at Elliott to see if his expression changed or if his eyes tracked them, but he continued smiling vaguely.

'Do you like that?' she asked him.

'What?'

'The *Love Island* thing. Do you like women who dress like that?'

'Um.'

'Do you like women who really make an *effort*? Or is that, like, toxic femininity?'

He frowned and said that he didn't feel *superior* to people who spray-tanned or worked out or got very made up, that he had plenty of metaphorical ways of spray-tanning himself, so what was the difference if it made them happy?

'I'm not trying to catch you out,' said Emily. 'I'm curious. Do men like that?'

'I'm sure some men do. It's not any of my business how people want to dress,' said Elliott.

'*People*,' said Emily. He seemed to be trying very hard not to say the wrong thing and it amused her. 'You know you can just tell me that you think it's hot or that it's a real turn-off because you think it looks trashy. You don't find it attractive?'

'It's hard to say,' said Elliott.

'Hahaha! No, it's not. Would you like to have sex with them? Hypothetically?'

'I think … Mostly I only want to have sex with people who are nice to me,' said Elliott. 'If we're being brutally honest.'

'Wow.'

'If someone's really nice to me that's an immediate thing and I'm like, Oh, also they're attractive.'

'What, so you never see someone who you're immediately … You don't sometimes just look at someone and think—'

'With *you*,' said Elliott.

'You looked at *me*?'

'Yes.'

'*Me?*'

'Immediately very drawn to you and I thought it was very obvious.'

'That's so weird.'

'You were pushing Arthur in the swing and I couldn't stop looking at you.'

'Wow. There's a kind of innocence about you, Elliott.'

'I can assure you there isn't,' he said. 'I'm just a different kind of bad.'

'When someone tells you who they are, believe them,' said Emily. 'Fortune cookie taught me that.'

— I think I've been relying on you to be the moral
and honourable one here and it's not fair, really.
— Why should you be moral and honourable?
You're a nihilist.
— I'm not a nihilist.
— Anyway, it's behoven … behooved … to me. To
be the moral one.
— Beethovened.
— I should be better than you, is what I'm saying,
Elliott. I'm setting a terrible example and
technically I should probably be
excommunicated.
— Do you … confess about me?
— Yes. No. I mean I would. It's been a while.
— Waow.
— There's this point, to go back to James, in all of
the late novels there's this point where the
characters who are up to no good sort of
embrace it. They have a conversation where
they're like … We're really bad, aren't we? Then
they start to feel superior. In their cruelty. That's
always kind of the turning point.

— Some vague memory of that.
— That's when they lose their humanity – when they choose to.
— Hmm.
— Something demonic about it.
— Well, it's been a blast as always, Emily.

41

'So many people say they're going to do things and then they just don't do them,' said Alathea. 'I can't stand it. I can't stand that I'm turning into one of them. It's deathly. So we're going to babysit for you and Steve, and you can go out, and then you can babysit for me and Elliott and we can go out, okay? We're going to do it next weekend, Friday and Saturday. Don't say no.'

'Oh,' said Emily. 'I'll check with Steven – that's lovely.'

'Don't *check*,' said Alathea. 'Tell.'

So it was agreed that they'd go on a staggered double date. *Parallel* dates, said Elliott, and Alathea said parallel would be simultaneous – separate but simultaneous – and she couldn't think of a single instance where that might be useful or felicitous; consecutive dates. On Friday they dropped Tomasz and Arthur round at Emily and Steven's at seven and went back to their house to get ready.

Elliott was trying to remove a whisker-length white eyebrow hair in the living-room mirror when Alathea came downstairs.

'You're wearing your hair up,' he said.

'That's interesting,' said Alathea. 'I wonder whether to widen my eyes and say *Do you like it?* or to infer that you don't and make a passive-aggressive comment about your powers of observation.'

'You're wearing your hair up!' said Elliott, joyfully.

'Better.'

'Going for a kind of older-sister-of-the-bride thing?'

'Yeah. I've seen it all. I'm happy for her in spite of it.'

'You're not sure about her husband to be.'

'He's just very boring,' said Alathea. 'I worry she'll get bored.'

'Speak now or forever et cetera.'

'Maybe not this year, or even next year … gradually.'

'But then they'll have kids.'

'And it won't matter anymore. Actually, on the subject of weddings,' said Alathea, 'Michael is getting married.'

'Who?' Alathea snorted.

'That guy,' said Elliott. 'Good for Michael.'

'He's invited me.'

'To *New Zealand*.'

'Yeah, of course.'

'Just you?'

'I'm not taking Dimitry on a long-haul flight,' said Alathea. 'I'm certainly not paying thousands of pounds for the pleasure. And the invitation was just for me.'

'Oh you're actually thinking of *going*?'

'Yeah,' said Alathea. 'I thought it might do me good.'

'Do you good?' said Elliott. 'Remind you of who you are aside from a psychoanalyst, a mother and a wife?'

'Yes.'

'A wedding guest.'

'You get to travel a lot with work and I don't. You're always getting reminded of who you are.'

'Yeah, but it's never good news,' said Elliott. 'I'm sorry, when is this?'

'Couple of months away.'

'Do we have the money?'

'I don't know,' said Alathea. 'Since the state is currently looking after our firstborn's education my feeling is we have plenty of money.'

'I just …' said Elliott.

Alathea held the electric car's key card over the drain. She licked her lips.

'Don't,' said Elliott. 'It's not even ours.'

'That's true. I'm playing with you. Of course I'm not going.' She gave him the key card.

'No, but *do*,' said Elliott. 'If you want to go you should go.'

'I just wanted to see how you'd react.'

'I'm reacting now and I'm saying you should go.'

'Don't be a martyr. I haven't even spoken to Michael in years.'

'I know,' said Elliott. 'I forbade it. Seriously, though, go.'

'Nah,' said Alathea. 'It would just be weird.'

They'd booked a table at Joel's, which had a Michelin star and a tasting menu. The lighting was dim and comforting, like Alathea's therapy room, which he had only seen once, when she needed help putting a chair together. The waiter greeted them like they were intimidatingly accomplished old friends he hadn't seen in a while and took their coats. He knew Alathea hated it if he hesitated or showed any uncertainty over matters of no consequence – *Do you want to go there? Are you sure? Are you okay? Would you be more comfortable if* … – a father issue, as she described it. So Elliott pulled out a chair and said, 'You're sitting here, Alathea,' which seemed to give her genuine pleasure.

'This isn't really your style, is it?' she said. 'You like places that have garden furniture indoors, but the food is *so authentic*.'

'What does that say about me?'

'Maybe nothing,' said Alathea. 'You're not a dick about it – almost as if it's not an affectation.'

'This is more of a *Michael* place, isn't it?' said Elliott.

'Oh *good*, I've really got to you.'

'Which is why I chose it. Hate that guy. Do you ever ask your clients for restaurant recommendations?'

'Hahaha! *Tapas*, you say?' said Alathea. 'The kind of menu where you don't really need to commit to any single choice. *Interesting*.'

'Also, I wanted to spoil you,' said Elliott. 'You look great, by the way.'

'Aw,' said Alathea. 'You're remembering why you fell in love with me.'

'Because you terrify me.'

'Uh huh.'

Alathea ordered two negronis and told Elliott that she planned to get quite drunk. She told him that they needed to establish a rule, for the night, that neither of them could mention the boys.

'Okay,' said Elliott.

'We need to focus on *us*,' said Alathea. 'You so much as mention them and within ten minutes we'd be comparing the photos on our phones we took an hour ago.'

They drank the negronis then ate baby beetroots and iced goat's cheese with two glasses of Sancerre in silence, aside from Elliott commenting that the cheese was very cold. Then he developed an unshakeable fixation that, to an objective observer, this might be taken for a first date which wasn't going well. He kept trying to think of something to say – something about politics, maybe – but felt that the only response it invited was *It's awful, isn't it? Yeah*.

'Are you okay?' said Alathea.

'Yeah, I'm good. Have you spoken to your mother recently?'

'No, not in over a week.'

'They doing okay?'

'Oh, who knows.'

Elliott took a gulp of wine and a forkful of summer truffle dumpling. 'These are really good,' he said.

'Mm. Perhaps we should have gone to see a horror film,' said Alathea. 'I'm concerned I don't have enough to say to you.'

'Yeah, what *is* that?' said Elliott. 'I have absolutely nothing to say for myself either. What do people talk about?'

'Most intelligent people', said Alathea, 'like to pivot between the highbrow and absolutely inane bullshit.'

'Right.'

'So, Adorno on gastronomic authenticity.'

'Great.'

'And then, self-consciously, I'd have to tell you about my new garden shears.'

'So sharp.'

'I love them. Then maybe I'd ask you if you had a favourite garden implement. Then back to Adorno. We all have our motifs,' said Alathea. 'Most artists pretty much wrote or painted or composed the same thing over and over again, right?'

'Refining it,' said Elliott.

'No, not always,' said Alathea.

'Mostly not, in fact,' said Elliott.

'Mostly trying to rediscover what was so good about it in the first place.'

They were given two small plates of Cornish lamb with wafers of fried potato and a glass of Malbec each.

'You're probably dangerously low on nicotine,' said Alathea. 'If you want to pop out and vape, that's fine – I'll flirt with the waiter.'

'No, I'm good,' said Elliott. 'I bought the extra strong liquid and I'm using it as eyedrops.'

'Do you think we've drifted apart?' said Alathea.

'Inevitably.'

'It's good that I still make you so nervous, though,' she said. 'I know you have a tendency to blame yourself for awkward silences.'

'That's true.'

'When you could just as easily blame me.'

'It would never occur to me.'

'But you've been more than usually absent recently.'

'I have?'

'Don't you think? You're far away.'

'Do I seem far away?'

'You've always been like that, but at the moment it's more like … where have you *gone*? Usually, with a client, that happens when there's something very specific they're not saying.'

'Since I hit my head?' said Elliott.

'Oh right, maybe it's long-term concussion,' said Alathea. 'Are you going to tell me or not?'

'Tell you what?' said Elliott. 'I don't know, Ally. I can't work and I feel played out. I'm not sure what the point of me is anymore.'

'No,' said Alathea. 'That's just your standard middle-class existential crisis. Go and volunteer for the Samaritans or something.'

'I'd be a *terrible* Samaritan.'

'A food bank, then. You still love me?'

'Besotted with you.'

'You know, when I first saw *Le Mépris* … I was probably about sixteen, and Godard makes such a big thing out of the *focal point* of the story being when the main guy insists on his wife going in the two-seater car with the producer and he'll take a cab. You remember that?'

'Vaguely.'

'Nouvelle vaguely,' said Alathea. 'That moment gets repeated over and over again, in montages, from several angles with a massively obtrusive soundtrack. And that's the moment Bardot's character irrevocably loses all respect for the protagonist – that *one* submissive gesture.'

'Yeah.'

'I remember thinking that was so silly. That anything might be so fragile and contingent. That you could lose someone based on … Eventually she just says, *You're not a man.'*

'I mean Godard does kill her in a car wreck,' said Elliott. 'Is *that* a man?'

'I thought it was great, but I also thought, *Ha! That's so daft.* But now it strikes me as dreadfully accurate.'

'Well that's a nice thought.'

'Imagine we've just met,' said Alathea. 'Imagine this is our first date.'

'I was.'

'What do you think of me so far?'

'I'm not sure yet.'

'I think you seem sweet and a little distracted,' said Alathea. 'But you're actually better looking than your photo, so good for you.'

'I'm thinking it's going to take quite a while to get to know you.'

'Are you going to tell me what's going on?' said Alathea. 'Do you want me to make a scene?'

'Like what?' said Elliott.

Alathea leaned over the table, picked up his glass of red wine and poured it into his lap.

'Oh my god,' said Elliott. He felt the wine soak through his suit trousers and boxer shorts. Alathea smiled at him.

'That was unfair,' she said. 'I didn't give you a chance to threaten me with anything.'

'I have limited options,' said Elliott. 'And I really like that dress.'

'All the better,' said Alathea. She looked at him severely. 'We should get you cleaned up. The bathrooms are lavish and discreet. Wait three minutes before you follow me.'

'Hey!' said Emily, springing up from the couch and dropping her Georges Simenon novel. She waved to Alathea and Elliott at the window and Elliott did a weird head waggle. She was wearing a knee-length Snoopy T-shirt and seeing them in eveningwear made her feel self-conscious about it, although it was almost midnight, so what the hell. She opened the front door and said *Hey* again.

'Emily, sweetheart, thank you so much,' said Alathea. She hugged her and kissed her on the cheek. She smelled of cigarette smoke.

'Where's Steven? Are the boys actually asleep?'

'He read to them. I think they're all in the same room. I haven't heard a sound for an hour. Did you have fun?'

'I'm shitfaced,' said Alathea.

'It was really lovely,' said Elliott. 'Thank you, Emily.'

'Oh, your trousers,' said Emily.

'Ha, yeah,' said Elliott. 'Clumsy.'

'Something I neglected to anticipate,' said Alathea, sitting down heavily on the sofa, 'is that I'm still going to be hungover when we're looking after yours tomorrow.'

'Yeah,' said Emily. 'That's going to suck.'

'Oh, no, I didn't mean that,' said Alathea. 'I just should have *anticipated* it, that's all.'

'Alathea really suffers,' said Elliott, sitting down next to his wife and rubbing her shoulders. She put her head in her hands and groaned, then leaned sideways until she was lying across the sofa. She kicked her shoes off.

'I shouldn't have had the last brandy,' she said, her voice muffled by the cushion. 'It was very unnecessary.'

'We'll reverse the order next time,' said Emily. 'Ally, let me get you some water.'

'It was so lovely of you, Emily,' said Alathea. 'Thank you.'

She kept the lights off and padded down the corridor into increasing darkness. The kitchen was illuminated enough by the moon. Her heart was beating fast and she felt like crying. She was filling a pint glass at the tap when she heard footsteps.

'I think Ally's gone to sleep,' said Elliott.

'Oh, hi,' said Emily. 'Don't touch the kitchen door – it's fucked.'

'I'm so sorry we stayed out so late.'

'That's not remotely a problem.'

'Are you all right, Emily?'

'Mmhm. Maybe you should all just stay over.'

'Right,' said Elliott. 'Long way home.'

'Hahaha. Are you drunk too? You're kind of swaying.'

'I'm pretty drunk,' said Elliott.

'But you had a good time?'

'Emily,' said Elliott.

'Drink this.'

'Okay, thank you.' He drank half the pint of water. 'Emily.'

'Speaking.'

'Are you okay? Are you angry with me?'

'*I just feel weird*,' she whispered.

'Okay,' said Elliott.

'I'm glad you had a good time with your gorgeous wife.'

'Yeah, it was good.'

'You look nice in your suit, even with the crotch covered in wine.'

'I don't wear suits very often,' said Elliott. 'I'm sorry you feel weird. You want out of this?'

'Out of *what*? I don't even know what this is. Out of what?'

'Ugh,' said Elliott. 'I don't know either. I'm tired and I'm drunk.'

'Kiss me.'

'I'm sorry?'

'Actually don't. I'm being ridiculous.'

'If there's something I can do to make this easier,' said Elliott.

'You can kiss me.'

'If you want to just go back to how things were.'

'How *were* things?'

'I don't know,' said Elliott. 'There has to be some way of dismantling it.'

'Like a bomb-disposal unit,' said Emily.

'I'm going to carry my family home one by one and get out of your hair,' he said.

'Okay, Elliott.'

She turned away from him and ran another glass of water.

When the plan was being made Emily had said to Elliott that she wasn't really sure what to do. Steven wasn't drinking and he honestly hated restaurants. So what is there? Bowling? Elliott said that a former postgrad of his had an exhibition opening – I mean even if you hate it, it's in a fun venue in the old industrial district and there's a bunch of free wine and this weird quartet are playing. Emily said that she supposed it might as well be something Steven could actively dislike.

The warehouse was filled by a six-by-six grid arrangement of large white plinths. Each plinth held an internal organ, brightly individually spot-lit. A heart, a liver, a pair of kidneys, a single lung. They weren't labelled and Emily couldn't identify everything. Each organ was connected to a pair of transparent wires filled with twinkling LEDs which led, in circuit formation, to a hole in the middle of the room. The organs had been motorised in some way so that they pulsed, twitched or inflated, quickly as if still alive. It was called *Functional Boundaries*. Emily felt completely flat and tried to compensate by drinking a lot of prosecco.

'Is there a brain?' she said.

'I don't know,' said Steven. 'Oh, there – look.'

They stood at plinth 4B and looked at the brain.

'I always forget how small they are,' said Emily.

'I think …' said Steven. 'I think I just don't really understand how information gets used in art. Do you know what I'm saying? If I wanted to know about anatomy or neurochemistry I could read a book and actually learn something about it instead of it being filtered through some … big ironic gesture.'

'Yeah,' said Emily. He was so resolutely non-fictional he probably *had* read books about anatomy and neurochemistry just to spite novelists. 'No, I do know what you're saying.'

'I don't know if that makes me a philistine.'

'No,' said Emily. 'I mean I knew you'd hate this, whatever it turned out to be, but that doesn't make you a philistine, and anyway, you're *my* philistine.'

She watched Steven walk around plinths 4C to 7A and back to her.

'It's good to have some time with you,' he said.

'Yeah,' said Emily. 'We don't have to stay.' She tried to think of something he might enjoy or appreciate and thought: exercise. 'We could walk home?'

'Seriously?' said Steven, brightening presumably at the thought of exceeding his step-count. 'It's over an hour.'

'I don't care.'

They cut through a luxury shopping centre nobody ever visited, which Emily called the Ghost Mall, to get to the towpath. The sun was setting and she felt buzzed enough by the sparkling wine to keep pace with Steven. Some kids smoking weed under a railway bridge ignored them. They were listening to music on a phone and Emily heard the words, which seemed to be something about a haunted jetty, which felt incongruously literary.

'What do we do when the boys get older?' she said, once they were out of earshot. 'Do we ever let them out of the house?'

'They'll be fine,' said Steven.

'Step over them under that railway bridge when we come to it,' said Emily.

'What?'

'Cross that bridge,' said Emily. 'I'm sorry. Failed play on words.'

'No,' said Steven. 'I'm sorry, I was being slow.'

He took her hand and she almost gasped.

'Is that okay?'

'Yes, Steven, of course it's okay.'

She heard the single, bright *ting* of WhatsApp, which she only used to communicate with Elliott – it was where he lived.

— How's it going?

She put her phone back in her pocket. 'Do you worry much about the future?' she said. 'You don't, do you? Not that there's really any time to think about anything.'

'What specifically?' said Steven. 'Resource scarcity? Climate change?'

'No!' said Emily. 'I mean the boys, us.'

'It's not like we're immune to those things,' said Steven. 'And it's not that far away. In *Scientific American* it said—'

'That doesn't worry me at all,' said Emily. 'I'd kill anyone who came near their resources with my bare hands. I mean assuming the ecological apocalypse doesn't arrive for a while and things just plod on into the dull grey future.'

'Right.'

'That's what I mean. Do you think we're going to be okay?'

'Are you unhappy?'

'Of course not.'

'With me?' said Steven.

'Why would I be?'

Steven quickened his pace a little and she squeezed his hand. 'I can't keep up.'

'Sorry.'

'Sometimes I feel like I'm shoring up a whole load of problems which aren't even going to become clear to me for years,' she said.

'Do you pray about it?'

'*Pray?*'

'What else is it for?'

It was just before nine-thirty when they reached the estate. Emily's legs felt heavy as they approached Elliott and Alathea's door. The four boys were in their pyjamas but eating popcorn out of separate bowls and watching *The Never-Ending Story*.

'Oh shit,' said Elliott.

'Elliott!' said Alathea.

Arthur ran to her and she picked him up.

'Sorry,' said Elliott. 'We were going to put them to bed before ten. Figured you'd treat us as badly as we treated you. Forgot how civilised you are. And Ally's too hungover to be disciplinarian.'

'What's *your* excuse?' said Alathea. 'They've been wonderful. Did you have fun?'

'It was good,' said Steven. 'Thank you both.'

'You really need to stay out very late and get blitzed next time,' said Alathea. 'For my sake. I'm fizzing with guilt here.'

'We had a really nice time,' said Emily. 'Finished all manner of sentences.'

'Where did you *go*?' said Matty, looking up from his popcorn.

'We told you! A gallery,' said Emily.

'Ah,' said Matty. 'Okay.'

Emily passed Arthur to Steven. She smiled at Elliott who seemed to be avoiding her gaze, which made her feel weird. She instinctively reached for her phone, because that's what she had started to do whenever she felt weird. Text Elliott to tell him she felt weird. Dear god.

'Oh! I missed a call from Mum,' she said. 'I must have left it on silent. I'll walk to the edge.' She nodded to the window.

'You don't want to go upstairs?' said Alathea.

'No, I like the night air,' said Emily.

'Shall I open some wine?'

'Tell her hi,' said Steven. Emily stepped out of the house and heard him say, 'She seems to really love that forest.'

'It's a good forest,' said Alathea.

Emily walked quickly to the perimeter fence a little way behind Elliott and Alathea's house. She dialled 'Home', but then felt that she wasn't far enough away from the houses, wanted to be among the trees. There was no stile, as if it had never occurred to the planners that anyone might want to take a walk outside the estate, so she braced herself against a post and tried to squeeze the toe of her shoe between the chicken wire to lift herself over. She scraped her shin on the top of the fence and landed awkwardly as her mother answered the phone.

'Mum,' she said, sadly.

'Oh dear,' said her mother.

'I think I've really fucked up my head.'

It was oppressively hot and close, as if a storm were about to break, and Emily's phone already felt sweaty against her ear. She circled a pale tree at the edge of the wood.

'Okay, darling,' said her mother. 'Have you made a doctor's appointment?'

'No,' said Emily. 'No, not that. I'm in love.'

'Ah,' said her mother.

'Mum?'

'I'm here, darling.'

'I don't know what to do.'

Her mother thought for a while. 'Sometimes,' she said, 'you'll meet someone who seems to be the answer to all your problems.'

'Yes.'

'And you need to remember that you have choices, at every turn. The path forks and you have choices.'

'It doesn't feel like I do,' said Emily.

'And you need to remind yourself that the choices you make are going to affect more than just you.'

'I know.'

'You understand that, don't you? Because that's a key part of being an adult.'

'I think I've let something really bad take root. I don't think there's anything I can do to get rid of it now,' said Emily. 'It's just grown rampantly over everything and I can cut it right down and it'll just grow back.'

'Emily, you need to take a deep breath,' said her mother. 'Stop trying to explain. You're in pain and you're frightened.'

'Yes. I'm sorry.'

'You don't need to explain anything and you don't need to apologise.'

'Okay. I'm so sorry.'

'I want you to go home, Emily, and hug your children and try to put things in some perspective. Will you do that?'

'Okay.'

'I don't want you to tell me anything about this person, because I don't want you to make it any more real than it is to you already.'

'It's real,' said Emily. 'It's real.'

'It doesn't have to be,' said her mother.

'I wish it wasn't.'

'Well that's something,' said her mother. 'We can work with that.'

Emily walked back around the tree and looked towards her house. The row of small identical detached houses was the only thing illuminated, like a charm bracelet. Somebody was coming towards the fence and she recognised the uncertain gait and the height of the approaching shape as his feet rustled through the lengthening grass.

'Emily?' said Elliott. 'Sorry. They sent me.'

'God, your voice,' she said. 'I love your voice.'

'Oh, Emily,' he chided her and handed her his hipflask through the fence. 'How did you even get over this?'

'I hurt my leg.'

'Poor thing.'

She took a swig from the flask. The metal spout tasted like licking a battery, but the whisky was sweet and drinkable. She took another sip.

'I prefer brandy really,' said Elliott. 'But I remembered that you like whisky.'

'My grandpa used to let me try it,' said Emily.

'What I'd really like, right now,' said Elliott, 'is to be lost with you somewhere. Like central France or something. The car's broken down. We don't know where we are.'

'Oh.'

'It's maybe miles to the nearest farmhouse where they hate English people. But I wouldn't even be fretting,' said Elliott. 'Which is very unlike me.'

'It would be so inconvenient,' said Emily, dreamily. She took another draft from the flask then screwed the lid on and handed it back to him.

'Better?'

'Much.'

'Let's head back,' said Elliott. 'I'm sorry we didn't get your children to sleep.'

— Do you think we're literally just feeding one
  another's need for attention? In a way that just
  increases our need for attention?
— No. I don't know. Okay – let's try science fiction.
  You're a psychologist on board a starship.
— And you're a kind of sentient mist we encounter
  in the Gamma quadrant.
— Hahaha
— I find it hard to even articulate what it is I love
  about you. And I'm the only psychologist so
  there's nobody I can talk to about it. I just stand
  at one of the viewing windows gazing at you.
— Oh that's mutual. So … I engulf the ship.
— But even though that's a really good thing as far
  as I'm concerned
— It makes the rest of the crew very sick.
— Yeah – they can't breathe, they're vomiting blood
  everywhere.
— It's gross. And the chief medical officer says
  everyone is going to die within 24 hours. So you
  have to choose: me
— Ol' cloudy

309

— or the wellbeing and ultimate survival of your crewmates.

— You.

— *Thank* you.

42

'You're shaking. Are you okay?'

'Because I'm here again.'

'You're here.'

'Last night I made a promise,' said Emily. 'To myself, to my children, to God.'

'Ah.'

'And now I'm here again.'

She was lying on her back on the futon in Elliott's half-converted attic. The futon had the texture of a sack of flour and she could feel the chipboard floor through it when she went up on one elbow.

Elliott turned to look at her and she leaned in to kiss him.

'Oh my god.'

'I'm sorry.'

'Don't.'

To feel wanted. To feel someone's desperation for you. She kissed him again.

'I'm not sure I can cope with this,' said Elliott. 'I can feel my psyche kind of splitting into two in real time.'

'That was very, very good, though, wasn't it?' said Emily.

'Yes.'

'Like being drawn into a whirlpool.'

They kissed for a little longer.

'I've been meaning to do that,' she said. 'This is a line, isn't it?'

'I don't think it's even a line if you've already crossed it in your head.'

'At this point …' said Emily. She kissed him again. 'At this point I … We can just keep this here, in this kind of pocket universe. Can't we?'

'I don't think we should have sex.'

'No.'

'I think that would destroy both of us.'

'So we could just dry-hump each other through our clothes?'

'Emily, that's so romantic.'

'Is that … Is there any way in which that's less of a betrayal?'

'I mean in a very real practical sense, yes and in a very real practical sense absolutely not.'

She climbed on top of him.

'Oh god, Emily,' said Elliott, 'please don't do that.'

'Because I just don't think I care anymore. Isn't that terrible?'

'It is.'

'You're hard.'

'Of course I am.'

Emily put her arms around his neck, pressed herself against him and started to move. He closed his eyes.

'Emily.'

'Elliott.'

'Don't stop.'

But after a minute she started to cry. She climbed off him and sat on the edge of the futon. He shuffled forward, put his arms around her and kissed the back of her neck.

'Oh,' said Emily, and stood up.

'Are you okay?'

'Yeah. Sorry.' She sniffed and wiped her eyes with the back of her hand.

'I know.'

'I didn't mean to start crying,' said Emily. 'I'm okay.'

'Oh god,' said Elliott.

'What?'

'Once … years ago,' said Elliott, 'when I first started seeing Alathea and we were just all over each other all the time—'

'Oh, I bet you used to really go at each other.'

'Once we were in bed and she just burst into tears and I was like, *Oh my god, what's wrong, are you hurt?* And she said, *I suddenly got this feeling that one day someone's going to take you away from me.*'

'Fuck,' said Emily.

'Which was weird because I didn't have the impression that she even liked me that much.'

Emily looked at the wall and started crying again.

'I'm not sorry,' said Elliott. 'About any of this. But I'm sorry it makes you sad.'

Emily shuffled off the futon and found her shoes in the corner.

'You're so fucking beautiful.'

'Shut up, Elliott.'

Before buttoning her shirt she walked to his shelves, picked out the *Collected Oscar Wilde* and flicked through to *De Profundis*. She scanned down a couple of pages.

'There,' she said. '*I forgot that every little action of the common day makes or unmakes character, and that therefore what one has done in the secret chamber one has some day to cry aloud on the housetop.* I mean he's quoting from Luke — if you had a Bible I'd have looked it up there.'

'Character,' said Elliott. 'People don't really talk about character anymore.'

'They do when someone does something bad,' said Emily. 'There are countries where they'd stone us to death.'

'That's true,' said Elliott, brightly, as if it was an interesting argument he'd not considered before. 'God, that's really true.'

'I saw a series of photos once,' said Emily. 'It was really disturbing. A man buried up to his neck. The rocks were these … rough, white fist-sized lumps — they looked like giant bits of popcorn.'

'Yeesh.'

'You could really *feel* it, you know? The impact. His dusty, bloodied face. And it wouldn't even take very long to fly there.'

'Four to six hours?'

'Isn't that weird? That you could get on a plane for a few hours and watch movies, have a snack and arrive at a place where they'd officially publicly torture and murder you for something you've *just done*?'

'I'm generally pretty down on this country,' said Elliott. 'But yeah, I guess we're okay.'

'Do you actually feel bad about this at all?' said Emily.

'I love you,' said Elliott.

'That's irrelevant. I love you too.'

'Did I send you that article about polyamory?'

'Yeah.'

'Did you read it?'

'Yeah. I don't know. I guess it might make a stupid person feel better about themselves.'

'It's insane to expect one partner to fulfil all your needs.'

'You told me sex wasn't a need.'

'Emotional needs as well as physical needs.'

'The point I took from it,' said Emily, 'is that it's based on honesty. There's a difference between being in a polyamorous relationship and just fucking someone else.'

'Hmm.'

'Would you tell Alathea?'

'I'd consider it,' said Elliott.

'Really?'

'I mean … No, probably not.'

'You still love her, right?'

Elliott thought for a moment. 'I mean yeah,' he said.

'I think that's an imbalance, for one thing,' said Emily. 'I'm not saying I don't love Steven. I'm not saying I don't feel guilty. But you're still crazy about Alathea. So that's different.'

'I'm crazy about you; I love her,' said Elliott, as if that explained everything.

'And it doesn't bother you, that it's completely immoral and tawdry, what we're even contemplating, and that it's a betrayal, and that we could hurt literally everyone we love in ways we probably can't even comprehend.'

'I don't know,' said Elliott. 'I think my capacity to not think about things is pretty vast. Maybe there's something wrong with me.'

43

— I hate myself.

— Agh. I know.

— Also I want to see you right now and I want you to …

— Emily.

— And also I hate myself.

— I shouldn't have let that happen. I'm truly sorry.

— No, it's me.

— It's not you.

But on Thursday she knocked on his door and he greeted her as if nothing had happened.

'All right, Emily?'

So casually that she wondered if Alathea was still in.

They ate Oreos and talked about French New Wave films and helped Arthur and Dimitry build a Brio train track and then they walked up and down the street with them in their buggies until they fell asleep.

Elliott lifted Dimitry's buggy through his front door then went to lift Arthur's but paused.

'Are you?' he said to Emily.

'Do you want me to?' said Emily. 'You don't have work or something?'

'The bruise hardly shows now,' she said. 'I mean your hair's in front of it anyway. Can we lie down if I absolutely promise not to do anything inappropriate?'

She told him about her brother, an engineer, who she hardly saw. Part of her had always assumed her children would be so irresistible to her family she wouldn't be able to keep them away, but actually people have lives, don't they?

'They do. It's hard to make time.'

'I'm sorry. I'm being so boring.'

'Stop it,' said Elliott, leaning his head on her shoulder.

'I'm talking to you about people you don't even know. I always do that.'

'Everything about you fascinates me.'

'Why?'

'Because you're perfect.'

'Shhh.'

'Everything.'

'I know,' said Emily. 'I don't get it.'

'I don't think Alathea and I were ever particularly interested in one another.'

'Of course you were. You just stopped trying.'

'Is there anything less exciting,' said Elliott, 'than *trying*?'

'Oh, trying is the worst,' said Emily.

'No,' said Elliott. 'Something drew us together but I don't think it was that we especially liked each other. This is an experiment, I suppose, in whether it's possible to love someone. If you love someone everything about them is interesting to you.'

'I think that's it,' said Emily. 'Laboratory conditions. The findings aren't transferable to the real world.'

'This isn't the real world?'

'It's not even close. When I'm with you I'm in some kind of nuclear bunker.'

'Hmm.'

'Do you know the old story about the bees and the snails?' said Emily. 'It's super weird.'

'No.'

'It's an old Chinese folktale. I had a big illustrated book of them when I was little.'

'Tiny Emily. What's it about?'

He rearranged himself in the bed so that he could lie with his head on her stomach and she laughed at him.

'I'm not a good storyteller,' she said. 'Five snails arrive at a beehive and start eating the honey. And the bee king is angry, but he tells them they can stay one night. But the snails say they're going to stay forever. They like honey and they're going to live on honey and they're going to stay in the bee kingdom and eat honey forever.'

'You're a great storyteller,' said Elliott. 'You just have low self-esteem.'

'There was a full-page illustration of the snails looking all stubborn. I loved it. The bee king insists they can only stay for one night, like that's more than generous. One night and all the honey they can eat in one night and then they have to go. But two days later they're still there. So the bee king loses his temper and tells the snails ... Are you asleep?'

'No! I'm just relaxing for the first time in about seven years.'

'Okay. He tells them they don't contribute anything, they don't work or offer anything to the bees, they just eat honey, and it's not acceptable. But the snails ignore him. The day after that, the bee king confronts the snails and says they're getting fat and they must leave. The snails say, *We are snails. We go where we like and we do what we like and right now we like honey, so we're staying here.* And the bee king tells the snails that if they stay they will die. Then he prepares his army and they sharpen their stings and get ready for battle. But the snails retreat into their shells so the bees can't sting them. It's very frustrating.'

'Yeah, I hate that.'

'But – and here's the good bit – the bee king tells the bees to seal the snails into their shells with wax, so they do it. And he says to the snails, *There. You snails were right when you said you would stay forever. You have chosen to stay and to die.*'

'That's …' said Elliott.

'I love the ending,' said Emily. 'Can you imagine being trapped in your own shell?' She made a face and pretended to fight for breath.

'Hahaha,' said Elliott. 'What's the moral, though? I mean …'

'Oh, it doesn't mean anything,' said Emily. 'It's not really an instructive story.'

●●●

— Don't do this to me don't do this to me don't do this to me don't do this to me.
— Hey. I'm here. I'm here. I'm sorry.
— No, I'm sorry. I'm losing it, Elliott. Can we start again?
— From what point?
— I don't know. I'm shaking. I can't stop shaking. I feel abject
— Don't feel abject. I think the best thing is if you make me abject. Think of me as the thing you hate most about yourself and then separate it from the symbolic order.
— I tattooed your name on my forehead and I'm very self-conscious about it.
— Simple as that.
— I feel *beyond redemption*
— Okay. We can start again from any point, Emily. Pick one.
— Okay. We're in your dining room. You've just picked up my pen and you start talking to me about pen-chewing and I say, 'What the fuck are you talking about?'

— Good.
— 'What the fuck are you talking about, Elliott? You're weird and I don't like you.'
— That works.
— I feel like I'm getting ill again.
— You sound perfectly coherent.
— I think I'm going to go and see Father Daniel.
— Your priest?
— I feel like I've been cursed.
— By me?
— No.
— Whatever you need to do.
— God I hate you when you sound breezy. Whatever I need to do.
— I'm sorry.
— Don't.
— I can never say the right thing when you're like this.
— Feels like something's malfunctioning? Is that all you really care about? Saying the right thing?
— Maybe. Do you think you're in the right frame of mind to speak to a stranger?
— He's not a stranger. Most of his job is talking to people when they're not in their right minds. You don't want me to talk to him?
— I don't have any desire to control you.
— You're worried this is all supposed to be secret and you don't want me talking about it?
— I don't want to influence you in any way.
— I'm getting my shoes on.

44

Emily had to look up her priest's number on the church website, which was a late 1990s HTML page with parallel text in Romanian and English. She deleted her most recent conversation with Elliott as if it would be sinful to use the same phone to call Father Daniel while any trace of her crimes remained on it. It rang fourteen times and she held her breath before he answered and sternly recited his own phone number.

'Father?'

'Who is this, please?'

'It's Emily.'

'Emily?'

'Your most useless parishioner.'

'Do you suppose that narrows it down? Emily, I am about to eat.'

'Oh no – I'm so sorry.'

'So if you could come to the point.'

'I needed to have confession, but it's—'

'At dinner time?'

'As soon as possible.'

'Are you dying, Emily? Could this maybe wait until before the liturgy on Sunday?'

'I'm not dying.'

'Good. Something terrible has happened?'

'In a way …'

'My sister is visiting and really …' He tailed off. 'Ugh.'

'I really don't want to put you out,' said Emily. 'I wouldn't ask if it wasn't urgent, I really …'

'It is fine. Emily, I will be at the church in one hour and if you are there you can begin by confessing your ill use of me.'

'Of course,' said Emily. 'Thank you, thank you so much.'

Father Daniel sighed and hung up.

Over an early dinner where the boys wouldn't eat their rice, Emily told Steven that she had to go to church, that it had been so long and she needed it. It was the truth, even though it felt like lying. Was that the real sadness of lying by omission? That eventually it became immaterial whether you were telling the truth or not? Anyway, it wasn't a short drive and she knew it was a big ask, but would he please let her? Without sighing?

She parked the eco-car outside a chemist and walked across the road to the courtyard. A woman was shaking out a doormat next to the church. She looked up. Emily smiled weakly before ducking through the low door.

The church was silent and empty aside from Father Daniel standing by a silver-backed copy of the Gospels, holding a wooden cross. She felt guilty that he had come out, unlocked the church, lit the candles and incense and put on his vestments just for her.

'Hi,' said Emily.

He frowned.

'O Lord God, the salvation of Your servants, merciful, compassionate, and long-suffering; Who forgives our evil deeds, not desiring the death of a sinner, but that they turn from their way and live,' he said. 'Show mercy, now, on Your servant, Emily, and grant to her an image of repentance, forgiveness of sins and deliverance, pardoning all her sins, whether voluntary or involuntary. Reconcile her and unite her to Your Holy Church, through Jesus Christ our Lord, to Whom, with You, are due all dominion and majesty, now and ever, and unto ages of ages. Amen.'

Emily looked at him.

'I am merely a witness. As you know. Now,' he said. 'Whatever have you been up to?'

Emily sighed.

'You impressed upon me that this was an emergency.'

'I haven't been here in so long.'

'True.'

'Are you not even going to acknowledge that?'

'Which one are you again?' he said, and smiled. 'We maybe have somewhat different concepts of time.'

'I'm so sorry,' said Emily. 'I've wanted to be here, I can't tell you how much I've wanted to – even just being here now I already feel … It's just the boys—'

'Your confessions are always very *protracted*,' he said. 'Try to be more like your husband.'

'I know that's a terrible excuse – I know I'm supposed to bring them, I know they're welcome.'

'Is *this* all you wanted to say? Oh dear.'

'I'm sorry,' said Emily. 'I prepared. I'm just embarrassed.'

'Well, good,' said Father Daniel. 'That means you're doing it right.'

'I mean it's worse than that. I'm worried I'm going to be excommunicated.'

'Hmm,' said Father Daniel. 'That tends to happen if you've been leading a heretical movement that gains traction with the Emperor. Have you?'

'I've been getting intrusive thoughts,' said Emily.

'Of what kind?'

'Sexual thoughts, violent thoughts. I'm ashamed to even say them out loud.'

'Ah, well,' said Father Daniel. 'You needn't. I'm sure I've had worse. You remember we've spoken about this, about thoughts. You're no more responsible for them than a conversation you overhear through a window.'

'But I don't feel like that,' said Emily. 'I feel like these come from *me*.'

'St Basil the Great says that the day you can tie a knot between two of your eyelashes is the day you can control your thoughts.'

'That's good,' said Emily, after a pause.

'You can gently repudiate them. Then let them go. Anything else?'

'I've been having strong feelings,' said Emily, 'for somebody else.'

'Strong feelings for somebody else,' muttered Father Daniel. 'You English are *terrible* at this. You could have murdered someone and you'd come to me saying that you had strong feelings ... Just tell me what you've done, Emily, if anything.'

'Okay. I fancy someone who isn't my husband,' said Emily.

'That's more like it,' said Father Daniel. 'You know, it

isn't wrong to find someone attractive, Emily. If you see someone magnificent looking, you can just say, *Thank you, God, for making somebody so beautiful*. Then you will feel absurd enough to forget about it.'

'No, it's more than that,' said Emily.

'You have *strong feelings* for them.'

'I feel horrible,' said Emily.

'What you mean is, you are tempted to commit adultery,' said Father Daniel. 'Has anything happened?'

'I talk to him constantly.'

'I see.'

'I love him.'

'Yes.'

'When I see him everything feels right and I feel known and accepted and loved.'

'Yes. I am trying to understand.'

'He has children too, he's married,' said Emily.

'Yes, so this is all something of a problem.'

'Uh huh.'

'Adultery is really a form of *theft*. It is the love which is supposed to belong to your family, to your children, and you are stealing it from them.'

'Yes,' said Emily. 'I see that.'

'And you love them.'

'I do.'

'Not that it matters, a chemical in the brain. You have an *obligation* to them.'

'I do love them.'

'I suppose that you feel very ashamed, as if you are the first person to feel like this, but that is not the case.'

'Mm.'

Emily felt a little fractious, as if the conversation wasn't going as badly as she'd hoped, as if the experience might pass over her and she'd walk away quietly, smugly absolved, none the wiser. Could she not be given penance – constant repetition for six months … seven years? *Abjection*, she thought.

'I'm getting angry,' she said.

'With me? Naturally,' said Father Daniel. 'This is not supposed to be fun. What do we do, Emily? We don't remain loyal to someone because they are a wonderful, beautiful person. That's monstrous. We'd kill each other trying to find the most wonderful, beautiful person to be loyal to. We do not do it for each other. We do it for Him.' He tilted his head at a large crucifix. 'Then it's simple.'

Emily said nothing.

'Too pious?' he said. 'If you love me, keep my commandments.'

'And if I can't do that?' said Emily.

'Emily, Emily,' said Father Daniel. 'What do you want? A new life? One without problems or travails, one without suffering or boredom? What do you want?'

'I want you to tell me what to *do*.'

'*Me?*' said Father Daniel. 'Perhaps you want a stern, puritanical authority who would tell you to stay with your husband even if he was a violent ogre. But you know that is not it. A marriage is no different to monasticism – same commitment, same sacrifice. Who can bear it? I can give you my opinion, which is that I think you would regret abandoning them, or causing this man to desert his own. What else can I do? Lock you in the church?'

'Out of it,' said Emily, sniffing. 'Would be more what I deserve.'

'We are free to lock ourselves out of it whenever we want.'

'I don't want to destroy someone else's family, hurt everyone I love.' She could feel her chin tensing and getting heavy.

'Yes, I would suggest that would be spiritually detrimental.'

Emily began to sob, with such abruptness that it sounded like a burst of cruel laughter and almost caused Father Daniel to lose his composure. For a moment he seemed about to take a step back before balancing on his feet again and rubbing the corner of the cross between his thumb and forefinger.

'There now,' he said.

She cried openly, without putting her hands to her face, her mouth open, like a child, she thought, like Matty or Arthur.

'I don't want to give him up!' she looked Father Daniel in the eye. 'Please don't make me give him up. I can't. I need him.'

'Good,' said Father Daniel. 'Good that you are not trying to hide. And what is he, really?'

'I have never loved another person as much as I love him. I'm madly in love with him. I love him, I love his soul, we're bound together with some force I can't even … Don't tell me I have to give him up.'

'Eventually he'll die,' snapped Father Daniel. 'Then what? We are not supposed to worship another person, you know this. You know that is not love. It is a void.'

'Then what?' said Emily, attempting to control her crying.

'Worse than that – it is *idolatry*,' said Father Daniel. He was close to shouting now. 'All of your stories which end with this bastardisation of love! It is nonsense, ruinous, you idolise it.'

'I don't!' Emily matched his volume. 'I know him. I love his flaws. I'm not idolising him.'

'No,' said Father Daniel. 'We are not for each other to know.'

'I want to run off with him and I know it would be difficult and horrible and wrong and I don't care.'

Father Daniel was quiet for a time.

'Is there,' he said. 'Anything else?'

Emily widened her eyes. Was that *it*? He met her gaze and they stared at each other for a few seconds.

'I put milk in my tea on a Wednesday,' she said, crossly.

'You mock,' said Father Daniel, 'but actually such basic instructions and observances are there for us because we cannot cope with anything more. Love one another! Ha! We'd rather die. So we fast and we pray. Or we're *supposed* to.'

'Well I haven't been doing *any* of that,' said Emily. 'Father, are you crying?'

'You are in great distress and it pains me.' He snorted like a bear.

'If I have to give him up I might hate you,' said Emily. 'For making me do it.'

'Good!' said Father Daniel. 'Good that you feel this.'

They were quiet again. Emily looked at an icon, one of a dozen on the wall next to her, of a man with a dark beard painting an icon within an icon on an easel depicting the Mother of God and the infant Christ. She couldn't read the writing. She stared at it until she stopped crying.

'Is there anything I can do?' she said. 'Is there anything you can do to take this away from me?'

'A special ritual? No,' said Father Daniel.

'What then?'

'You can walk away and change nothing and carry on,' he said. 'Or, the moment you wake up, you stand, you go to your corner and you pray for mercy, on yourself and on everyone else. You do that every day. Read the prayers out loud. Read Psalm 51. It doesn't matter if you feel nothing but tiredness and annoyance. Maybe that's all you'll ever feel. You do it anyway.'

'Okay.'

He squeezed her hand. 'You'll try?' he said, and his voice sounded higher, like a young boy, like Matty entreating her for something.

'Yes,' said Emily. 'Okay.'

She knelt, facing the floor, and felt a heavy cloth being placed over the back of her head before Father Daniel quite roughly tapped out the shape of a cross.

45

She hadn't managed to sleep until four and resented her phone's cheerful alarm at six in the morning. Arthur didn't stir beside her so she carefully climbed out of the bed and sidled out of the room. Who am I? she thought. How do I feel? Bad. Very, very bad.

She went downstairs and lit a candle in her icon corner, picked up the dessicated prayerbook she hadn't opened in over a year and turned to the service of Matins.

'In the name of the—'

Her voice sounded stupid. She felt stupid. She flicked through the pages and felt that there were far too many. She imagined messaging Elliott. She'd say, *Get a load of this, Elliott, I'm *praying*!* And Elliott would say, *That bad, eh?* and she'd say, *Hahaha! This is what you've reduced me to.* And he'd say, *Maybe I should try it too.* And she'd say, *Yeah, why don't you come over?*

She unlocked her phone and hovered over the WhatsApp icon, then held her finger down on it until it started to wobble and a tiny X appeared in the top right corner. She pressed it and her phone asked her if she was sure she wanted to delete the app and all data associated with the app and she pressed Okay, which seemed suitably ambivalent.

For a couple of seconds she felt decisive and powerful and as if she'd just shrugged off a wet, heavy coat. Then she thought: our conversations, our photos, the archive of our private jokes. No. No, no, no. She tried to reinstall the app and it came back blank. She started to google 'how to restore WhatsApp messages' and then threw her phone under the bed. Fuck's sake.

'Have mercy on me o God according to thy great mercy …'

Every other Friday Emily and Alathea's days coincided. Emily was happy to go along with whatever Alathea suggested, even if it was a National Trust property, where the boys would howl through every dim and over-furnished room. She might have expected to feel more awkward about spending time with Alathea, but she didn't. It felt like a way of being close to Elliott, and anyway Emily loved Alathea and if anything it disturbed her how easy and natural it felt.

Alathea texted to say there was a new soft-play centre a half hour's drive away and Emily said she hated soft-play centres, but Alathea said this one was different: it was an *organic* soft-play centre or something and it served healthy snacks and didn't have rubber toy machines and the play equipment had been specifically designed to be stimulating and educational.

'It sounds even worse,' said Emily.

'I'll drive.'

* * *

Every traffic light turned red as they approached and Alathea started growling. Dimitry was grousing in his baby seat.

'He's *so* cranky today.'

'It's hot.'

'That's true,' said Alathea. 'I'm also cranky. Something in the air. Elliott was in a weird mood this morning.'

'Oh?'

'No idea what's going on with him at the moment. He smashed the French press against the tap, accidentally, obviously, but then he just sat on the kitchen floor. When he sits on the floor that usually means he's very disturbed about something.'

'That's funny.'

'Like he stops observing basic protocols. Do you know what's up with him?'

'Do *I*?'

'I mean he really likes you,' said Alathea. 'It would neither surprise nor bother me if he confided in you.'

'Oh,' said Emily. 'I mean, yeah, I like talking to him a lot. I love both of you a lot.'

'I feel like he might actually tell you things he wouldn't tell me.'

'God, I don't think that's true.'

'Which I don't mind at all,' said Alathea. 'To be completely clear. I think it's really sweet that you get on so well.'

'I can … talk to him?' said Emily.

'God, no,' said Alathea. 'Just keep an eye on him for me.'

'Of course.'

They drove to the next set of traffic lights in silence. Three cars got through and it turned red just as they approached.

'Fuck's sake,' said Alathea. 'Dimitry, hush, sweetheart, we'll be there soon.'

'How's work?' said Emily, once they were moving again.

'Is that something friends do?' said Alathea. 'Ask about how work's going?'

'Sure,' said Emily. 'Then the onus is on you to come up with an amusing anecdote about something that happened at work recently rather than just saying, *Yeah, fine.*'

'How exhausting,' said Alathea. 'No wonder I haven't bothered with it until now. Also confidentiality. How's *your* work?'

'Yeah, fine,' said Emily. 'I had to break up a *fight* yesterday.'

'Ooh, was there blood?'

'Nah. This girl's already been excluded from one school and it was her first day and she went in hard, I guess.'

'Ugh, that's dreadful,' said Alathea.

'You know how you want to rescue someone sometimes? Like you can see exactly the pattern they're working to, that they're just doing it over and over again in spite of themselves.'

'That's not unfamiliar.'

'But actually there's not very much you can do.'

'That also resonates.'

'You know what my priest said? One of our parishioners is a therapist and he was talking to him and he said, *Our jobs are quite similar, really – we tell people how they could change their lives for the better, look outwards, be more loving, more*

considerate, more deliberate; and they say, yes, that sounds like very
good advice, and then they leave our office or church and forget it
instantly. And then he said, *But at least I get to bury them.*'

'Rather morbid,' said Alathea.

'Wouldn't you like to bury your clients sometimes?'

'Maybe we *should* have the option to have our funerals
presided by a psychoanalyst,' said Alathea.

Emily clipped Arthur into his reins to negotiate the car
park. Alathea carried Dimitry. Once inside and through the
gates she ran to keep pace with the children, whose speed
tended to outstrip their stability. There was nothing to
immediately distinguish 'Lottie's' from any of the other
soft-play centres she'd visited, but there were posters
framed in Perspex informing them of the centre's mission,
which seemed largely based around sustainable materials.

They were both dressed in leggings and T-shirts, which
Alathea called the Uniform of Having Altogether Given
Up.

'Stop it – you look ridiculously good in everything,' said
Emily.

'Yeah,' said Alathea, tucking in her T-shirt. 'It's weird –
Elliott says he really likes it. Gets very handsy.'

'Uh huh.'

Emily kept one hand on Arthur's bottom to help him
climb a tall foam staircase. He squealed with laughter as he
reached the top and then teetered precariously over the
edge before throwing himself into her arms.

'Oof. This is actually really sweet,' she said. 'I'm so negative all the time. And they're really happy here.'

'If we make it an hour, max,' said Alathea, 'we won't burn out.'

'Once I spent an entire day in this big warehouse-sized soft-play with Matty,' said Emily. 'We had breakfast, lunch and dinner there. I completely lost my mind.'

'I'll get us some coffee,' said Alathea.

While Alathea was visiting the centre's built-in café both Arthur and Dimitry approached Emily and started climbing her knees.

'Hello, you two,' she said. 'Shall we go to the trampoline?'

Alathea returned with two cardboard cups of black coffee while they were waiting for the trampoline to clear. It was supposed to be one child at a time, but nobody took any notice except for them.

'Elliott used to take Tomasz out all the time,' she said. 'I was working on my doctorate for the first year and he was good about that. So he'd go to playgroups in church halls, park meet-ups, baby sensory, all that stuff; he probably did a few full-day soft-play hells too. Pretty much every time he'd come back with another young mum's number.'

'Hahaha, what?'

'Yeah – he'd always find somebody to take a shine to, or they'd just glom onto him, *Why don't we take them to lunch or something?* I mean god, everyone is just so impossibly bored you latch onto whatever's going.'

'Haha,' said Emily. 'I *never* got picked up at a stay-and-play. I'm a little disappointed.'

'It wasn't something systematic. He'd act very confused by the whole thing. The thing about Elliott: I used to think he was just someone who refused to take any responsibility for their affect, but actually I've come to the conclusion that he has a desperate and voracious need for everyone to be in love with him.'

'Ha!' said Emily. 'I mean everyone wants to be loved, don't they?'

'Liked,' said Alathea. 'But this is different.'

'All anyone wants is to walk into a room and feel certain they're loved – it's like the easiest part of parenting – you just let them know you love them!'

'Do you know you meet roughly eighty thousand people in your life?'

'That sounds high.'

'That includes people you barely exchange more than a couple of words with. But it's around eighty thousand. And Elliott is driven by the need for all eighty thousand to be infatuated with him. And I know he'd never do anything because he knows I'd kick the shit out of him.'

'Good,' said Emily.

'But I know what he's like. And he's oblivious. Or he pretends to be. I got this letter once …' Alathea seemed to weigh up whether to continue. She took a sip of her black coffee and looked over at the ball pool. 'You know I'm not entirely sure what the difference is between this and any other soft-play centre. I suppose everything's recycled.'

'A letter?' said Emily.

'This was years ago,' said Alathea. 'It arrived at the house, hand addressed to me. I mean that's rare enough and even when I picked it up I had this feeling … I opened it at work. It said, *Dear Alathea Broughton, You don't know me, but the fact is Elliott and I are very much in love. I don't want to say anything hurtful and believe me I never thought I'd find myself in this position.* That kind of shit.'

'Oh my god,' said Emily. 'Oh my *god*. What did he say?'

'I never told him,' said Alathea.

'Seriously?' The skin around Emily's skull felt tight, as if she had been laughing hysterically. 'You didn't confront him?'

'I wrote back to her and arranged to meet for a coffee the following week,' said Alathea. 'Sweet woman. A post-doc. A lot less forthright in person than she was in writing.'

'I suppose people tend to be,' said Emily. 'Arthur, that's *too* high.'

'I told her … I made something up. I had options – I could have just slapped her in the face before we sat down and walked out. I told her that Elliott and I had an arrangement and that it was fine, but that we had clear rules. And if Elliott hadn't told her about those I was sorry but she was in danger of getting very hurt. If she got too close. And she smiled, and I hated her then, because she pitied me.'

'Jesus, Ally,' said Emily.

'Babe, this was years ago,' said Alathea. 'Don't look so upset.'

'No, it's just. I'm sorry.'

'Did you know that in some states of America you can sue the person your partner's having an affair with? It's called Alienation of Affection.'

'No?' said Emily, who had read several articles about it.

'I mean you can ruin them, basically,' said Alathea. 'Hundreds of thousands of dollars. You can financially destroy them for the rest of their lives. I think if people have never been *really* poor they have a romantic notion that that's not really important, that as long as they have love … and you can imagine how long *that* lasts once they can't afford their heating bill.'

'Mm.'

'I established fairly quickly that nothing had actually happened,' said Alathea. 'Nothing physical. And the more she talked, the more I realised … he'd been stringing her along, certainly, but almost out of politeness.'

'Were they … meeting up or just talking or what?' said Emily. 'I mean what was it that gave her the idea?'

'Similar research areas, a couple of meetings, then a lengthy text and email correspondence. I think she felt they had some kind of deep spiritual bond and of course he did very little to disabuse her of that.'

'Dear god.'

'There's something so *obliging* about him I'm surprised he's never been convicted of accessory to murder, you know? *Elliott, honey, I just need you to help me dispose of a body – I don't know who else to turn to.* I mean he's also a vampire and needs the attention until it gets out of control and then he's terrified.'

'Once he makes you into a vampire too,' said Emily, 'I mean *them*.'

'Right. So I'd thought I might need to threaten her, go to her supervisor, whatever, but within half an hour I felt like I had the measure of the whole situation and that it was best to leave it. I told her she was going to be okay, that this had happened before and it would happen again, and that I wished her very well.'

'And that was that?'

'Didn't hear another peep out of her.'

'And Elliott?'

'He never showed a single sign of anything having changed,' said Alathea. 'And I'm not sure how aware of it he even … I think to him it was a footnote, if that makes sense.'

'Sure.'

'What you need to watch for,' said Alathea, 'is when *you* become the footnote.'

'Agh,' said Emily.

'Has he told you about his mother?'

'No,' said Emily.

'Oh,' said Alathea. 'I maybe shouldn't say anything, then. He doesn't like to talk about her, but you two are close so I wondered if he'd told you.'

'What happened?'

'She was quite troubled. Left when he was eleven. He has some contact with her now – we don't really see his parents much at all.'

'He actually hasn't mentioned her at all.'

'No. I've always felt it accounts for how he *is* with women. That sounds rather melodramatic. He can't say no to anyone, can't control himself, really, because every encounter is another chance to repair that relationship with his mother. That's the brief abstract.'

'Dear god,' said Emily.

'Except with you,' said Alathea. 'It's honestly a massive fucking relief to see him have any kind of uncomplicated friendship with someone of the opposite sex.'

'I'm an uncomplicated gal,' said Emily.

'Well, you're straightforward,' said Alathea, 'which helps. Can you promise me you won't tell him I told you *anything* about this?'

'Of course,' said Emily. 'God, of course.'

Once the boys were asleep and Emily had finished marking mock exams she wanted to write to Elliott and ask him about *the way he was with women.* She remembered that she'd deleted WhatsApp and kicked the skirting board. She stood in front of her icons, lit a candle and said nothing.

She saw Elliott at the school gate the next day and tried not to look at him. She crouched to the ground and adjusted Matty's collar. Once the children were inside she turned with the buggy and made to cross the road, all but closing her eyes when she felt a hand on the side of her arm.

'Hey,' said Elliott. 'You disappeared. I was trying to talk to you last night.'

She started walking and he kept pace. 'You were?'

'And our … There was a little grey circle where you used to be.'

'I deleted the app. Arthur, you can either get out and walk or stay in the buggy, it's up to you.'

'Oh,' said Elliott. 'Why would you do that?'

'Remember how you've felt quite ambivalent about this from the start?'

'Well, that was something I *said*, yeah.'

'I've been weighing it up, and I think you were right — we can cut each other out.'

'It never occurred to me that you might think I *meant* it.'

'Controlled explosion.'

'Okay,' said Elliott. 'I'm not sure I agree.'

'So we stop. Completely this time, no trial period.'

'How does that even work?' said Elliott. 'We live opposite each other for god's sake.'

'I barely see most of our neighbours,' said Emily.

'And Alathea?'

'Okay, look,' said Emily. 'It doesn't need to be weird. You and I just need to stop spending time together.'

'Emily,' said Elliott. 'What have I done?'

'You haven't done anything.'

'Then don't do this. Please don't do this.'

'*We've* barely done anything. Which is all the more reason to stop now.'

'I'm not entirely sure how to—'

He stepped into the road to let three women past on the pavement. One smiled and nodded and he apologised. He was always apologising, especially when there was nothing to apologise for. They waited until the women were out of earshot.

'I'm not entirely sure how to live without you. Is what I was saying,' said Elliott.

'You lived quite well without me before you met me,' said Emily.

'I feel like I'm talking to an AI.'

'I've made up my mind.'

'Where's Emily? This is like invasion of the body-snatchers.'

'I think both of us are going to have to learn,' said Emily, 'to live without each other because the alternative is worse.'

'No,' said Elliott. 'No, I promise you, this is worse.'

46

It didn't work, but then nothing worked, neither the course of Prozac nor the six free CBT sessions she trialled going to once a week after work, nor the open safety pin she kept in her pocket to jab herself in the thigh with whenever she thought about him. She wrote to David to say she'd like to get more involved in the committee and he wrote back, *Great! That's great! See you at the next meeting!* She followed Father Daniel's regimen of prayer, went straight to her icon corner when she woke up, but a smile would play on her lips as she began to speak, quietly, as if her prayer were a mockery, an affront.

Sometimes it would come back to her like a tide, like the moment you remembered someone you loved was dead and that your base level, the very foundation of your background mind and functionality depended, it turned out, on temporary amnesia. Which was to say you no longer had a foundation. But *it* was never anything, so what was there to mourn? And if there *was* anything it was unacceptable, selfish to the point of mental impairment, only less forgivable. There really oughtn't to be any sympathy, not from anyone.

She tried to rotate it to various angles, she read obsessively, both online and the books her counsellor recommended. She turned it and turned it: it was an adaption disorder; she was drying out from an addiction; he was a limerent object; it was an anxious-insecure attachment style; she was a covert narcissist; they both were; she was being tested by the devil; someone had put a curse on her; she was possessed by a demon; God, please take this from me, I don't want to feel this way any more. And God would say, Remind me who you are again?

Are you really just supposed to have showers and go to work and live with yourself?

The breeze whipped up the dust of the bark chips and she shielded her eyes.

'Arthur,' she said, 'don't try to climb that.'

She deleted all of her social media and downloaded a sobriety app which gave you a little clock that counted seconds, minutes, days, and gave you chips for abstaining. She chose the label *Codependency* from a drop-down list.

The way Elliott used his e-cigarette … He said that he was like Darth Vader and that he could no longer breathe or talk without it, but really it was as if he were trying to breathe himself out, just exhale his whole soul, release it into the air. And, no shit, maybe every addiction was like that – you're trying, really, really hard to get something as far away from yourself as possible, and that something is yourself, so of course it doesn't work, which is why you keep doing it. And it felt like the same thing. That they had dedicated so much of their time to collaborating on a project, painstaking research and blueprints and tests; that they had built something together and that that thing had turned out to be a sublimely conceived and constructed trap. No, not so much *built* something, a cage or a prison, as collaborated, perfectly, on a fiendishly effective piece of programming; a long project, painstakingly conceived, designed and executed, line after line of code, text after text, call and response. Correcting any imprecisions in the other's data, fine-tuning their expectations and delivery until their souls were running in absolute parallel, enmeshed forever, ineluctably. Fuck. That over hundreds of thousands of words, he had given her a disease to which he alone was the cure … that it was both. And perhaps, if that was the case, you could achieve the same damnation with literally any other person if you were willing to put the work in. Or lacked the will to resist. She listened to a podcast by an American Orthodox priest she'd always liked. She listened to his episode on Hell. *If you are relying on somebody else, if you're demanding some kind of a reaction, if you're dependent for any sense of your own happiness or security … that's Hell. That's already Hell.* She steadied Arthur on the roundabout and told him that she loved him and with her other hand she took out her phone. Knowing that he was there, that he was still there, that he was waiting. You've built up forty-eight days. Do you really want to reset the clock back to zero? Don't do it, don't do it, don't do it.

● ● ●

— Hey.

• • •

— Hey you.

• • •

— Tell me a story.

•••

— Okay. Emily met the love of her life when she
was 26 and it was very good – let's go and have
way too many cocktails; let's go find some
bridges to walk on; let's go wherever I don't care,
a community centre in a depressed town; you're
so fucking great. They were artists. It was the
best year, both of them agreed on that, although
it was hard to tell if one or either of them wasn't
exaggerating because when you love someone
you want to say things which will make them
happy; which is maybe a desperate form of
manipulation should you wish them to associate
you with being happy, or at least if it is you and
you alone that you want them to associate with
being happy, a sad and ugly project. This is a
problem if you question it too much, so they
didn't. One night in her flat they were taking it
in turns to read aloud to one another from The
Cloud of Unknowing and Fear and Trembling,
respectively, and they would watch one another
read, standing naked in front of the bed, and
each would feel the other watching more than

listening and how much he/she loved her/him which would amplify/magnify how easy it was to love him/her or, that is to say, how safe it felt to love the other in return. And then Emily said that she was probably going to have a brandy and milk as a nightcap and he said that that was like something out of a Raymond Chandler novel and she said she'd make him one too. And when she got back to the bed holding two opaque glasses she said, What if we broke up, right now, and never saw one another again? And he said, Emily, what are you talking about? And she said, It could be our next project; it would be exhilarating, and he said, I don't think I could live without you and she said, Me neither, which is why it would be exhilarating. And he took out his phone and started deleting photos of her and blocked her on numerous social networks and she did the same, and she said, I think I'm going to cry and he said, I feel so completely terrible, and she said, I feel like I've been shot several times in the stomach and he said, Yes, that's it exactly, and she said, I feel so alive and so dead at the same time, and he said, Are we actually going to do this you can't actually be serious about this.

— That's a sad story, Elliott.

— Now you.

— Okay. There's a YouTube video of every episode of Friends at once, overlaid and overlaid and overlaid until it looks like a thousand distended holograms of a Klimt painting and sounds like the audience reaction to a stand-up routine in Hell. I thought that might make a good reference but it actually only has 8.5k views so maybe not; what I was wondering is if that's how God sees the world. A tsunami, your ability to compartmentalise. Jealousy, an avalanche. I'm sorry, that's awful. It is 22 minutes and 27 seconds long, the same length as the longest episode of Friends minus ad-breaks, and I wonder if that's how God sees the world too, as 22 minutes and 27 seconds long. Except that it all maybe coalesces into. Except that it maybe makes. Except that all it would really take to …

••●

— That's also sad.
— You go again.
— I'm out of ideas.
— I'll give you a prompt.
— Okay.
— Tell me a story set on a lifeboat.

…

— The lifeboat is spacious and seaworthy and the
  water is calm. This presents a problem for the
  writer in that nobody has to be thrown
  overboard. If the story is to function at all,
  characters will have to provoke one another into
  getting thrown overboard or want to be thrown
  overboard and the reasons will be complicated
  and sad.
— But as the days pass and we're reduced to
  drinking seawater you become delirious enough
  to unlock the rusty chain securing me to the
  railing. In my pocket I have a single Polo mint
  twisted into the end of its tube, plasticised foil

and a scrap of paper wrapper, and I give it to
you. Our crewmates start whooping and
hollering and waving their arms and we look to
the horizon which is completely fucked up and
drunk on the sunset. A ship is coming to rescue
us. Two ships. But then the ships start exchanging
fire and soon they both sink. And now we have
more people on the lifeboat and this really
changes the whole dynamic.

— We couldn't agree on a course anyway and now
there are eight more people with strong
opinions, and somebody smelled the Polo mint
on your breath so we are both being shunned.
They lock us in an empty supply cupboard and
we're like, so what? Then we find a trapdoor in
the supply cupboard and we drop down to a
storage space.

— There are bottles of water and tins of tuna steak,
there are vacuum-sealed flatbreads and cans of
fruit and tomatoes and packets of salted crackers
and we just start tearing at everything and
opening the bottles and the cans and pouring
the contents into our mouths and I remember
once hearing a fable about a man stuck at the
bottom of a well with a lampworm or
something, some giant worm, and when he got
rescued, starving and emaciated, they gave him
such a lavish feast he ate himself to death in a
matter of minutes and I'm about to tell you this
because it really stayed with me since childhood
but then I realise that you're already dead and so

am I, stiffened, eyes closed, tomato puree around our mouths, and it's maybe not the way I would have chosen to go but I'm glad, given the circumstances, that we both made the decisions we made.

● ● ●

— I'm blocking your email address and your
number.

● ● ●

— Please don't do that again. I only feel okay when
  I'm talking to you.

• • •

— I have to.

●●●

— I'm not even sure which of us is speaking any
more.

47

Concentrate. You're the only one responsible for this. Resist the urge to go looking for absolution. Sit with what you've done then start gradually clearing it up.

With the house to herself, Emily was entering student names and numbers on a spreadsheet for consideration by the widening-participation programme and waiting for the morning's second load of laundry to finish when she heard someone thumping on the front door with such urgency she assumed something must be wrong with one of the boys and stubbed her toe on the radiator in her hurry to get down the hall.

'Elliott, hi,' she said. 'You know, I'd been thinking …'

She hadn't seen him in six weeks – quite how he'd managed to avoid her altogether she wasn't sure, but he'd clearly taken her request to heart. He'd lost weight and hadn't shaved and had a wild look in his eyes.

'Emily,' he said. 'My aunt died and I just inherited twenty grand.'

'Oh god, Elliott, I'm so sorry,' said Emily. 'Come in.'

'Oh, yeah, I liked her a lot,' he said. 'But these things happen. Run away with me.'

'What?'

'Passport, wallet,' said Elliott. 'We'll chuck our phones.'

'I can't chuck my phone. Why don't you come in?'

'And our keys. No, bring them and we'll just put them in the liquids bin.'

'I think you need to sit down and maybe have a glass of wine,' said Emily.

'We don't need luggage – we can buy clothes wherever we end up.'

'Elliott. Have you been drinking?'

'Where should we go? Paris?'

'No,' said Emily. 'Somewhere cheaper and weirder.'

'Yeah! Like you always said. Latvia. We'll just look at the flights when we get to the airport and choose somewhere and I can buy tickets on my phone.'

'So best not to chuck your phone,' said Emily. 'I don't think you're thinking straight, Elliott – this isn't something that people do.'

'I am just so sick of everything.'

'You could see a counsellor?'

'Oh yeah, I'll get Ally to recommend someone. I love you and I can't take it any more.'

'But you have to.'

'I can't. It's killing me. You still love me?'

'I don't know.'

'Jesus, don't say that. Run away with me. You don't *know*?'

'I don't.'

'When did *that* happen?'

'I have to be sensible about this, Elliott.'

'God, I forgot how *pragmatic* women are,' said Elliott. 'That was a *real* fucking oversight.'

'I think this is … You're not willing to *tell* your wife or your children that you're leaving them, but you think you're willing to actually *leave* them. So you're thinking, what if you were just pathologically selfish?'

'Yes!'

'Ignored the repercussions. Faked your own death. You'd regret it within a day.'

'Do you know, some people go their entire lives without meeting someone like you?'

'I'm a dime a dozen.'

'That's from *Peanuts*.'

'Ha – yeah, I think that's where I got it,' said Emily.

'Snoopy overheard Charlie Brown saying it and it haunted him, lying on top of his kennel, for nights. They used it for a song in the Snoopy musical in 1982.'

'Oh god, they did as well.'

'The musical was called *Snoopy!!!* With three exclamation marks.'

'Snoopy!' Emily shouted. 'Maybe the only musical to ever have three.'

'It was so awful. I love you, Emily.'

'I'm sorry.'

'You're sorry. Okay.'

'I don't know what else to say.'

'All of this was different,' said Elliott. 'I thought it was possible for both of us to … It was different.'

'What do you *want* me to say? Love is something strong and mad and we both should have been a lot more careful.'

'You could maybe have *not written to me constantly for a year.*'

'We were writing to each other.'

'If it's just a case of turning a tap off for you.'

'That's completely unfair.'

'I've pretty much transferred everything over to you in my head.'

'I never wanted you to do that.'

'Like I've converted everything into an obsolete currency.'

'I'm sorry. You're really angry with me.'

'No. God, whatever, just come with me.'

'Ugh.' Emily slipped her shoes on and took her handbag off the coat peg. 'I'll come to the airport, Elliott, but because I'm *worried* about you, not because I'm running away with you.'

'That'll do,' said Elliott.

'How were you *planning* on getting to the airport?' she said. 'Was all this just a ruse to get me to take you?' She scrolled through the estate's car-pool app on her phone. Any grand gesture usually foundered on practicalities: an ultimatum followed by an awkward wait for a bus; a declaration, but then you were, after all, in the same room and someone needed to come up with an excuse to leave – *I should go* … So much of life felt like bidding a tearful goodbye to someone then realising you were both walking the same way anyway.

'You really don't have to.'

'It's fine – I'll drop you off. Oh, all the cars are out.'

'I'm gonna call an Uber.'

'That'll cost hundreds.'

'I don't care. And I want you to have a drink.'

'So I can make bad decisions?'

He ordered four double gin and tonics in the pub by the Departures entrance. The retail units were rectangular slots, replaceable, but this one had been done up to look like an old-fashioned boozer.

'Love airport bars,' he said. 'They exist completely outside of time. Have you read Bergson?'

'No.'

'Me neither, but he'd have loved airport bars too. And the deeper you go into the airport' – he slid two of the glasses to Emily and the drink lapped the sides but didn't spill – 'the further you go into this … *mise en abyme* where nothing really matters—'

'The thing that's worrying me—'

'Drink.'

Emily sipped her first gin and tonic. 'Oh, this is really good. The thing that's worrying me is eventually you have to get on a plane.'

'Drunk.'

'And then you arrive at your destination.'

'Still drunk.'

'And eventually something starts mattering again.'

'You're overthinking it. We'll be completely untraceable. And it's possible to delay things mattering *indefinitely*.'

'That's not even half true.'

'You're all that matters to me.'

'I shouldn't be.'

'Emily, seriously, don't leave me in this – I'll get stuck permanently. Throw a rope down.'

'What's a rope in this analogy?'

'It's an analogy where you've left me in a pit with a broken leg and you've just about managed to scale out of it.'

'Nice. What's the rope?'

'Tell me you still love me.'

'I don't … That's not how I feel about you any more.'

'Well in that case you need to make me understand why.'

'I don't want to say something that's going to hurt you.'

'You've already driven off in the Jeep. You'll get back to base camp and tell them I fell in a ravine.'

'I was very sad for a long time,' said Emily.

'Practically *weeks*,' said Elliott, bitterly.

'And then I started to wake up and get used to it and I thought maybe you'd started to get used to it as well. It's been *months*.'

'It's been exactly fifty-three days,' said Elliott. 'Emily' – he ran his hands through his hair and seemed to try to pull out his fringe – 'I will never get used to it, I will never stop loving you and you will always be the first person I want to tell about … anything. Major award, terminal illness.'

'And that's not *healthy*,' said Emily.

'Why are you so interested in *health* all of a sudden?'

'Is it a bad thing to want to avoid things which are unhealthy?'

'Have you joined a *cult*?'

'I haven't joined a cult.'

'Because I always suspected that somewhere out there there's a cult which, for whatever reason, is solely dedicated to hating me. They project a big image of me and just hiss at it. They finally got to you?'

She almost laughed and caught it in time. Elliott was still holding his head in his hands on the dark wooden table. He looked up at her. 'Where is it? I'm trying to find it. I can't accept it's not there.'

'How's Ally doing?'

'Oh,' said Elliott. 'That's clever. Are you wearing a wire?'

'I'm genuinely asking.'

'God, I hate what this has turned me into,' said Elliott, draining his first gin and tonic and taking a swig from the second. 'I'm being such a little bitch. She's fine, thank you.'

'The last time I spoke to her properly,' said Emily, 'she told me about some complicated situations you'd got into with other women and said she thought it was partly to do with your relationship with your mother.'

'What?' said Elliott.

'I'd have asked you about it but we weren't speaking.'

'Okay, well, all of that's bullshit,' said Elliott.

'She's making it up or she's wrong?'

'I haven't got into *any* "complicated situations" with anyone,' said Elliott, crossly. 'This is the closest I've ever been to a complicated situation. We can talk about my mother if you like – I might need a couple more drinks.'

'No, I'm sorry. Of course not.'

'Do you remember once you said to me, *What do I do? Tell me what I should do?*'

'I said a lot of things.'

'Did you mean *any* of them?'

'Of *course* I did. For fuck's sake, Elliott, stop being so *mean* to me.'

'I'm sorry. I'm so sorry. Tell me what I should do.'

'You'll wake up from this, sooner than you think, and I'll be like a bad dream.'

'No. You won't.'

'I think if you're not happy there are things you can do about that,' said Emily. 'But not with me.'

'Okay,' he said, finishing the last of his drink and making a face. 'That's fairly unequivocal. I'm going to get on a plane now.'

'Elliott, where are you *going*?'

'Why would that matter to you?'

'Because I'm your *friend*.'

'Emily,' he said. 'We have never been friends.'

His chair scraped as he stood and turned away, picked up his rucksack and slung it over one shoulder. She was too cross with him to say anything, felt close to tears and didn't want to give him the satisfaction. And the thought that this was what it had come down to made her dig her nails into her knees. So she watched as he picked his way through the clustered groups drowning their pre-flight anxieties and then walked unsteadily over to the auto-mated passport scanners. She didn't look away until he had disappeared through the entrance to security; he paused before the fold, as if he was considering turning around for a moment.

48

You could have just said yes – you could have just got on the plane, even if you were going to come back the same day. You could have told him you still loved him. At least give him that. She jabbed herself in the thigh with the safety pin in her pocket. She had taken the train back from the airport to save money and was approaching the three-mile nature walk back to the estate when she saw Alathea carrying Dimitry on one shoulder and struggling with an overstuffed tote bag.

'Thank god,' said Alathea, grabbing her arm. 'Emily, I'm so sorry – I haven't seen you in weeks – I've been so busy.'

'Oh god, no, you don't ever need to apologise about that,' said Emily. 'It usually takes me about a year to respond to a text message.'

Alathea looked unusually pale. Her hair was tied back and her eyes were red.

'Are you free now?' she said. 'Can we get a cup of tea? I need someone I can talk to.'

'Oh. Sure,' said Emily.

'And that's *you*, worse luck for you.'

'I'm absolutely free.'

She followed Alathea to a little tearoom called the Cobweb by the overpass where the city guttered out into Criterion Gardens, an incongruously perfect suburb in an industrial wasteland. It was the kind of tearoom she didn't think existed anymore – a raisin-scones and butter sort of place with floral armchairs. Alathea put Dimitry in a high-chair and he immediately stood up.

'Don't, baby,' she said. 'Mummy's fucking exhausted. The thing about highchairs' – she turned to Emily – 'is some-one needs to develop one with a containment shield.'

'Could make a killing.'

'Ugh, I love them to bits but I *hate* the prospect of being on my own with them for four days,' she said. 'I'm the worst.'

'Elliot …'

'He's at a conference in *Paris* for the weekend.'

'Ohh,' said Emily. 'Right. He said he was on his way to the airport – I saw him …' She paused. Why would Elliott tell her he was on his way to the airport without telling her where he was going? Also, *was* he going to a confer-ence or was that a cover story for trying to elope with her? She was relieved when Alathea didn't show any sign of pursuing this or even of having noticed.

'Which is really just a weekend's hard drinking,' she said. 'Which I could do with myself, to be honest, if it wasn't … Dimitry, calm down, honestly.'

'He said his aunt died.'

'Oh yeah, Aunt Lauren died,' said Alathea. 'It's sad. She had a good innings, though.'

'Right. Ally,' said Emily. 'Are things okay? You look like you've been crying.'

'Fucking hay fever,' said Alathea. But her voice sounded thicker than usual and she looked into the corner.

'What's … wrong?'

'I wasn't going to say anything,' said Alathea.

'Oh god,' said Emily. 'Ally … I.' She braced as if someone was about to saw off her leg in a temporary military hospital, glanced around for something to bite. The menus looked pretty thick.

'Oh what's the point,' said Alathea. 'I was unusually late and it turns out I'm up the duff again and it was very much unintentional.'

'Oh *wow*,' said Emily. 'Wow wow wow wow.'

'Yeah,' said Alathea.

'Wow. I mean, *fuck*. Haha. Sorry. That's *huge*.'

'This is pretty much how I reacted,' said Alathea. 'You're a good friend, Emily. Thank you for not saying congratulations.'

'I mean *obviously*, congratulations.'

'No, I meant it. We'll have to move, of course – we're bouncing off each other as it is.'

'Oh,' said Emily. 'No. Wow.'

'I know, right? I'll really miss you, Ems. You're one of the least insufferable people I've ever met.'

'You too. God, Ally.'

'Emily. And my parents can bloody well help this time,' said Alathea. 'Naturally. You know when a rich person says they're broke what they *mean* is they may have to dip into their third stock portfolio.'

'Ha.'

'But they've made their point now.'

'Their point?'

'Or we've made ours. It's difficult to say. We'll get a proper house, with a big garden, a tree house. The kids'll go to good schools. We'll probably have an au pair. I've not told them yet, but my folks are going to absolutely *love* it. It's completely humiliating. Jesus, listen to me, sorry, Emily.'

'No, it's cool,' said Emily. 'I respect my superiors.'

Alathea widened her eyes and laughed. 'Elliott's actually taking it better than I thought he would.'

Emily's head felt hot and she thought she must be blushing severely and thanked god it was a hot day. 'Oh, Ally,' she said.

'I think we're both equally scared shitless – how do we make this work? How do we work with it? How can we love another one as much as … I mean it wasn't part of our plan, but then what *was* our plan, really?'

49

It was raining on Saturday morning, but Emily said she would take the children to the park anyway and give Steven a chance to rest.

'Or if you need to visit your mother,' said Emily. 'Or we could all go, I mean …'

It wasn't that she expected gratitude, but he just said, 'If you're sure?' and walked slowly back upstairs as if in pain. She hadn't slept. She'd cried for an hour and then completed thirty-six levels of *Toon Blast*, which was like *Candy Crush* but somehow more passive, until the sun came up.

They walked with their hoods up, Arthur breaking into an uneven run intermittently until Emily scooped him up to carry him. She gave Matty the half-inflated football.

'Why are we going out when it's so horrible?' he said.

'We need some exercise,' said Emily. 'All of us will go mad otherwise.'

They saw a squirrel with its head in a coffee cup by the first line of trees.

'Look!' said Matty.

The squirrel sat up and the cup fell around its shoulders.

'Hahaha!'

'Little cup-head squirrel,' said Emily, absently.

'Photograph it!'

She tried to hold Arthur in one arm and take her phone out with her free hand, but by the time she had the camera open the squirrel had shaken the cup off. It seemed to shake its fist at them before scampering away. For a moment she felt that it was a shame because she could have sent the photograph to Elliott and said Hey, check out this squirrel, but then she remembered that she wasn't talking to him anymore and felt sad.

For a while she would look him up, but his social media seemed to have gone cold, which she supposed she understood. Most people she knew went through periods of swearing the whole thing off then got right back on it within a couple of months, tweeting about how much the break had improved their mental health. She couldn't say for certain that looking him up gave her much of a dopamine hit anymore – she just dejectedly flicked through images of him feeling nothing but detachment from the room around her, sometimes from her own children. She downloaded an app which cut off her access to all social networks.

'Mum, I'm getting really wet,' said Matty. 'Can we go home?'

'We've only just got here,' said Emily.

She tried to put Arthur down by the gate to the playground but he cried and held his arms out to her.

'Oh, Arthur,' she said, picking him up again. 'Maybe this was a mistake.'

'I told you it was a mistake,' said Matty. 'One: It's raining.'

'Emily?'

She turned with a start. Magda was walking her bedraggled dog.

'Awful, isn't it?' she said.

'I know. I don't know why I insisted on taking them out.'

'You could just take us *home*,' said Matty, taking his younger brother's hand and walking him towards the row of trees by the fence.

'I wondered,' said Magda, quietly, 'how you were coping.'

'Oh, fine,' said Emily. 'Why do you ask?'

'Do tell me to go away,' said Magda. 'But I couldn't help but notice you getting rather close to Elliott over a ... certain period.'

'Oh,' said Emily. 'What?'

'And I hate to even bring it up. But I couldn't sleep last night – I kept thinking, I ought to say something, I ought to say something. And here we both are, so it's clearly meant to be.'

'I suppose I have got rather close to him,' said Emily.

'There's a certain cupidity ...'

'Cupidity?'

'I do know him quite well, actually.'

'Oh really?'

'We were friends. It's a bit of a sad story. He worked at the same faculty as Bob. Fifteen years ago, maybe. And it was a small scene, Criterion Gardens was far more bohemian at the beginning. We had a lot of soirees. He didn't live here – Bob would pick him up, or else he'd walk for hours and turn up on our doorstep.'

'I'm sorry, what?' said Emily. 'Magda, he told me you were a mad old woman who tried to cross through his garden.'

'Is that so.'

'That's literally all he said about you. You were a stranger who asked if you could take your shopping through his garden and when he said no you got all weird.'

'Oh, well, I suppose that's as good an excuse as any. Perhaps we'd all like to distance ourselves from anyone who's helped us. We took him in, you might say. Charming and volatile young man, something quite vulnerable about him, and talented, of course. He must only have been in his late twenties. He seemed very alive, twice as alive as most people you meet.'

Emily had never seen Magda quite so animated, in a rush to unburden herself, she supposed, and yet she found it hard to take the words in, as if a soundtrack were swelling in the background. Arthur and Matty crouched over a puddle, seemingly transfixed by something in it. She took a couple of steps backward and sat down on the short backless bench at the edge of the park so she could still see the boys. Magda followed, sat next to her, took her hand and started to gently circle her palm with her finger.

'We'd have people to dinner and it inevitably turned into some kind of party. Elliott would always still be awake when the sun came up, still talking,' she said. 'Bob – despite his poetry, he was very much a social realist – Bob would say something like *art is the selective recreation of reality* and Elliott would tell him to piss off and they'd go round in circles. It was all rather loose, I rarely saw him twice with the same woman — it's not unusual, the carte blanche we give to artists, they fall in love easily — and I felt very protective of him so I'd vet them — *I don't think she's right for you at all.* One night he fell asleep in my lap. I remember stroking his hair.'

'Oh god, Magda,' said Emily.

'Yes, yes, it was like the inappropriate relationship with the son I never had et cetera,' said Magda. 'Bob was very well connected. He put him in touch with some influential curators, wrote effusive references for grant applications. Even helped him hang his first exhibition. Really he was a mentor to Elliott.'

'Why would he keep this from me?'

'We fell out. We always tended to be quite critical of the idea of the nuclear family, which is rather funny if you look at the place now. To come to the point, Elliott had an affair with a married Cultural Studies lecturer — they were often at our house. I'd make up the sofa bed for them. They made each other laugh a lot. It ended rather horribly — her husband tried to kill himself, as it happens — and Elliott disappeared.'

'That's *horrible*,' said Emily.

'Well, who's to say?' said Magda. 'These things happen, and removing himself from the situation was probably quite sensible. Bob had to cover his classes for half a term.'

'Hightailed it out of there,' said Emily, quietly.

'*Mum*,' said Matty.

'And then it was almost a decade later he got back in touch, quite established by this point, ostensibly to pass on his condolences — he *did* love Bob, he wasn't ungrateful. But also so that I could approve his application for his family to move here. I should apologise,' said Magda. 'I didn't mean to withhold this from you. I don't like to make assumptions and I don't like to get involved in other people's affairs. I could have told you something and I opted for discretion. But I am sorry.'

'No, no, I get it,' said Emily. 'I wouldn't have listened if you *had* told me anything – it's just … Why did you fall out the second time?'

'I assumed he might have settled down a little after meeting Alathea – she was pregnant when they moved.'

'She is again.'

'Oh, how lovely. But then … Well, I'm glad you're all right, Emily.'

'You haven't answered my question.'

'Perhaps it was all a misunderstanding. I saw something and I assumed there was a strong enough foundation to our friendship for me to give him a piece of my mind, mistakenly, it turned out. He was mortified and cut me off.'

'He just charms people,' said Emily. 'Serially.'

'Well doesn't everyone in their way?' said Magda. 'I've always felt that charm is rather a basic evolutionary principle. If you want shelter, food and comfort it would serve you well to be charming.'

'I felt as though he loved me,' said Emily. 'It was all a bit stupid.'

'I don't doubt that he loved you,' said Magda. 'He's not calculating. He's probably been deeply, mortally in love with over a hundred people. There's nothing in it for him, really, he's just at the whim of … that's what I meant by cupidity. So I'm telling you not to feel stupid.'

'I'll take that under advisement.'

'We can love anyone,' said Magda. '*Anyone*. We just close our eyes to their flaws, ignore anything that doesn't correspond to our image of them and get on with it.'

Arthur sat down in the puddle.

'Oh, Arthur.'

'I should let you get them home,' said Magda. She took Emily's hand. 'You're still very raw, aren't you? Do you know marathon runners say that twenty miles is the halfway point?'

'They do?'

'You're doing admirably, is what I'm trying to say.'

Her phone shook in her pocket. Her mother had texted. *Hi darling, please can you reply just so I know you're okay? Thinking of you all xxx.* The thought of trying to respond in any depth exhausted her so she just wrote *I'm okay, mum xx.*

What was it, that closeness and distance, that ease and caution between them? How could you explain your relationship with your mother to anyone else? And why would they even care?

She admonished the boys for not taking their shoes off at the door and was about to run after them when she noticed Matty had left a muddy footprint on a postcard in the porch. She picked it up. It was a deliberately tacky photograph of the Eiffel Tower, out of focus with pink flowers in the foreground.

'Elliott,' she said, out loud.

She turned it over. It was addressed to her, and it occurred to her that it was the first time she had ever seen his handwriting: it was neat, flowing and loopy, exactly as it ought to be, oddly familiar. In lieu of a message on the left-hand side he had copied out a quotation:

> Thou art so true
> that thoughts of thee suffice.
> — *Donne*

For a moment she thought it was sweet. He was telling her that he was okay, that he hadn't drunk himself into a Parisian gutter, and that he still thought about her and that was enough; it melted something in her.

'Oh, Elliott,' she muttered.

But then she wondered why it felt familiar. Had they, in their endless messaging, talked about Donne? Had he said it to her before? No. They talked so often he'd barely have had a chance to think about her anyway.

'Mum!'

'I'm coming.'

'I can't open the juice.'

Or had she seen it somewhere else? Her hands shook as she opened her wallet and checked behind a wedge of loyalty cards for where she'd folded the pink post-it note that had fluttered to the floor from the shallow wardrobe the first time she'd opened it. The note between two fingers, she fumbled her wallet and dropped it on the doorstep and didn't stoop to pick it up until she'd peeled the scrap of paper open.

Thou art so true that thoughts of thee suffice. She held it next to the postcard. It was unmistakably the same handwriting.

50

It was unusual for Alathea to text her and so, once Emily recovered from the vestigial twinge of disappointment that it wasn't Elliott, she scraped the onion she was dicing into a bowl and put it in the fridge and went to get her coat. *Emily are you free I need to talk to you urgently, come over, please? x* It was the *please?* which made her feel faintly nauseated and she crossed the road as if being gently reeled in against her will.

Alathea took her through to the utility room off the kitchen. She had put in a low table and four square wicker chairs with comfortable oblong cushions. A cold glare through the window.

'This is nice.'

'Oh it was *full* of junk – I'm cosmetically enhancing it to try to trick someone into buying the place,' said Alathea. 'We've been back and forth to the dump twenty times.' Then she groaned and stroked her stomach.

'How are you finding it?'

'I didn't really get morning sickness with Tomasz *or* Dimitry,' said Alathea. 'Part of me thought people were just making that up, but Jesus. I suppose, that being the case, I deserve it. Our thoughts always come back to punish us. It's probably a girl.'

'You poor thing,' said Emily.

Alathea had prepared a saucer of six yellow truffles which could have been marzipan or lemon – Emily wasn't really in the mood.

'Are you in the right headspace to receive information which could potentially hurt you?' said Alathea.

'Am I *what*?' said Emily.

She put her hands on Emily's waist.

'Oh,' said Emily.

'Sit down. We're going to play a game where we stop lying to each other.'

'Lying?' said Emily.

'I know everything, Emily, sweetheart, absolutely everything to the last bloody yearning text message, so you don't need to try to pretend anymore. Take a big deep breath. And let it out.'

Emily sat down heavily and closed her eyes thinking *don't cry, don't cry, don't cry* which was really as much use as thinking *don't fall* when you've already lost your balance.

Once they were seated opposite each other and the room began to spin a little slower, Alathea took her hand and began to run her finger over Emily's wedding ring.

'We can be civil, can't we?' she said, quietly. 'There's really quite a lot at stake for both of us.'

Emily nodded.

'You have such pretty hands. Long, delicate fingers.'

Alathea let go and put her hand to Emily's cheek and began, gently, to divert her tears with her thumb. Emily felt the tiny cold stream track past her ear.

'When we talked, in the soft-play,' said Alathea, 'I wasn't really being honest with you.'

'I'm so sorry,' said Emily.

'You're quite something,' said Alathea. 'I can see how he got into trouble with you. I mean I could always see that. You have a certain quality … You remind me of *him* if anything.'

'I didn't—' said Emily. 'Nothing—'

'Breathe.'

'I didn't do any of this to hurt you and I didn't mean to get so lost.'

'I know.'

'I just shut it out, I *did* feel guilty, I *did*.'

'Shhh,' said Alathea. 'I understand.'

'But the more I shut it out the easier it was to shut it out and I'm so ashamed and I'm so sorry.'

'There's no need for you to say things like that,' said Alathea.

'I felt very drawn to both of you.'

'Hmm. I am going to tell you something and you will probably stop crying,' said Alathea. 'You will probably hate me and feel a combination of disgust and relief.'

'I could never hate you,' said Emily.

'We'll see,' said Alathea. 'The first thing I should say is I don't exactly have a … blotless copybook here, so I'm not one to judge.'

'I'm sorry,' said Emily. 'I'm so sorry.'

'Please stop crying,' said Alathea. 'I don't like seeing you so upset. Years ago I had this friend, you know? Another therapist, and we were close … actually, it started because he came to see me, but that very quickly became unwise.

We met for drinks occasionally – we were colleagues, we talked about our practice. We had this tacit agreement that we weren't going to ruin that or blow up each other's lives – we really valued each other. As much as anything else it was so useful for me to have someone I could run ideas by, you know? And it didn't hurt that I fancied him, but that was irrelevant – everyone has crushes. And Elliott … was *such* a dick about it. He was always super jealous and one day he emailed the guy from *my* account when I left it logged in one night and told him, from my perspective, that I was selfish, that I was a dangerous person and that I was sorry for giving him the wrong impression and that we shouldn't see each other again. Please don't reply, and ignore me when I try to get back in touch with you – something like that.'

'Oh.'

'It was a while before I found out he'd done it – as far as I knew the guy had fallen off a motorway bridge or something. So what do you think I did?'

Emily widened her eyes and shook her head.

'You're so adorable. There was a woman I knew he liked – an artist he'd worked with and I knew they still talked occasionally. I mean *all* of these little things. You know them. She was called Ziva. And I sent Ziva a message from his phone telling her that I, Elliott, had complicated feelings for her and didn't really know what to do about it. And she wrote back straight away to say that she was so *relieved* that I, Elliott, had said that … I had to be careful, Emily. If I said anything that she'd *ask* him about that would ruin it and I just wanted to push it that little bit further here and there. So I kept it fairly subtle and minimal and told her we had to be careful and deleted the exchanges and just let things develop. Months passed and they'd made plans to meet, so then I told him.'

'God,' said Emily.

'I know, we're like *The Twits*, right? He was furious, but. We made up, he saw the funny side. The thing is it felt like a sort of natural extension of destroying each other's stuff – I know he told you about that. So a few times … We wouldn't exactly go out of our way to look for—'

'Victims?' said Emily.

'People are people,' said Alathea. 'We'd never let things get too far out of hand. It was more, when the opportunity was there, which very occasionally it would be. I really admire anyone who can make a genuinely open relation-ship work, but even *they'd* probably admit things get a little screwed up sometimes and people get hurt. And we tended not to go that far; our main thing was hurting each *other*. The thing is we'd *agreed*, after we'd moved here – we have children now, for goodness' sake – we'd agreed to leave that behind. Only things, never people. Too messy, too danger-ous. So this – you – it was a bit of a surprise for me.'

'I'm sorry.'

'No no no,' said Alathea. 'If anything I'm the one who should apologise. What I'm saying is, all the time you've been writing to him …' She paused, watching Emily carefully.

'No,' said Emily.

'He's actually very busy despite his air of nonchalance. And you're maybe one of … a couple of women he was writing to? Also you're something of a two-person job, Emily. Some outsourcing was inevitable.'

'No.'

'I don't mean to say', said Alathea, 'that it was never him. Or that it wasn't him at least ... half the time.'

Emily shook her head.

'There's probably some way of uploading the whole cache of messages and attributing them if I can find someone more technically savvy than me. It's probably about a terabyte by this point, isn't it?'

'I don't believe you,' said Emily, quietly.

'If you'd like a full *record*, if you'd like to know exactly which exchanges were with him and which were with me. These are vegan, by the way,' said Alathea. 'I got them from that new pop-up shop. Very sweet.'

'I'm fine, thank you.'

'*If this is hurting you we can just stop*, that was one of mine ... *Sometimes I feel like I don't know who I am* ... I'm trying to remember some of the things you told me.'

Emily closed her eyes and cried silently. Then she composed herself and looked at Alathea.

'He *loved* me.'

'Yes,' said Alathea. 'Don't worry – I'm not trying to ... lord it over you.'

'Yes you are.'

'A bit, maybe,' said Alathea, 'you can probably admit I deserve that. Do you want to know something funny?'

'No.'

'Yes you do. I fell for you too. Which certainly wasn't my intention.'

'Alathea.'

'You're *really* angry, aren't you?' said Alathea, and shuddered. 'Of course you are. I took no pleasure in seeing you so vulnerable – I felt sick with myself. I miss talking to you, actually. Eventually I stopped and decided I needed to take a different tack. Which is this. Just grasp the nettle.'

'You miss sock-puppeting me.'

'The really ridiculous thing is that after a while, when I told you I loved you, I *meant* it.' She took Emily's hand in hers again and Emily felt too exhausted to take it back. 'Oh god, you've gone all limp like I've drained your life force or something. I *did* mean it. I'd imagine falling asleep with my arms around you.'

'He knew,' said Emily. 'He knew it was you the whole time?'

'Not at first. He's a heavy sleeper and he's scatterbrained. I tried to sort things out my own way, but it was a bit of a non-starter, so it seemed best to get involved directly, push things just too far for him so he'd panic and have second thoughts about you. Which is just him, that's what he's like. So sometimes I'd take his phone when he fell asleep or pick it up when he'd left it on the … hob or something.'

'At what point?'

'Oh, I don't know. I only started when it became clear to me that this was different and that he was crazy about you and that I was losing him. And I didn't really have a clear plan and I definitely didn't mean for it to go on this long.'

'He was *okay* with you doing this to me? is what I'm asking,' said Emily.

'Try to see it from his perspective,' said Alathea.

'Oh I'm trying.'

'He probably just wanted to keep talking to you and keep things as they were, more or less, and gradually he had to accept more and more little contingencies—'

'Like you impersonating him.'

'Which, if he objected to—'

'He wouldn't …'

'You can take on a *lot* of water before the ship sinks. I mean you *were* basically having an affair with my husband,' said Alathea, 'so you understand that as well as any of us.'

Emily got up and steadied herself on the back of the chair, then she leaned over and took one of the truffles.

'Okay,' she said. 'Okay.' Then she put the truffle back on the plate and started pressing her thumb into the palm of her hand.

'Look, we're all going to walk away from this, by some miracle, probably thanks to your god, Emily – I expect it's some small consolation to know your prayers didn't go unheeded – and everyone is going to be okay.'

'Okay.'

'We'll exchange Christmas cards once a year.'

Emily nodded.

'I'm not trying to be shitty about this,' said Alathea. 'And I'm not trying to be fucking … *magnanimous* about it either. But I think if we choose to we can all just shrug it off. We can both go and throw up now, if you like?'

'Sure.'

'You're being quite monosyllabic, Emily.'

'I don't have very much to say.'

'Ems.' Alathea got up, quite suddenly, and put her arms around Emily, and Emily didn't stiffen or push her gently, firmly away; she found, curiously, that it was quite easy to hold Alathea tight, as if she was comforting her, as if she could afford to let her believe that she, Emily, could accept her forgiveness, love her, forgive her as well, as if she could afford to let her believe that she could love or forgive herself. Although whether the gesture was sincere on either side it was hard to say.

'I do really regret it and I'm sorry. I didn't mean to deceive you.'

'Alathea,' said Emily. 'What exactly *did* you mean to do?'

'Hmm,' said Alathea. 'No, that's fair. I just mean I'm sorry for hurting you. I like you.'

'I think I'd like to go now,' said Emily, standing.

'Of course – like I said, we can put all this behind us.'

'Yes, what a valuable learning experience,' said Emily.

'Yes, that will be all, have a good one.'

'What an opportunity to grow.'

'Haha!'

'Well, take care of him, whoever he really is,' said Emily. 'He's profoundly unhappy, which I suppose you're aware of.'

'Oh,' said Alathea. 'We rub along okay, you know? It's funny that you don't seem to have much concern for *me* in all this. Injured party and all that.'

'Sometimes I don't think I care very much about anyone,' said Emily.

'Well, not many people would admit that.'

'I'm trying to be more honest.'

'Bonne chance.'

'I'll let you get back to …'

'Yes, yes, let's get on with it,' said Alathea. 'I've got about a grand's worth of new light shades coming.'

51

As Emily approached her front door she could hear a high-pitched whine, like the moments after an explosion in a film, but it didn't feel like anything she needed urgently to stop. She felt as though she could live with it forever if need be, everything a little muted and dream-like, nothing that could ever really infiltrate her forcefield again.

Steven was sitting at the kitchen island answering emails. He looked up and nodded.

'Steven,' she said. 'Tell me what you're thinking.'

'I'm not thinking anything.'

'Because the thing is, Steven, you're actually killing me, this is killing me, and if you don't start talking to me I am actually going to die.'

He raised his eyebrows and, although he was staring at the white tiles on the far wall, it felt like the most he'd said to her in a year.

'Does that make sense?' said Emily. 'Does that make sense to you? Or is it one of those things I say that doesn't make any sense?'

Outside a single magpie had perched at the top of a tree and she kept looking out of the window until she saw a second.

'Do you understand,' Steven said, 'how hard I'm trying?'

'*No*,' said Emily. 'No. I don't.'

He hunched his shoulders and stared into his cup of tea.

'For a long time now,' he said, then he seemed to give up and closed his eyes.

'Steven, talk to me, for a long time what?'

'I feel like I lost you years ago and I'm sad and I don't know what to do about it,' he said quietly.

'Why? When?'

'I feel like … You've been through something difficult and it's used up any of the love you had for me. But so what? It would be nice if we got on a little better, but that's not the priority.' He seemed to shrug it off and took a sip of his tea.

'Ugh,' said Emily. 'Don't stop now. I don't know how you can put this all on me. Do you think I can't tell how much I *annoy* you?'

'You don't annoy me.'

'I'm *always* annoying to you, I *constantly* annoy you. You sigh and you give me withering looks. That's what I've come to expect from you. That's *all* I've come to expect from you.'

'I know,' said Steven, 'that with the boys … I know how hard you've struggled. I know that. But do you think it's been easy for me? Do you think nothing affects me?'

'I was *ill*.'

'I know.'

'Do you think I *wanted* to be ill?'

'Why are we even … Why say something like that?' said Steven. 'Yes. I think you wanted to be ill. Is that what you want me to say?'

'It would be a start. Do you have any idea what it was like?' said Emily, 'I couldn't trust my own perceptions, I couldn't trust my own mind, everything I thought kept getting presented back to me as something I was *wrong* about, everyone was attacking me and I was supposed to— A time when I was supposed to just be full of the joys of motherhood, to be so *disappointed* in myself? Do you know how hard it was?'

'Yes, you told me, at great length, all the time, night and day.'

'Oh, I never shut up, right?'

'When I was walking up and down the hallway trying to get the baby to sleep at 3 a.m. Until I wanted to beg you to stop talking.'

She laughed coldly.

'But I didn't, because I was frightened of making you even more angry. For such a long time – *years* – it was like living with a hostile stranger,' said Steven.

'It?'

'The situation.'

'*I* was like a hostile stranger?'

'Yes!' said Steven, looking at her for the first time, his eyes wide. It was the most animated she'd ever seen him. 'Yes, you *were*, okay? You were angry and unpredictable and you'd say things that didn't make very much sense and it was scary. For months, for years, relentlessly. I was scared of you.'

'Fucking hell, Steven.'

'What was I supposed to do other than make a good go of it, for your sake, for Matty's sake, for Arthur's sake? And maybe that meant retreating into myself.'

'I don't feel like you had very far to retreat.'

'For a long time,' said Steven, 'my job has been to keep things together.'

'Your job. Do you want a long-service medal for sticking with me?' said Emily. 'Seeing as I've been so hellish?'

'I wasn't going anywhere.'

'I know you weren't. The thing is, it sounds to me,' said Emily, 'to go back to something you said earlier, that *you've* been through something difficult and it's used up any of the love you had for *me*.'

'You don't feel loved?'

'No, I don't. I feel a great deal of indifference from you bordering on contempt. What *are* you trying hard to do?'

'I'm not a martyr,' said Steven. 'I love you. I'd like a kind word every now and then, that's all.'

'Does it ever occur to you that's all *I'd* like too? That that would be enough? To be treated like more than a *problem* you've been saddled with.'

'What's the verse, Emily?' said Steven. 'Seventy times seven. The four hundred and ninetieth time I tried to say something kind or loving or tried to put my hand on your shoulder and you shook me off like I was a … The four hundred and ninetieth time is when I started feeling like it might be better for both of us if I just stopped.'

'*Steven*,' said Emily.

She went to him and sat on his lap and they both wobbled on the stool until he braced with one of his legs and put his arms around her.

'Don't fucking *say* things like that to me,' she said.

He had his face pressed against her shoulder and her neck and he was crying and he rocked back and forth with her insofar as that was possible on the chrome stool. She said *just be kind to me just love me I'm so sorry* and then she looked at the counter and said, 'Oh god, the boys' swimming stuff I thought I'd packed it.'

'Emily,' said Steven.

'It's okay, I'll run in with it.'

'There's something I have to tell you.'

'More? I think I'm just about at capacity for catharsis.'

'No. Something else. Alathea.'

Emily's head felt very cold. 'Alathea what?' she said.

'She kissed me. I mean I kissed her. It's been killing me.'

Emily laughed, a little too loud.

'This isn't how I thought you'd react,' said Steven.

'No, no,' said Emily, 'I'm sorry.' She slid down to the kitchen floor against a cupboard and laughed again.

'I need to tell you everything,' said Steven. 'She'd come round after work. The school's on the way home from her practice. She'd bring me a coffee and at first it was just ... It would be about half an hour, then she'd drive off. She'd ask after you. She'd try to make me laugh. She said she was determined to get below the surface and I said, *Well, good luck.*'

Emily smiled at him. There were tears in his eyes. She felt the way she felt with Matty when he cried because he'd ruined a drawing.

'It's quite a deep surface,' she said.

'I didn't think much of it. Bit puzzled when she lived just across the street. To be honest I liked the attention. But gradually she started ... confiding in me or something. Things about Elliott. He comes across as all nice, but she showed me some of the things he'd broken in a rage. Can't even imagine him in a rage, really, but you don't know with men, do you?'

'Steven.'

'So eventually I started talking to her about … you know, if she needed help. People she could talk to.'

'Oh, Steven.'

'And she said she didn't know. She asked me not to say anything to you. I don't know why, but I just did what she said. It felt like a very delicate situation and I wanted to respect that. She was worried he'd try to take the children or something. She felt trapped.'

'God,' Emily muttered. This was, she supposed, Alathea trying to sort things out her own way.

'But she was so grateful, Emily. And she started coming round a bit more frequently. She'd sit on my desk, always just for half an hour on her way home. And the last time … I'm very sorry. It was unacceptable and I'm sorry. I'll respect … however you want to proceed.'

'Why are you sorry?' said Emily. 'You haven't *done* anything.'

'We kissed,' said Steven. 'Briefly. I stopped it. I could have stopped it earlier. I could have backed away before it started.'

'Oh, babe, so what?' said Emily.

'Emily.'

'Come here. Don't pace.'

'I think you're supposed to be very angry,' said Steven. She stood and put her arms around his thick waist. He'd always felt impossibly firm, like a human sandbag. 'Everything I read said that I should expect you to be very angry,' he continued. 'That you're not is kind of scary, to be honest.'

'Has this been torturing you for a while?'

He nodded.

'Steven,' she said, wiping her eyes. 'I think it's just what they're like. Both of them. They need something to hold over each other.'

Steven's face contorted. 'I thought … I was going to lose you.'

'Shh.'

'I thought …'

She stroked his head and said, 'Not ever. Not ever, not ever, not ever, not ever.'

52

It was raining heavily and Emily hadn't brought an umbrella on the school run because it was just too much to manage with the buggy. She hated hats and found hoods restricted her peripheral vision so much it almost induced a panic attack – how on earth were you supposed to make sure your child wasn't darting into oncoming traffic? That was the most fundamental rule of being a parent: don't let anyone literally kill them, and hoods made that completely impossible for the sake of keeping your head dry. So she did her best to embrace the sensation. She thought of monastics wandering the desert thanking God for the raw blisters on their feet. Arthur gazed out of the misshapen plastic cover at the rivulets working their way down in a small cataract onto Emily's left boot. She put Matty's rucksack onto his back and then held him to her waist.

'Hey!'

'I love you,' she said.

'Yeah, yeah,' he said.

'You know it. Have a good day.'

She ran her hands through her hair and was about to turn for the gate when she saw Elliott hand in hand with Tomasz. She watched as they walked all the way up to the infant school door and Elliott had a word with the teacher. Their imminent house move, maybe, a few days off towards the end of term, would that be okay, great, thanks.

It would be nice to feel nothing at all when she saw him; it would be nice to hate him or take some pleasure in cutting him dead, but something close to pity kept her waiting until he turned and caught her eye. He approached, looking at the ground.

'I wondered if you were going to say goodbye,' said Emily. 'Oh, you look sad.'

'Emily.'

'What is it?'

'You're looking great.'

'Oh really? Thank you. I had my hair completely soaked with rain in case I ran into you.'

'Do you want to—'

'Get some *brunch*?'

'I owe you a huge apology.'

'You don't owe me anything – we never owed each other anything.'

'I should have come to talk to you days ago, I just—'

'I imagine you've been very busy. Shall we walk? They'll lock the gates soon.'

'I'm the actual worst,' said Elliott.

'No it's fine,' said Emily. 'What you've done has hurt me more than I believed I had the capacity for, but I don't want to hurl insults at you. I can't be bothered.'

'Emily—'

'I just wanted you to know that you've broken and humiliated me. I'd have done this via WhatsApp but then I wouldn't have been sure I was talking to you.'

'No, that's exactly it – she's exaggerating,' said Elliott. 'You were talking to me, every time. She's just trying to hurt you. I caught her with my phone *once*.'

'When? How long ago? Stop – you'll get soaked.'

A minivan tore through a puddle ahead of them and sent a wave over the pavement.

'Thank you. I don't know. Months.'

'But this is just *you*, isn't it?' said Emily.

'She found out what was going on, she found a way in, she found a way to break it.'

'This is just charming, vacuous you. That's presumably why she went after Steven?'

'Yeah. *About* that,' said Elliott.

'I don't really want to know,' said Emily. 'You do this all the time and it's just some kink you both have and it's so gross I could actually kill you.'

'Emily, I need you to know that this was different.'

'No,' said Emily. Different than it was with the woman who lived in my house before me? I don't care. You'll say literally anything to stop someone thinking badly of you, that's your *only* motivation, that's your entire personality.'

'That's … fair. None of this was by design. I mean we've got carried away with things before, but this was different and she went in on Steven *because* it was different.'

He sounded like a politician, leveraging his desperation in service of a point; the desperation, at least, felt real.

'I've been in love with a Magic 8-Ball,' she said.

'Because I loved you. I'm still in love with you. I always will be.'

'It's meaningless.'

Emily put her hand in her coat pocket. The postcard from Elliott was wet at the corners, and the little pink note with the same quotation on it in the same handwriting, the one she'd kept in her wallet for the last year folded up behind a supermarket loyalty card. She had thought to present them both to him as some kind of coup de grâce, but now that she was standing in front of him it felt unnecessary.

'Please. What she's given you is a horrible distortion – don't let her.'

'You've *both* given me a horrible distortion.'

'She's angry—'

'I don't blame her.'

'No, sure, me neither. But don't let her take something that was real. It was real,' said Elliott. 'I don't expect you to ever talk to me again and I hope you never have to spend much time even *thinking* about me again, but you need to hear that this was different, that you changed me, that I've never been loved the way you loved me before and I've never met anyone I thought could … save me before you. Even if you don't believe me.'

'Okay,' said Emily. 'And you need to hear that I don't believe you.'

Elliott stopped walking.

She turned around keeping one hand on the buggy. 'Where are you going?'

'I need to get some shopping,' he said.

'Oh. "Save you." Elliott, for goodness' sake, that's so tired.'

'You don't know anyone,' he said. 'You can't take anything anyone says at face value. It's all too easily falsifiable. All we ever do is try to present ourselves in as good a light as possible. You can't tell the truth.'

'You can *try*,' said Emily. 'Oh, my god, you can try.'

'I miss you.'

'That's really all that's asked of us.'

'Emily.'

He looked so despondent she almost wanted to tell him to forget everything, talk to me whenever you want, draw me right back in, I don't even care. She tested him, like a dog, to see if he could meet her gaze.

'God, Elliott, this fucking rain,' she said. She turned around so that the buggy was braced against her back and took his hand and drew him towards her. She kissed him once on the lips and then turned around and started to walk back up the hill.

— When it's over
— Don't
— WHEN IT'S OVER
— Okay, can't ignore all caps
— Are you going to go really distant on me?
— Why do we have to talk about this?
— Are you going to suddenly develop this absolute respect for boundaries and propriety?
— Nothing is ever over.
— When one of the things I *love* about you is your lack of boundaries and propriety?
— Nothing ends.
— No, this is one of the exceptions. Do you ever think about your exes, just generally?
— It's not like there've been dozens. No. Not much.
— Right. Benign indifference.
— I don't think I'm capable of thinking about you with 'benign indifference'
— But you will.
— If I have to.
— Okay.
— Won't like it.

— No me neither.
— Just for the moment though … imagine I
  blindfold you
— And also I blindfold you
— We're both blindfolded. We say, 'I want to show
  you something special.'
— In unison?
— Just out of sync. And you take my hand
— And you take my hand
— And we just set off like that.

53

There should be, Emily felt, some punishment, because how was it endurable otherwise? But, if there was going to be, she supposed she would have to choose it herself. And if that was the case she might just as well choose nothing at all.

It was Saturday and Steven had taken the boys swimming, then probably for ice cream. Possibly for more than one ice cream because he was a soft touch. With them, with her, with everyone. That was who he was, really. The wind was raging and the trees were hysterical. She parked the electric car, one of the shabbiest in the fleet, on the muddy verge and walked to the low stile at the foot of the hill.

She had taken to re-watching the entire series of *Quantum Leap* on her phone at night. One headphone in her right ear so she'd hear the children if they woke up. It was funny that Ziggy, Al's sparkling handheld device, had prefigured the smartphone in some way, at once more and infinitely less helpful. What do you think about that, Elliott? Do you like my little observation? Ziggy says there's a 67 per cent chance he's not even thinking about you any more.

Lord, take my ingratitude and delusions, wound me with compassion.

'Hi, Mum.'

'Sweetheart.'

'This isn't really the weather for a walk.'

'Take that attitude in this country and you'd never leave the house,' said her mother.

'I guess.'

'You sound so American sometimes.'

'I only like American telly,' said Emily. 'I hate the English accent.'

'Ha!'

Her mother rearranged her bag and took out a flask. 'Do you want some of this now?'

'No,' said Emily. 'I want to earn it.'

She tried to help her mother over the fence, but she brushed her off. 'Save your energy for ten years' time.'

They walked the hill path in silence for a few minutes. Her hair kept whipping her eyes and she'd forgotten to bring anything to tie it back.

'You're right,' her mother said. 'It's a horrible day. It's giving me an ear-ache.'

'The boys really resent me taking them out at the moment,' said Emily. 'The other day …' She paused and it developed into simply not finishing the sentence.

'So?' said her mother. 'Are things okay?'

'I'm a bit worried about Matty,' said Emily. 'This morning I found a Kinder Egg capsule and I opened it and he hadn't even put the toy together.'

'I'm not sure that's really cause for concern,' said her mother. 'Maybe he's growing out of them.'

'I feel like I've been neglecting him.'

'Emily,' said her mother. 'I've seen neglect. Don't be absurd. There's a horrible trend at the moment—'

'Emotionally.'

'Absolute rot. To pathologise every shortcoming. It's nonsense.'

'Maybe.'

'And, as you know, I was asking how *you* were.'

'I'm actually really struggling to be very present with anyone. I feel like I've made everything into a lie.'

'That's hard,' said her mother. 'It's hard to feel numb.'

'I don't really know what to do. I'm *ruminant*. A bipedal ruminant.'

'Do you know, Emily, I'm not sure there's very much you *can* do.'

'Well that's helpful.'

'Eventually your brain just does it for you.'

'I'm trying to find joy in the smallest things, but I think doing that means I find dread in the smallest things too.'

'Was that thunder?'

'I didn't hear. I'm trying to bear in mind that if I'm suffering it's because of what I chose to do.'

'Hmm.'

'And that we're wrong and sinful and selfish, and, if we're not suffering from some external cause, we bring it on ourselves. And that there's a point to that, that it's maybe the only one. And that I should *count it all joy*.'

'Bible stuff?' said her mother.

'Yes, it's from the Epistle of St James. I'm trying to see it as the answer to everything.'

A border collie ran towards them, stopped suddenly and darted off again. *Hey – hey, look at this!* It circled them as if it thought it might try to herd them but then gave up and ran back up the hill.

Her mother sighed and nodded, took her bag off her right shoulder and transferred it to her left.

'And how's that going?'

Acknowledgements

For exceptional editorial insight and patience I want to thank Georgia Garrett, Anna Kelly and Luke Brown. I'm also lucky to have friends who read full drafts or kicked ideas around with preternatural generosity; my heartfelt thanks to Ruth Gilligan, Anna Metcalfe, Susannah Dickey and Miles Bradley.